West Falls Revisited

a novel

D. H. Schleicher

PRAISE FOR D. H. SCHLEICHER

Then Came Darkness

"The catharsis of emotional writing in this book was incredible…I laughed. I cried. I had to take breaks because some scenes tore me to pieces. It's dark, gritty, and I love it." – *Lo Potter Writes*

"Tense and brooding…like *(The) Grapes of Wrath*, only creepier and with a lot more murder…a delightfully dark read." – *Margaret Adelle, booktuber*

"A page-turner with a dark slant, morally gray characters who were flawed yet likable, realistic and multi-faceted with certain twists I didn't see coming." - *Jenna Moquin, author*

"Historical fiction at its finest. D. H. Schleicher is a master with words…I found myself holding my breath several times." – *Gina Rae Mitchell, book blogger*

CONTENTS

AUTHOR'S NOTE ABOUT CONTENT

This novel covers difficult subject matter, and over the years the residents of West Falls are directly impacted by events such as the Catholic Church sexual abuse scandal, the COVID pandemic, and an array of other violent acts, illnesses, and trauma. The depictions deal more with the psychological impacts rather than dwelling on overtly graphic details, and some characters still find glimmers of hope through the darkness.

Passing gossip, real events, and real people inspired certain aspects of the novel, however, West Falls and its inhabitants are amalgamations of those inspirations and works of fiction.

To my potential readers, above all, be kind to and protect yourselves. Make your decision to enter the town of West Falls accordingly.

PROLOGUE

1875-1876
Elizabeth

Elizabeth Laurel Van Elms could see the future.

"We will live here," she said at the foot of the hill on the east side of the swampland. She planted a stake in the ground. The sun's bright aura blanketed the clear sky and cast the hill and everything around it in a hot seasonal glow.

With her family inheritance, her husband had purchased this large swath of land and the marl pit at the base of the waterfall. Though only ten miles from the city, once across the river and beyond the confines of Hampten, it might as well have been another world, wild and untamed. Ripe for cultivation. The marl pit would be their source of livelihood and would provide for the farms being plotted around the falls.

Elizabeth imagined a large, square stone house at the foot of the hill from which they could survey all of their land, this West Falls. She was nineteen, confident, and full of ideas. She was matched by her ambitious husband, Franz Van Elms, twenty-six, who treated her as an equal in decisions.

When Elizabeth was two-years-old, she was struck by a ravenous fever. It left her partially deaf and temporarily blind. It was in that period of blindness she began to have her visions. She saw this hill. The falls. The gorge. She heard the hawks and other birds, the sound of the water flowing over the edge and emptying into the pond. She could even smell the air, the land, and the swampy fecundity of it. As she grew, her hearing partially recovered, and her eyesight fully returned. Her visions continued, however, and they were her little secret. She told no one of them.

Elizabeth wondered, though, could her husband see it in her eyes, in her body language, when they stepped foot on this land? Whether by miraculous foresight or some kind of earthly intuition a woman had that a man could never understand, when she declared they would live here, he did not question it.

In the days and months to come, some men labored to build the stone house at the foot of the hill while others rerouted some of the pond water, creating a little stream, and uncovering more of the marl pit for excavation. When Elizabeth saw the shape of it, she knew instantly something was lurking in that marl pit, and just as she would be birthing her first child come spring, so too would this marl pit birth the ancient fossils of some fantastic beast. If only she could carve her visions into the past to know what it was.

The house was complete before the first snow that winter. In its comforts she prepared for their child. At night she dreamed of the lineage to come, the generations of Elms who would inhabit this house.

We will live here.

We will love here.

We will hate here.

We will die here.

We will wait for you to come.

The visions and faces came to her like music. She couldn't understand all she saw. It filled her with the most immense sense of fantastic melancholic longing; longing to know them all, love them all. She wanted to be with them in every moment. The good and the bad. The joy and the sadness. She wanted to know what they dreamed of, all of her descendants in this West Falls.

In the following spring Elizabeth had a son, healthy and strong. She took the baby down to the marl pit, and they watched as the men uncovered a most wondrous sight: the giant jaw bone of some fearsome creature the likes of which no human had ever seen. The men were shocked, thinking they unearthed a dragon or demon. They were relieved to see her there, as they were used to her visiting the work site, but had not seen her in some time as she had been temporarily housebound from the birthing of the bouncing child she now held in her arms.

"There is nothing to fear," she told them. "My husband has told me of the struggles to keep the pit free of water after it storms. We need to re-excavate at a different point that will drain the water into the stream more effectively. It will leave this section, then, completely covered by water, which I determine is best to keep this creature at bay. Cover it at once."

What she did not share with them, nor with her husband, was that she knew one day the falls would no longer run. The progress of the town would demand a new conquering of the water. She saw it in a dream, and in that dream she saw them unearthing the creature, and others. A great excavation site would arise that would bring West Falls newfound fame. She also saw a boy and a girl, Robbie and Laurel, living in her house and visiting the site.

When her firstborn son was a little bit older, she showed him where she carved those names into the stone block in the corner of the basement. She said their names aloud to him.

"Who are they, mama?" he asked.

"We shall have to wait and see," she said.

There was more to her vision. Yes, there was that flash of wonder at the discovery of those fantastic beasts, but it was soon followed by heartbreak and despair. She held her hand out to them – these children – in her dreams. She saw the boy in the woods, alone, at night. She could feel and hear his heartbeat. It pounded.

"Take my hand," she called to him.

He paused, a stick breaking beneath his foot. A hawk calling out above. He looked around. Did he hear her? No. He shoved his hands in his pockets, and walked on.

Robbie. Darkness. The heartbeat stopped, and she shot up in bed, drenched in sweat, tears streaming down her face. She could only whisper her prayer for comfort. When she closed her eyes again, she saw beyond the darkness, then beyond the stars. She saw footprints on a strange rock, not of this earth. She felt her descendants there, too. The girl. The prayer contained a minor change in tone.

We will live here.
We will love here.
We will hate here.
We will NOT ALL die here.
We will wait for you to come.

EPISODE ONE – SOME/BODY

November 2019
Monday (Veteran's Day) Afternoon
Sam

Their son Henry was born under the dark storm clouds of rising Trumpism, about eight months before the election. He was also literally born under storm clouds in the middle of a rare winter thunderstorm. Sam thought when Henry was a baby, and he and Val still lived in the city, that those ear-shattering screams in the middle of the night were Henry asking his fathers, *why did you bring me into this world when that lunatic was going to become president?* Everyone still thought Trump wouldn't win, but somehow baby Henry knew the inevitable, and so he screamed into the existential void from his crib. Or maybe it was gas. Hell, all babies woke up screaming in the middle of the night. Maybe throughout all of history babies channeled the anxieties of their community through their nighttime cries.

The entire world seemed to be increasingly on edge, but it wasn't that Henry was a particularly anxious baby or kid. He was almost four now. He was charming and clever and more often than not smiling. When Henry was two, Sam and Val made the decision to leave the city and do what any self-respecting parents throughout most of modern America history had done: they found a better school district. So, they moved from a blue working-class city to an even bluer, progressive suburb along the high-speed line.

At the time of the move, Henry had just finally started to sleep through the night. But in the new home, a one-hundred-year-old colonial full of character with modern updates – original hardwood floors with trace borders, a vented hooded chef's stove – Henry started waking up screaming at the top of his lungs again.

"I'm not above hiring someone to do a sage burning ceremony to ward off the ghosts here," Val said in that super-serious-but-actually-joking voice of his.

Sometimes Sam wondered if it was Trump anxiety when Henry was an infant, was it ghosts bothering him now? Eh, the house was beautiful and perfect with or without ghosts. It was just part of the transition. Eventually Henry stopped waking up screaming, and instead just started climbing into their bed when he could maneuver the space, or sleeping on their floor when he couldn't. Maybe the ghost was a homophobe and refused to come into Sam and Val's room and couldn't bother Henry there. A bigoted ghost, a kid who slept on the floor. *To each their own,* Sam thought to himself.

They settled in the town of West Falls, which was a dream. It was walkable, with a thriving business district with award-winning restaurants and boutiques, a festival for every season, a weekend farmer's market from spring to fall, multiple parks, and beautifully maintained older homes on mature tree-lined streets. Henry would go to a top tier public school, and Sam and Val were still just a fifteen-minute train ride from the city where they maintained their corporate careers, both of which increasingly allowed them to work from home. Oh, and the history! A gorge with a lovely little creek at the bottom and exposed marl pit containing a rich deposit of dinosaur bones still being excavated.

They knew, however, they lived in a comfortable little bubble. Every once in a while there would be a tiny pin poking the bubble from the inside, testing its elasticity. Just a few days after they moved in, they walked down to the Saturday morning farmer's market for the first time, and they noticed a Confederate flag inside the window of a neighbor's house, ironically across the street from a house with a *Hate Has No Home Here* sign. It seemed inexplicable to see a Confederate flag in a northern state, but this was the Trump era after all, a chaotic time of *anything goes*. On many of the social media community pages there was light chatter around this. How it was a shock and a *disgrace*, which gave Sam and Val comfort that their new community had their backs. The Vaughans were a bit of a nightmare for Trumpers – gay, interracial, and with a blonde-haired, blue-eyed son born through a surrogate.

Another pin poked the bubble this weekend.

Veteran's Day fell on a Monday, giving most an extended weekend, and came with a pleasant temperature warm up. This prompted them to take a walk down to the park straddling three different small towns, whose leisurely shaded paths rambled around the small lake. This was formed when settlers dammed the branch of the larger river that subsequently stopped the falls which gave the town its name and originally emptied into the gorge. The lake was murky and sometimes smelled, stagnant from the damming and polluted with goose feces and sewage runoff from the local Catholic high school. But it wasn't so bad. It was peaceful, and it was their lake now. There was chatter on the social media community page, *Under the Falls,* about potential plans to dredge it, sue the Catholic diocese, control the geese population, or even undo the damming and bring back the real falls to let nature take its course. Concerns about how that would impact the dinosaur bone excavation site in the gorge usually shot that last idea down.

Henry playfully sprinted ahead of them in little spurts, joyous to be jacket-less in autumn, chasing away the immigrant geese that plagued the lake year-round.

"Henry!" Sam called out.

"I know," Henry called back. "Watch the goose shit."

Sam shook his head. Val laughed.

"He learned that from you," Val said.

As Henry darted from the patches of shade into shafts of hazy sunlight, Val knotted his brow – a habit that over the years created deep, stately vertical lines running half-way up the center of his forehead – and mused, "Our literal golden boy." Even in this town, Val sometimes got looks, especially when he was alone with Henry, and this blonde-haired, blue-eyed child called him, a half-Black, half-Asian man, "Daddy."

As they came around the bend to where a street bridged over the lake and cut the park in half, they saw police cars, whose sirens silently strobed their lights, parked at the foot of the path heading into the woods. Local teenagers frequently partied up in those woods, usually harmlessly.

Henry was mesmerized by the lights of the cop cars. He had play cars like that at home.

"What's going on?" he asked his fathers.

"Probably some kids caught with pot up there," Sam said.

"What's pot?" Henry asked.

Val nudged Sam's arm with his sharp elbow.

"What?" Sam said to Val. "It's going to be legal in this state soon."

Henry saw some ducks on their side of the lake and was quickly distracted. They walked away from the scene with no further investigation, not giving it another thought.

Until later that night, after Henry was tucked into bed and Val was watching his latest streaming epic fantasy drama, when Sam checked the latest posts on *Under the Falls*.

"Anyone know what the cops were doing up in Stabler Woods this afternoon?" a woman asked the community. He recognized her name and profile picture. She frequently posted questions along the lines of, "Why was there a helicopter over town today?" or "What was that smell by the overpass?" or "Who else heard that boom just now?"

Like most posts, this one was playfully victimized by some funny gifs and sarcastic replies. "Must be aliens," one joker responded. "Was this following a loud boom?" someone else jested. "Damn geese again," posted another. Many assumed, like Sam did, some kids were probably caught smoking pot or drinking. Maybe there was a minor scuffle. But then one person posted the truth, heard second-hand, from their cousin who was dating one of the cops on the scene.

It wasn't just some kids partying up there in the woods.

The police were up there because some kid had found something.

Not something. Some body.

≈

Sunday – one day before the body was found
Carl

Carl Strong wished only to make things good again. Things didn't even have to be great. Just good. Good like Robbie Elms was.

"You're good boys," Robbie's mother would tell them, "I know that, no matter what you did."

He hadn't been back home in years. Stepping off the train from the city at West Falls, he had been previously blind to the progress. Walking the streets, the trees were more mature; some were gone, and some new ones planted. Some houses had fresh coats of paint, maybe an extension, new fences, new roofs or a covered porch. A few new constructions were here or there, as if the most blighted properties had been surgically removed like growths were removed to heal a patient. But the essence of the town was, if anything, brighter and recovered – the antithesis of Carl, someone who never recovered. The blocks spread out before him the same, but everything was just slightly different. Better, most would say, though there were always those stricken with the nostalgia sickness.

Carl walked through those fabled streets of his childhood under the shade of the trees. He knew where each piece of uprooted sidewalk threatened to trip those newer to town, who foolishly looked up at the massive tree limbs or at the houses speckled with sunlight and shadow, unaware of the hazards at their feet. West Falls was a marvel of American residential architecture: old cozy Dutch colonials three in a row, a Victorian on a corner, then another block lined with brick Cape Cods and eclectic craftsmen and bungalows. He walked literally over the river (well, creek) and through the woods (Stabler Woods) down to the pike. He could've walked this blindfolded, even though peculiarities not seen before, like rainbow flags outside a vegan bakery, kept reminding him some things had changed. On the pike there was still the Rialto Theater, the once fabled hangout spot and last reported location of Robbie Elms. It later turned into a smut house before being shuttered, only to be revived now as a thriving community theater and stood as a reminder of change – good change – while across from it stood a reminder some things never changed. *Connie's Place.*

Carl Strong stepped inside the old bar with confidence that surprised even him. Jim Croce's "I Got a Name" was playing, and the music was pleasantly loud and the air pleasantly cold like outside. He took a big, deep breath with calm familiarity, which was like a tonic itself, which is to say nothing of the tonic he was about to order at the bar from the smiling young bartender.

"You look kinda familiar," she said to him.

"Well, kinda like this town…this song…I guess. I'm an oldie but a goodie. But it's been a long time."

"Well, we love the oldies in here. I'm Amie. What can I get you to drink?"

"Is Connie around?" Carl asked.

"Connie's away for the weekend. Who can I say is asking for her?"

"I'm her cousin…well, long lost cousin I guess…and indeed, like this old song, I gotta name. Carl." Oh, how this young woman didn't know how much this song meant to him, how perfectly melancholic and appropriate it was to be playing when he stepped into this bar, how bullied he was as a kid, called everything by everybody except his own damn name. How Robbie was the only one who called him by his name and defended him.

Amie seemed genuinely surprised. "Wow, I never knew she had a cousin Carl."

"Well, I don't see why you would."

"I'll tell her the next time she's in that you stopped by. She got your number and all?"

"Mmm, don't worry too much about it. I'll be in again. We'll run into each other sure enough. How about that drink now? What's on tap? And don't tell me you gotta list of thirty artisanal locally brewed beers I can peruse…or that you're brewing your own out back, and *would I like a sampler's flight?*"

Amie laughed. "Well, we do carry some of the local stuff. Gotta keep with the times and all, but we've got what we've always got. You can head downtown to the strip if you want all that other stuff."

"Eh, screw the beer anyways. G'head and give me a whiskey, whatever you got on the top shelf. Make it a double. No ice."

"I like a man who knows what he wants. Coming right up, Carl."

Carl was pleased with himself, surprised at how easily he could seem so normal, or affable at least.

Amie politely chatted with him between serving the few other customers in the bar, real old-timers who were probably sitting in those same seats when Carl was a kid, remembering the days when you could smoke inside and didn't have to huddle out back or on the corner, like some homeless person, to catch a drag. Carl felt he could be like them, just relax, enjoy a moment with a drink or a smoke, letting the troubles of his day mute themselves, even if only for a second. But he wasn't like them. He couldn't enjoy any moment, and he couldn't have just a drink or two. He ordered more whiskey. Amie asked if he wanted anything to eat. He said,

"Nah, thanks though." More whiskey.

When one of the old-timers snuck outside, presumably to catch a smoke, leaving a full beer behind, Carl followed him and asked awkwardly if he could bum a cigarette.

"Do I know you?" the old-timer asked.

"Nah," Carl said, "I'm just passing through." But the truth was this old-timer lived in the house on the corner of Carl's old street, and Carl used to cut his lawn. The guy was probably busy doing the math in his head, thinking, *this looks like that kid who cut my lawn in the 90s, and stole cigarettes out of my car...but this guy also looks about twenty years older than he should be if he was that kid.*

They smoked their cigarettes silently and then walked back into the bar. Well, Carl stumbled. Amie had a look of concern on her face.

"Sure you don't want something to eat?" she said. "The stuff is real good here. I'm not just trying to upsell you."

"Nah, my stomach is a bit torn up. Got this condition. I'm all good. Can I settle up?"

"Sure, the first one was on the house with you being Connie's long-lost cousin and all." She placed the bill on the bar in front of him.

Carl fumbled through his jacket pocket and pulled out some crumbled bills he tried feebly to straighten. He placed them down on the bar and said, "Keep the change."

"Thanks, hun," Amie said.

As Carl passed the old-timer who gave him a cigarette, the guy had a look on his face as if to say, *it is you, you little shit.* He shook his head as if in disgust. "Take it easy, kid," he muttered under his breath.

Carl nodded and limped onto the street. He headed towards Stabler Woods where he and Robbie Elms used to play. Robbie also played there with his other friends, the ones who routinely shunned Carl. Friends like Hank Carter. Word was Hank had taken over his father's auto repair business and built a McMansion monstrosity in the newish development that had required clearing a small portion of the woods. The back of Hank's house apparently butted up against the new edge of the woods, and he had a double-tiered party deck overlooking near where Robbie had been found back in the summer of 1993.

It was getting dark now. The paths through the woods were still roughly the same, but instead of continuing through more woods and the former secret kid hangouts, Carl now stepped into the backyard of Hank Carter. Hank even had a fire pit in the middle of the grass. All the lights in the back of the house were on, and flood lights lit the back deck. Carl stood next to the fire pit looking up into the house.

Hank had married the girl he dated senior year of high school, Sheila. He was a second-string football player, and she was a popular cheerleader. She was considered out of his league, but they had stuck to each other like glue. Carl watched as she paced back and forth behind the sliding glass doors to the deck, nursing a beer bottle. She looked sad and frumpy in her West Falls Middle School sweats, a far cry from her shining days in high school. Word was she was the receptionist at the middle school. She and Hank had no kids, though apparently he coached pee-wee football.

He wondered, did she or Hank ever think about Robbie when they gazed out into the woods, or was their McMansion their little fortress protecting them from the past? Did Hank ever get teary-eyed and vulnerable when they drank and tell Sheila about what happened? Or did they drink to forget, like Carl did?

Oh shit. Sheila was suddenly still and staring straight at Carl. He could see her mouth moving, "Haaank!"

Then suddenly there was Hank, passing his bottle of beer to Sheila, sliding open those doors and marching out onto the deck. He placed his hands arms-width apart on the railing, like a bird of prey spreading his wings, and peered down with squinting eyes at Carl standing in the middle of his backyard.

"Can I help you with something?" Hank boomed with a

drunken air of superiority.

"Fuck you, Hank Carter," Carl was surprised to find himself saying with a false sense of bravado. But it was almost under his breath, both a yell and a whisper.

Hank leaned back with his chest puffed out. "Speak up, I didn't hear you!"

Carl coughed and then yelled louder and clearer, "Fuck you, Hank Carter! And fuck your wife, too! And this fucking house!"

"Oh, you gotta lotta nerve coming back here after all these years, and to *my house!*" Hank turned and grabbed the baseball bat propped up against the grill. He charged down the stairs while Carl stood his ground.

Carl started to shake as Hank rushed towards him and then stopped short, acting like he was going to swing the bat but then decided at the last minute not to.

"You think you can hide here in plain sight? You think you can just erase what happened?" Carl yelled, his voice growing hoarse.

"Robbie was my friend, too," Hank said through gritted teeth.

"I'm not even talking about that!"

"Oh, you fucking lying piece of shit!" Hank swung the bat and struck Carl hard in the shoulder.

"Hank, no!" Sheila screamed from the top of the deck.

"G'head, keep swinging that bat," Carl taunted.

"I'll kill you with my bare hands!" Hank shouted as he threw the bat down and swung a fist at Carl's face.

Carl fell to the ground, hard.

"Stop it, Hank!" Sheila wailed.

Hank got down and pounded Carl with his fists numerous times in his face and ribs.

Sheila was crying now. "Hank, he's gonna call the cops!"

Hank breathed in heavily through his nose and lifted himself off Carl, who was trying to shield his face with his arms. "This piece of shit ain't calling nobody," he said, looking back up at his wife. He turned back to Carl who was slowly, unsteadily coming back up on his feet. "Now get the fuck off my property."

Carl wiped the blood off his nose. It was enough that it slapped against the fire pit, leaving a pulpy red splatter. He placed his hand under his swollen lower lip. "You know I was always telling the truth. But g'head and die with your denial." Carl stumbled back into the dark cover of the woods.

≈

Sunday Night
Amie

It was closing time after a mostly slow and uneventful shift. Usually, on the nights her mystery man was able to slip away, Amie would get a text before midnight asking, "Need Company?" She always replied, "Yes." There was no pre-text tonight, which is why she looked surprised when he came through the door, later than usual. He wasn't looking his normal, charming self.

"Why do you look so shocked?" Hank asked her.

"Did I miss your text?" she asked.

"No, sorry, it was literally a last-minute opportunity to slip out without Sheila noticing, I just completely forgot to text you." His tense shoulders slacked a bit as he sat down at the bar. He smiled softly, "Still want company?"

"Of course," Amie replied. "But it was a real slow night, as you can probably tell."

Hank looked around at the empty bar.

"So, I'm almost done cleaning up."

"Hey, no problem. I don't even need a drink. Just finish your stuff and we can get right to it." He winked at her.

Amie slapped the wet bar rag at him, "This guy, such the romantic."

"I don't know what you see in me." He said this often, mockingly, but it sounded more real this time to Amie, like he was really wondering.

"What's got you so down, Romeo?"

Hank placed his hands atop the bar, revealing his scraped and blistered knuckles.

"Holy shit, Hank, what happened?"

"I don't wanna talk about it."

"You sure you don't need a drink?"

"I've had enough already."

"God, you didn't drive did you?"

"No, I walked."

Amie proceeded to wipe down the rest of the bar and put away some of the glasses. "Well, you know you never have to explain anything to me. But if you wanna talk, we can do that, too. My night wasn't nearly as eventful, but I did have this weird guy come in this afternoon. Maybe about fifty. Sickly looking guy. Claimed to be Connie's cousin."

Hank shook his head and wanted to laugh. "Honey, that's the guy that met the other end of my fists tonight."

Amie looked stunned, again. "You gotta be kidding me."

"He must've got loaded up here and then wandered into my backyard. Fucking Carl Strong."

"How the hell do you know him?"

"He's Connie's cousin for chrissakes! And he ain't no fifty. He's same age as me…not even forty. He's just used up as hell."

"Drugs?" Amie prodded.

"You name it." Hank said.

"What was he doing in your backyard?"

"Trying to start shit."

Amie had never seen Hank turn so red, look so upset.

"Shit," she said, "I'm sorry, had I known, I woulda…"

"You woulda what? Don't worry about it. How could you know? What would you have done, not served him? Called the cops? For what?"

Amie sighed. "Let me just go get my things from the back,

and we can get outta here."

As per ritual, they walked in a bold little statement to their relationship, hand in hand and mostly in the dark, to Amie's apartment, a little one bedroom over a storefront on the main strip. The woozy glow from the vintage street lamps lining the sidewalks outside streamed in through her bedroom window and illuminated their love-making. But Hank couldn't keep it up tonight, not a usual problem for him. After a frustrating ten minutes of false starts, he rolled off her and said, "I'm sorry." He almost looked like he was going to cry.

"Aw, don't worry about it," she said as she laid her head on his chest. "You had a rough night. You got a lot on your mind."

Hank sighed deeply.

"Look, I know this isn't how we normally roll," Amie said. "We like to focus on the physical, and I love that, but you can talk to me if you want."

"I know. You always say that."

"We're both just lying here naked with each other. This flimsy sheet barely covering us. Go on, be vulnerable with me. Say what's on your mind."

"I'm not one of your emo-hipster boyfriends from Portland."

Amie rolled back onto her pillow. They were both just staring at the cracks in the ceiling now. "Fine, then I'll just be straight-up with you. Why the hell did you have to beat the shit out of that poor guy? What did he ever do to you?"

Hank snickered. "Oh, like you really wanna know."

"I do. What would possess a guy like you to beat on a poor guy like that? Are you just a bully, Hank Carter?"

"Don't start with me. And let me tell you, Carl Strong is a piece of shit. A drug addict. A liar. An all-around waste of a human being. Hell, he's barely even a human being."

"Seemed like a nice enough guy to me. Sure, sad and clearly fucked-up, but..."

"Look, years ago he spread some pretty horrible lies about

me, and then after all these years he has the nerve to come onto my property and disturb me and my wife?"

"Oh, *your wife*. Heaven forbid anyone disturb Sheila."

"Don't start with me, Amie."

Amie was sitting up on the edge of the bed now with her back turned to him. She grabbed her vape pen from the bedside table and took a long hit. Sadly, she thought this would be the only pleasure she got tonight. "And what kinda childish shit…he spread lies about you? When you were in high school?"

"Middle school if you really wanna know. He was always a little shit. I was stuck doing altar boy shit with him for a few years. And one day he claims he was abused by this priest, which was a flat-out lie, and then to top it off, he claimed I was, too. Which was an even bigger lie because if anyone had tried to touch me like that, I would've killed them!"

Amie turned back to him. She placed her hand on his chest. "Jesus Christ, are you serious?"

Hank sat up so they would be eye to eye. "Oh, don't go getting that look in your eye. *That pity look*. This is why I don't ever talk about this shit. Because people immediately think, 'Oh dear, did poor Hanky-boy get diddled by a priest?' It's complete bullshit, and I'm not gonna have you sitting there looking at me like that. And by the way, that poor priest he accused – that man was a saint. He did so much for my father and me when my mom got cancer. He rallied the whole church around us. That's the kinda guy Father MacShay was. And for that lying little weirdo to go say something like that about him…I should've killed Carl back then."

Amie didn't want this kind of drama. Why did she always attract this kind of drama? She was born in the city and left the city after high school because of drama, and she moved all the way across the country to Portland…where she found more drama. And she left there, too, after a few years. She picked West Falls as her next stop because it was close to where she grew up, but she had never heard of it back then, and it seemed so nice and progressive and charming.

There was also a silly notion, she knew, a romantic one, regarding the dinosaur bones she soon learned West Falls was famous for. Growing up she had wanted to be an archaeologist, like Lara Croft. Lame, she knew, but it seemed like fate that she should find her way to West Falls, and now here was more drama. Hell, sure, there was bound to be some with Hank being married, but not something like this. Sheila was willfully oblivious, so Hank being married was bad news in name only. What the hell was Amie supposed to do with something like this – Hank's melodramatic past, his violent side? Like always, Amie felt like she asked for it. She turned back towards the wall and continued to vape.

"Why can't you just smoke a cigarette like a normal person?" Hank asked her.

"It's filthy," she said.

"It's honest."

"I don't even know what you're talking about anymore."

"And this is exactly why I don't talk and normally just stick to what I'm good at, which apparently tonight I'm not even good at that." Hank stood up and slipped on his boxers, shirt, and jeans.

"Go home to Sheila. I sure hope that Carl guy doesn't press charges against you." Part of Amie kinda hoped he would. God, what the hell was she gonna tell Connie about all of this?

≈

Monday Night - after the body was found
Sutton

Sutton and Connie were enjoying a long weekend getaway at a charming little B&B on a wine trail when she first got the courtesy call from the West Falls sheriff Sunday night. Her office manager, who monitored the town's social media pages religiously for hubbub, had already texted her that afternoon about the gossip posted regarding the police presence in Stabler Woods. Sheriff Jim

Van Patten Jr. confirmed it was a body.

"Sutton, I have to tell you something," the sheriff said after relaying the bare minimum of facts. "What I'm about to tell you extends beyond the normal courtesy call we make to the mayor in situations like these."

Sutton was standing on the heated patio of a restaurant, two glasses of wine into dinner. Connie was still seated at the table inside. "What do you mean, Jim?"

"The body did have ID on it."

"And?"

"Sutton…it's Carl Strong."

Sutton took a deep breath. She wanted to gasp, but for some reason couldn't. She was focused completely now on the giant heat lamp's oppressive radiation enveloping the one side of her body. She thought the sleeve of her sweater might catch fire, or her hair, the gray strands in danger of becoming ashes. She stepped away from the heat lamp, but there was just another one ready to burn her other side. She felt flushed and light-headed.

"Mayor Jackson…are you still there?" the sheriff asked.

Sutton stepped off the patio into the cold darkness. "I'm sorry," she said. "I presume you still need next of kin confirmation?"

"Yes."

"Let me tell her. We were going to head back to town in the morning, but we can leave tonight."

"No, it can wait for the morning. You should both get some rest…if it's possible."

"Has the cause been identified?"

"The circumstances are still being determined. There appears to be multiple injuries, perhaps not all from the same incident, and drug paraphernalia was found on his person."

Sutton looked down at the ground and shook her head. The change from intense heat to sudden cold was making her sniffle, which in turn was triggering a few stray tears. "Ok, thank you, Jim,

I'll let you get back to it. I'm sure our offices are already in touch. Let's control the local spin on this one as much as we can."

"Of course," the sheriff replied mechanically.

"I need to collect myself and then get back to Connie," Sutton concluded. "Text or call me if anything else emerges before the morning. We'll see you tomorrow."

"Take care of yourself, Sutton, and Connie."

Sutton placed her phone in the pocket of her long, flowing button-down sweater which she held closed as she stepped back onto the patio. She grabbed the glass of wine she had placed on a table out there and quickly knocked back the rest. She checked her eyes in the reflection of the glass patio door to insure there were no more stray tears, and then went back inside the restaurant and sat down at the table across from Connie.

"You look like you've seen a ghost," Connie said with a worried smile.

"Connie, they think they've found your cousin's body," Sutton said.

Just at that moment the waiter appeared with their entrees. He could sense the somber tension as he placed the meals down. He smiled politely and asked awkwardly, "Is there anything else I can get you ladies right now?"

"More wine," Connie said. "We decided to do the whole bottle."

The waiter nodded his head. "Wonderful, of course. I'll be right back with that for you." He stepped away.

Sutton reached her hand across the table. Connie took her hand in hers. Sutton offered her a soft, sad smile.

They pecked at their food. They drank the rest of the wine. They passed on dessert. Sutton hugged her as they huddled in the cold outside the restaurant waiting for the car.

Back at the B&B, while removing her make-up sitting at the antique vanity, Connie asked, "Where did they find him?"

"Stabler Woods," Sutton said as she began to pre-pack their

bags so they could depart as quickly as possible in the morning.

"I didn't even know he was back in town."

As they later lay in bed together, they both stared at the ceiling, not touching.

"The crown molding is really impressive," Connie remarked. "What do they call this kind? Dental?"

"You don't have to pretend to be interested in this stuff just for me," Sutton said.

"I really enjoyed this weekend with you."

"Me too."

"I'm not going to have to ID the body, am I?"

Sutton sighed. "I'm afraid so." She turned on her side so her eyes focused on Connie. "But I'll be right there with you."

"Was it something other than drugs?" Connie asked, turning on her side to face Sutton now, their breaths merging in the small space between them.

"They don't know yet. I'm assuming there will be a full autopsy. We can find out all that tomorrow at the station."

Connie rolled onto her back again and stuck her fingers in the front of her thick blonde hair. She breathed in and out deeply a few times. She freed her fingers from her hair and then turned on her side again towards Sutton. She said, "I guess I'm lucky to be with someone like you, who already understands all the history. I wouldn't even know where to start."

"You can say nothing, or you can say everything. We can talk about wine or dental crown molding or what we're going to do about the Ramble Lake funk. I'll be here no matter what." Sutton kissed Connie gently on the forehead. "We'll get through this together."

Connie began to cry. "I don't wanna talk about Robbie again."

"I know, I know," Sutton said as she caressed Connie's hair.

After Connie fell asleep, Sutton rolled back to her other side and texted her office manager to reschedule tomorrow's meeting with the university board about the latest archaeological excavation at the gorge. It was going to be a long week.

≈

Tuesday
Connie

Connie unplugged over the weekend as she promised herself she would. She had hoped Sutton would, too, but knew as mayor Sutton never really could. While Connie's phone was off, she missed a series of texts from Amie on Monday morning about Carl's drop-in at the bar and Hank's subsequent scuffle with Carl. She didn't see the texts until the drive home.

"Shit," she said from the front passenger's seat while Sutton drove. Her head was throbbing from all that wine last night. She gulped down half a water bottle. Part of her wished she had driven, then maybe she wouldn't have seen these texts until after the visit to the police station.

"What is it?" Sutton asked.

"Amie texted me on Monday morning that Carl stopped by the bar on Sunday," Connie said.

"Oh, we'll have to tell the police."

"I know, but that's not all."

"What else?" Sutton asked.

"Hank Carter apparently got into a fight with Carl on Sunday night," Connie said.

"How does Amie know that?"

"Oh, c'mon. I know you like to stay above the local gossip, but they've been sleeping together for almost a year now."

"You'll have to tell the police that, too." Sutton said.

"That's hearsay from Amie," Connie shot back.

"They need to question Hank."

"If they're doing their job wouldn't they already be doing that?"

"Have you suddenly forgotten I was a former prosecutor?" It

was a shockingly rude question in the moment, as how could anyone, especially Connie, forget that fact given the high-profile and personal nature of the case with which Sutton Lynn Jackson made a name for herself?

Connie imagined Sutton interrogating her and finding out about Connie's past relationship with Hank. Her stomach was completely in knots now. Denial had allowed her to wake up, eat a decent breakfast, and calmly get in the car for the ninety-minute drive back to West Falls. Watching the cold, flat farmland unfurl outside the window, it hit her all at once. It was like the panic grew out in those wide-open fields overnight, and when it saw her in the car cruising through, it sprung up to devour her.

"You have to tell them everything," Sutton said. "I can be there in the room with you."

"No," Connie was definitive, hoping her directness would redirect her panic and allow her to gather her thoughts.

The last text from Amie was, "Are you okay?"

Connie responded to Amie's text, "I'm heading back to West Falls now with Sutton. I'm sorry I didn't respond earlier, I was unplugged. Thank you for telling me. We'll talk soon." She didn't want Amie to reveal anything else about Hank and his potential involvement, at least not in writing, before Connie talked to the police this morning.

Connie was surprised Amie was up that early and responded immediately. "Okay. Hugs."

At the station, Sheriff Jim Van Patten Jr. personally escorted them to the morgue to identify the body. Connie couldn't help but think how much the sheriff looked just like his dearly departed father Detective "Slim" Jim Van Patten. Just seeing him brought back a flood of memories.

Sheriff Van Patten explained before having the coroner unveil the body underneath the white sheet atop the cold metal slab, "Now, I need to warn you. There are some injuries to his face and upper body."

Then, of course, there was seeing her little cousin, Carl, lying there, bruised and battered, his eyes shut, his body now eternally cold.

"It's Carl," Connie said after a deep breath. She wanted to reach out and touch his face but she held back. She thought about how she wished she had been there for him more, especially recently, but also back then.

Back then all the kids picked on him. All the kids except Robbie Elms and Hap Wolinski. Connie used to babysit Robbie, and he would invite Hap over to play, and sometimes she had to bring Carl along, too. Carl stayed intermittently with her and her father when his parents would be out of town on benders, or when they were home and just couldn't be bothered with him. Robbie and Hap were nice to him when she brought him to Robbie's house. She suspected Hap succumbed to peer pressure at school and would join in the teasing of Carl there, but not Robbie. He was always nice to Carl no matter where they were.

Hank Carter certainly was one of the worst offenders and had all kinds of horrible nicknames for Carl. Connie used to yell at him to get off their lawn when he shouted those terrible things at Carl. She thought Hank was a punk whose bad behavior people let slide because his mother was battling cancer. When she started dating Robbie's older brother, Freddie, she tried to get him to beat up Hank, or threaten him at least. While Freddie agreed Hank was a punk, he was Robbie's friend, and Freddie didn't want to get in the middle of that little kid drama. Plus, Hank's mom had just died.

All this time had passed. All that had changed. Freddie went god knows where. Connie's father left her his iconic hometown bar when he passed. Sutton retired from prosecuting criminals to become mayor and restored West Falls to its former glory after over a decade of hard times. Connie thought Hank had changed over time, too. She had changed. But maybe some things never would. Hank Carter hated Carl Strong with a unique passion. Now Carl was dead.

After her moment with the body, she told Sheriff Van Patten about the texts Amie sent her.

"Would you allow us to look at your phone?" the sheriff asked.

Sutton stepped in, her hand on Connie's arm. "She'll send you screenshots of the texts she referenced. If you require any additional information you believe is housed in her phone that is pertinent to the case, we'll require a warrant."

"Of course," Sheriff Van Patten said. "I am so sorry for your loss, Connie. Thank you for your cooperation as we continue to investigate. We'll keep you posted if any of the leads pan out."

"Thank you, we'll be in touch." Sutton spoke for both her and Connie, and then lead Connie out of the station.

Connie didn't mind. She needed a drink and wanted to get the hell out of there.

≈

Wednesday
Sam

Sam and Val both had to go into the city for work today. Val had to go in an hour earlier than Sam for a special meeting so he walked to the high-speed line and took the 7:30 train while Sam dropped Henry off at daycare and then drove to the high-speed line to catch the 8:30 train. On these days, provided their meeting schedules allowed, Sam and Val would make it a date to grab lunch together at the upscale taco place that sat conveniently between their two office buildings which were seven blocks apart from each other. It gave them something to look forward to, and it had become a little in-joke that Henry could never learn of these mid-week, mid-day dates because he was obsessed with tacos and would be so jealous they went to this place without him.

"Henry must never learn of Center City Taqueria," Val would say with his theatrical mock seriousness.

"We'll take this secret to our graves," Sam would say.

Today Val ran late from a meeting and was flustered when he got to the table. Sam had taken the liberty to order for them already knowing they were tight on time.

"Thanks. Today might not have been the best day for this." Val said.

"We can get the tacos to go if you want," Sam said.

"No, no, the waiting will be the same amount of time," Val conceded. "Oh, hey, you know those two young ladies with the pink and black hair and 1950s' style glasses who are usually on the train with us when we take the 8:30?"

"Yeah, of course," Sam said. "The Twins Who Aren't Twins, Just Creepily Alike and With the Same Questionable Fashion Taste."

"The Single White Females in Mom Jeans, yes." Val laughed. "Well, at any rate, I ran into them on the 19th floor today when I was trying to find a conference room for a last-minute face-to-face with strategic sourcing. *Apparently they have very lax dress code down there.* I had no idea they worked at the same company I did. I felt like such an elitist."

"Because you always assumed they worked somewhere…less professional?" Sam wondered.

"I don't know, I just felt kind of bad," Val said. "Anyway, they were nice and acknowledged me at the coffee bar. Watch, tonight I'm going to realize they live across the street from us."

"*They* don't live across the street," Sam was eager to point out. "They share an apartment on the main strip above that boutique olive oil shop."

"Now we are definitely being elitist."

"No, *you are*," Sam insisted. "I'm not. They really do live there. I saw them walk home from the train station one night."

"Well, anyway, they were talking about that body found in the woods on Monday."

Sam put his drink down and raised his eyebrows. "Oh, did

they identify who it was yet?"

"I don't know. I didn't catch much of what they said."

"That reminds me," Sam continued. "I wanted to check out *Under the Falls* to see what people were saying about it this morning but I forgot."

"You're obsessed with *Under the Falls.*" Val shook his head from right to left repeatedly.

"It's important to know what's going on in the community and what our neighbors are saying."

Val scoffed. "It's a straight-up gossip page."

"People really help people on there, too," Sam insisted. "Like the time people bought all those Christmas presents for that single mom in need."

Val rolled his eyes. "I'll just have to take your word for it."

Sam's face grew somber. "It gives me chills thinking about that body they found."

"That's your White Privilege talking now, Sammy."

The waiter placed the spread of tacos before them, a welcome relief from the conversation that preceded.

"Mmm, looks delicious," Val said, eyes wide. "Henry would love that one." He looked at Sam with a mischievous smile.

They both said in unison in deep voices, *"Henry can never know about this."*

On the train ride home after work, Val listened to some podcast while Sam stared blankly out the window at the world zipping by, thinking about that body in the woods. They were sitting facing backwards, which always gave him a headache. Before reaching West Falls, the train briefly went dark underground before rising back up into the ashes and rambling through Hampten, one of the most crime-ridden and depressed areas in the state. Sam's mind meandered from thoughts of the dead body to Val's earlier off-handed comment about his White Privilege. Sam had never thought about himself that way. Being gay he identified as a minority, but he was also white, grew up middle class and well-adjusted about an hour north of West Falls, and never really had much trouble in his life.

Val, on the other hand, grew up in Hampten. His mother was the daughter of Chinese immigrants who owned a restaurant that was always barely scraping by and went belly-up during the Great Recession. All of that side of Val's family had passed away or moved out west, his mother now famous for her awkward video calls once a month to speak to Henry. His father was a small-time drug dealer who was in and out of jail, and disowned Val when he came out as gay in his teens, which was perfectly fine with Val as his dad had never been around anyway. He was apparently still living in Hampten, less than five miles from where they now lived, but he might as well have been living on the moon – or dead. Val rose up out of all of that by being smart and never looking back, though Sam often wondered how much of it weighed on Val every time they took the train to the city with his hometown just outside the window and considered a cancer on the region. Maybe that's why Val always kept his earbuds in and his eyes forward.

That night after dinner, during *Lounge (on the couch) Hour*, Henry peered over Sam's shoulder while he surfed the *Under the Falls* social media page.

"What are you looking at?" Henry asked in his silly voice, his head cocking back and forth.

"Just catching up on the news around town," Sam said.

"I can read what it says, you know."

"Oh, you can? Well okay, mister, what does it say?"

"It says Daddy and Daddy should make tacos for dinner tomorrow…and every day!"

"Oh, it does, does it?"

Val chimed in from the loveseat catty-corner to the couch, "I think it says it's time for Henry to go to bed."

"Mmm…" Henry jumped off the couch and did a few wandering laps around the living room furniture before finally coming to a pensive stop at the foot of the stairs. "I'll go to bed if we have tacos tomorrow," he announced after giving it much thought.

"And brush your teeth, too?" Val asked.

"Two nights of tacos!"

"The master negotiator."

"How about," Sam chimed in, "Tacos tomorrow and hibachi the next night?"

Henry's eyebrows lifted and he tilted his chin up. "Take-out or with the funny chef?" He was weighing the deal.

"Um, obviously with the funny chef."

"Wait, wait, wait, who said I would agree to this?" Val asked them.

"Oh, I'm not feeling so tired," Henry said with a little giggle.

Sam looked over at Val with *your turn* eyes.

"Alright, you rascal," Val said as he leapt up from the loveseat and acted like he was about to tickle Henry. "It's a deal. Now up to bed." He chased Henry up the stairs. Their boy's kid-wild laughter echoed through the house.

Sam settled in with his laptop and began to scan the one-hundred and forty-two comments to the original thread about the body in the woods from Sunday night. It must've been close to a record for largest thread, although it seemed nothing would ever top the close to two-hundred comments of people piling on that poor lady who complained about the July 4th parade earlier that year. He seemed to find a sweet-spot in the conversation about two-thirds of the way down the thread. It was somebody posting a link to a news article identifying the body as thirty-eight-year-old former West Falls resident Carl Strong.

"That's so sad, I hope it wasn't foul play," someone commented.

"It was probably drugs. Carl used to be the town derelict before he moved away. Surprised he didn't die on the streets of Hampten years ago." another said.

"Carl Strong was trash. Always was. Came from trash. Died

trash," wrote Hank Carter, whose name Sam recognized as the owner of the auto repair shop on the pike.

"It's not polite to speak ill of the dead," someone replied.

"Hank is right-on," another said. "Anyone who knew Carl knew this guy was no good. Still a shame, but Hank has very good reasons for saying what he did. Sadly he ain't wrong."

"I feel bad for Connie and the rest of the family. Carl was always the black sheep," the chorus continued.

Sam scrolled down some more. Someone asked about the last time a body was found, which lead others to chime in about the body of a young boy that was found in almost exactly the same spot back in 1993, and many asked if anyone remembered the name of that boy.

"Yes," Hap Wolinski, a friendly neighborhood handyman who fixed Sam and Val's leaky bathroom sink when they first moved in, jumped in. "That boy was Robbie Elms. He was my best friend. He was murdered on July 4th, 1993."

"Oh Hap! I had no idea!" someone said.

Hap continued, "I still think about Robbie every day. As does anybody who knew him. It will always haunt me. We were all supposed to go to the fireworks show together that night, but Robbie was mad at us over something silly and refused to go. I'll never forgive myself for not making him come with me. He would still be alive today."

"So sad…I'm so sorry…Oh Hap!" the chorus lamented.

"Carl was friends with Robbie, too. Some say Robbie's death is what lead him to drugs," Hap added.

Then Connie Strong, respected local small business owner put an end to the thread, "I understand the desire to speculate, but my family would appreciate it if you could keep your speculations to yourselves and let the police do their jobs. If any of you think you have a serious lead on what happened to my cousin, I encourage you to contact the authorities. I've asked the moderators to shut down this thread. Thank you all who have expressed your sympathies and concerns."

32

EPISODE TWO – BONES

Thursday Morning
Amie

Amie slipped down to the corner coffee shop around 10am, when it usually wasn't crowded after the morning rush dissipated. She sat down at the back corner table beyond the barista station and cash register with her steaming mug of local blend with extra milk and sugar. She was the only customer there and could see anyone come in through the front door from that vantage point. She had been up late last night closing the bar, and she enjoyed the feeling of the warm coffee in her hands as she took nervous little sips, trying to wash away the cobwebs from her mind with a slow drip of caffeine. She was on edge about everything. She almost dropped her mug and leapt out of her seat when Sheila Carter walked through the door.

Sheila avoided eye contact with Amie while she ordered a coffee. She looked disheveled, her heavy winter coat with its faux fur collared hood practically hanging off her. Her hair was frazzled and tied loosely in a ponytail. She wore old sunglasses. Amie couldn't pretend she didn't see her, so she just stared at her head-on.

"Have you seen Hank?" Sheila asked Amie in a slow, calm voice that reminded Amie of her mother's voice when she was addicted to painkillers.

"Not since Saturday night," Amie said while she remained

seated and Sheila stayed standing at the coffee bar.

Sheila laughed under her breath.

"I swear Sheila, I haven't seen him," Amie continued. "I thought I would see him last night, but I didn't. He never texted me or anything."

The barista handed Sheila her fancy iced coffee drink topped with whip cream and caramel. Sheila took a plastic straw and jammed it into the plastic cup. "We're supposed to use reusable straws now, right? And you're supposed to fuck my husband every Wednesday and Sunday night, right?" Sheila sipped the coffee. The barista went wide-eyed, pretended she hadn't heard that and turned to wipe down the other side of the counter.

Amie didn't know how to respond, so she said, "Do you want to sit down and talk?"

"No, I'd rather yell at you from this counter." Sheila sipped more coffee, like a kid would a milkshake. "Just what the hell did you tell the cops about Hank?"

"Nothing, Sheila, I swear. Yes, I told Connie about her cousin stopping by…"

"And about what Hank told you that night? About the incident?"

Amie took a deep breath. "Yes."

"So, Connie told the cops?"

"I can't speak for her."

"So, you and Connie don't tell each other everything, don't share all your secrets? You two don't talk about Hank?"

"I don't know what you want me to say, Sheila."

"I am not the bad guy here!" Sheila threw her arms up, almost sending her coffee drink flying in the process. "Why they hell does everyone act like I'm the bad guy for wanting to know what the hell is going on with *my husband?* Who is fucking *my husband?* Who is talking to the cops about *my husband?*"

"What can I tell ya…you're right. You're not the bad guy. Maybe your husband is just a son of a bitch."

Sheila waved her arms around again like some wounded bird. "If you hear from him, tell him to come home. To call me. Tell him to do me at least *that* courtesy before he goes to the cops." She dropped the coffee and it spilled all over the floor, a sticky, white-foamed mess.

The barista turned around at the sound of the plastic cup hitting the floor.

"I'm sorry," Sheila said to the barista. "I'm sorry." She looked at Amie. She looked up at the ceiling. "I'm sorry!"

"Miss, it's okay," the barista said. "I can get you another one."

Sheila waved her hand dismissively. "Fuck it." She turned and walked back out onto the street.

From the kitchen came a man carrying a brown to-go bag. "I got two breakfast biscuits, one with burnt bacon!" he announced loudly, even though Amie was the only one there. So much for enjoying a solitary coffee while waiting for her order. She left the mug on the table and took the bag from the man.

"I feel like I should help you clean up," she said to the barista.

"Don't worry about it," the barista responded.

"What a piece of work!" the man said loudly, apparently having heard everything from the kitchen.

Amie sidestepped the spilt coffee and left.

Back at her apartment, Hank was still in bed, but awake and sitting up. His legs were slung over the side, hands bracing the edge of the mattress, fingers gripping the sheets. It looked like he had been sitting there for ages, staring pensively through the open bedroom door contemplating an entire lifetime of wrongdoings.

"I thought you might be hungry," Amie said from the living room, holding up the bag to him.

"Thanks," Hank said. "Was that Connie you were on the phone with this morning?"

"Yeah."

"Have they identified how he died yet?"

"They told Connie he had a lot of drugs in his system, enough to overdose. He also had a pretty bad blow to the back of his head."

"Well, I only punched him in the face and the ribs," Hank said. "He walked away from my house on his own accord. If he slipped and fell in the woods and bashed his head…how is that my fault?"

"No one is saying it is."

"I bet the cops are. They've been out to get me for a long time."

"You sound paranoid."

"Why don't you just turn me in?"

Amie shrugged and threw the brown bag on the coffee table. "I'm not even hungry any more. Sheila was in the coffee shop. I told her I didn't know where you were, and I hadn't heard from you since Saturday."

"*The conspiracy thickens.*"

"You need to get your shit straight, go down to the station, and clear this up. If it all happened how you said it did, then you've got nothing to be afraid of."

"*If*…what do you mean *if?* That is how it happened. I'm not letting the cops take me down over some dead junkie."

"Oh, and when did you and Connie have a fling?"

Hank laughed, the same under the breath sarcastic laugh his wife had. "She tell you that? That was a long time ago. Before Sheila and I got real serious. Connie probably still thinks she took my virginity."

Amie walked into the bedroom and knelt at the bedside face to face with Hank. She took his hands in hers. "Look, I don't understand about all this stuff that happened in the past, but don't make people chase you. You can end this drama."

"Will you come with me to the station?" he pleaded with those sad brown eyes of his, like a lost dog.

"Wouldn't it be better if Sheila went with you?"

Hank nodded. "She did witness the fight."

"She wants to back you up, Hank."

"She hates me."

"But she'll back you up if you ask her to go with you."

He nodded again, slowly.

Amie said, "We all want to do the right thing."

≈

Thursday Night
Sam

It was a long day at work with endless conference calls about a mobile app advertisement that had to be pulled due to a complaint from a VIP customer about the model in the ad showing too much of her legs. Sam wanted to take a stand on principle that they were not going to grovel at the feet of one extreme customer with outdated views on what was appropriate and what was not. The model in the ad was lifting her young child with her legs in a playful, family-friendly image that was on brand and would offend no reasonable person. The complaint was escalated high enough that Sam was overruled.

Sam reenacted the details to Val at the dinner table over the much-ballyhooed tacos promised to Henry, who listened along intently as if he understood everything.

"Can I see the picture?" Henry asked.

Sam handed Henry his phone with the offending ad on screen.

Henry regarded it thoughtfully and cocked his head, his mouth still half-full of ground beef and taco shell. "Can I be in the pictures?"

Val laughed. "Henry can be a model and we can both retire early. Become stage parents." He passed Sam another beer, noticing the empty one Sam had been waving around while dramatizing the high points of the incident.

"I really shouldn't," Sam said.

"You really should," Val said.

Henry had commandeered Sam's phone and was now swiping all over the place.

"It's just so disheartening," Sam said.

"I don't know why you are always shocked by these types of things," Val said. "It doesn't surprise me at all. The world isn't nearly as progressive as we would like it to be. It's still the stone age for many people, and they have a big voice right now."

"Hopefully their last gasp. I guess I'm just more of an optimist."

"If that's what you want to call it. I'd call it being naïve, and maybe a little…"

"Don't say it, Val."

Henry put the phone down and was looking back and forth at both his parents. "Say what?" he asked.

Val approached Henry with his hands contorted to be claws. In a funny monster voice he said, "Don't say it's almost time for a bath!" He went in for a tickle and Henry squealed.

"Can I watch just one episode of *Paw Patrol* first?" Henry volleyed back as his opening offer after recovering from the tickle attack. "I should let these tacos digest."

Sam laughed at his son's echoing of Val-like logic and phrasing.

"Okay, just one episode, and then bath time," Val said.

Henry clapped "Yay!" and climbed down from his chair and went into the living room where his tablet was on the couch.

Sam took a long draught from the beer bottle before putting it down on the kitchen island. "You've called me out on my White Privilege twice in the past two days," he said to Val.

"Look, believe me, I get your frustration," Val said. "You just have to learn to pick your battles, especially these days. My people have been doing that for hundreds of years. We're just a little bit ahead of you on that front, that's all." He walked over to Sam and kissed him on the cheek. "I'll take Henry duty again. You enjoy that second beer and relax a bit…simmer down."

Sam gave him a begrudging "thanks." He wanted to say back to Val, "Aren't we – meaning, you, me, and Henry – YOUR people?" Sam wanted to live in a world beyond labels, but hell, he worked in marketing which was all about population segmentation and targeting. Maybe Val was right; maybe Sam was naive. But he'd rather be naive than too hardened to expect anything could ever get better.

Sam cleaned up the dishes, and Val took Henry upstairs after the *Paw Patrol* episode was over. Sam grabbed a third and final beer and sat down at the kitchen island with his laptop. He went on *Under the Falls* to see the latest on the Carl Strong investigation. Someone posted a link to the latest local online newspaper article. Apparently a "person of interest" was questioned at the station this afternoon. The medical examiners had still not yet ruled out homicide.

There was more chatter about the murder of Robbie Elms. Hap Wolinski posted an image of an old picture. "This was taken earlier that summer in 1993 at the opening of the town pool. That's me on the left, Robbie Elms, and Carl Strong. Behind us are Robbie's older sister Laurel and brother Freddie, Connie Strong, and my older brother Pete. It's hard to believe just a few weeks later Robbie would be taken from us."

Everyone in the picture was smiling, even Carl. The three younger boys were soaking wet and had their arms around each other's shoulders. Freddie had his arm around Connie and looked like he was about to lean in for a kiss while she tried to move away from him and laughed. Laurel was smiling, but also looked like she might've just rolled her eyes, probably at Freddie or Pete whose eyes bugged out in a goofy manner.

"I can't believe they never caught the guy who did it," someone commented.

Hap responded, "They did, kinda. They got him many years later on another charge. He's in jail today but not for Robbie."

Someone else posted a link to an article in the local paper from 2008 about the trial of a man named Darrel Strayer:

Today in court at the sentencing of Darrel Strayer was a somber and surprising scene. Strayer was convicted of multiple counts of child sexual assault and possession and distribution of child pornography. Prosecutor Sutton Lynn Jackson made a bold statement when she walked into session this morning with friends and relatives of another alleged victim of Strayer's.

Fifteen years ago, in the summer of 1993, the town of West Falls was torn apart when the body of twelve-year-old Robbie Elms was discovered in Stabler Woods. He had been sexually assaulted before receiving blunt trauma to the back of his head and left for dead. Robbie Elms was a beloved son and brother, straight-A student, former altar boy and star Little League player. His brutal murder sent shockwaves through a community which hadn't had a single homicide in decades.

At the time, evidence began to mount pointing towards West Falls resident Darrel Strayer, but formal charges were never brought forward.

Contacts from the West Falls Police Department expressed the frustration at the time, as it was clear to many on the inside that Strayer was the culprit. Unfortunately, a highly public investigation initially had multiple credible suspects, muddied the water, and thwarted detectives from securing the necessary evidence to put forward charges.

The lead on the case, Detective "Slim" Jim Van Patten made a vow to Robbie's parents, Vera and Burg Elms, he would eventually bring Darrel Strayer to justice.

Today was that day. Detective Van Patten never took his eyes off Darrel Strayer, and he was eventually able to gather credible evidence against Strayer on child sexual assault and pornography charges, and put a stop to Strayer's heinous criminal activities which had culminated in the systematic stalking of young boys over the years on his routine commutes up and down the high-speed line from West Falls into Hampten.

Strayer's defense attorney, Diana Strand, unsuccessfully argued the West Falls Police Department, and Detective Jim Van Patten in particular, had been holding an unfair grudge against her client for years in the wake of the Robbie Elms murder and systematically harassed and entrapped her client, painting Strayer as the victim of mistaken identity and an overzealous police conspiracy.

Detective Jim Van Patten, who along with his son, Officer Jim Van Patten Jr. and Prosecutor Sutton Lynn Strong, encouraged the friends and family of Robbie Elms to attend the sentencing today. The families of the current victims were allowed to provide statements in their plea to impose the maximum sentence on Darrel Strayer. All were given express instructions not to mention Robbie Elms or the previous case for which Strayer was never prosecuted.

It was especially striking to watch these adults, who were children at the time of their friend Robbie Elms' murder, listen to these statements and the judge's sentencing. Many of them were exceptionally poised and well-spoken when questioned after the hearing by reporters. One couldn't help but look at Robbie Elm's childhood friends and think about the type of adult Robbie could've grown up to be.

Darrel Strayer was sentenced today to thirty years (ten years for each sexual assault conviction to run concurrent with the lesser sentences for each of the pornography charges). He will be eligible for parole after serving half of the thirty-year sentence.

"Nothing will ever bring Robbie back, and it's tragic to know this monster was allowed to roam the streets and harm more innocent children," one of those childhood friends, who asked to remain anonymous, was quoted as saying, "but there was justice served today."

"We will forever miss our Robbie," his mother Vera Elms

said. "I'll never be at peace. But at least now I know this monster is behind bars. I hope his other victims can find some peace now."

Sam closed the link, tears forming in the corner of his eyes. The last message on the thread was, "Hey, Hap, isn't this scumbag coming up for parole soon?" He finished off the beer and wiped the tears from his eyes. He scrolled back up to the picture of Robbie Elms and his friends and siblings at the pool. He thought of how Henry had probably stood at the same spot at some point last summer. He turned and noticed Val was already downstairs on the couch watching TV. How much time had passed?

"How was he tonight?" Sam asked.

"Huh?" Val asked.

"Henry. Did he go to sleep okay?"

"He was out like a light as soon as his head hit the pillow."

"Did you leave the new nightlight on for him?"

"Shit…"

"No worries, I'll go get it." Sam closed his laptop and quietly padded up the stairs.

The door to Henry's room was always left open just a crack. It was all darkness on the other side, but he could hear the calm wheezy cadence of his son's breathing from the far corner of the room where he slept on his bed. Sam opened the door half-way and reached in to grab the small remote control resting on the built-in shelf which ran to the edge of the doorframe. He pressed a button, and the kaleidoscope nightlight on the bedside table turned on and cast colorful shadows of dinosaurs gently circling up the walls and ceiling of the room.

Upon hearing the white noise of the machine, Henry sprang up and pretended his arms were dinosaur claws. "Rawr!" he said to Sam, and then he smiled and laid back down, instantly returning to dreamland.

Sam smiled and closed the door.

≈

Friday Morning
Connie

Connie met with the funeral director early in the morning at West Falls Cemetery.

"They still have not released the body," she explained to him. "Hopefully soon."

"Don't worry, as soon as we're given permission to take your cousin's remains, we'll take care of everything from there," he told her.

After they discussed more of the logistics and burial plans, the funeral director left Connie amongst the graves on the hill under the grim gray skies, her hair and scarf fluttering in the blustery wind. She looked down at the empty plot, and then at Carl's parent's graves and her father's, all in a row. There was an empty plot for her, too. She wondered how Carl would feel about being laid to rest here. There would be no Catholic ceremony, and no priest to pray over him. She made sure of that. He would probably rather be buried out there in the woods, where he laid dead, but that type of thing hadn't been legal for a long time.

She walked amongst the rows of tombstones, past the grave of Detective Jim Van Patten Sr. and found the marker for Robbie Elms. Maybe Carl would feel some sense of solace being close to Robbie once again. Atop Robbie's tombstone, held down with a rock, was a printout of an old picture of Robbie and Carl in their Little League uniforms. Underneath was handwritten, "I miss you guys – Hap."

Next to Robbie was his mother's grave, Vera, who passed away after a battle with pancreatic cancer in 2016. Connie thought back to that time in 2000 when Vera had the séance at her house. It was both tragically sad and comical, as the woman leading the séance was obviously cuckoo, and she tried to convince Connie she could talk to her father, who wasn't even dead yet. She remembered how hard she and Vera laughed about it afterwards, hysterical over-tired laughter.

"God, Connie, I am so sorry," Vera said to her between laughs and tears. "I mean what a lunatic that woman was! Remember when she tried to talk to the bird, too?"

Connie could never forget the look on Vera's face after she calmed down from laughing and wiped away her tears, a sudden look of wistful, hopeful sincerity. "I want to thank you and that insane medium. That was the most laughter in this house in over seven years. Robbie used to make me laugh like that all the time, even during all those hard times with Burg."

"Maybe in some crazy way we did conjure him tonight then," Connie offered.

Vera nodded and patted Connie's hand. "I'm sorry things didn't work out between you and Freddie back then, but I'm glad we stayed friends at least."

"Me too, Mrs. Elms," Connie said.

Connie couldn't understand how Vera could stay in that old, empty stone house overlooking Ramble Lake all those years. First Burg moved out, then Robbie was murdered, and then in another few years both Freddie and Laurel moved away, too.

The night of the séance, while they sat on the front porch looking out onto the lake, Vera said to Connie, "I know it might sound strange to some people, but it brings me comfort to be able to look out across the water and into the woods where Robbie spent his last moments. I sometimes imagine him still being there, and maybe he's calling out for me, and I want him to know I'm here. He can always find me here."

Connie wondered, while looking at Vera's final resting place, if they held a séance at the old Elms house today, would they find her still there?

Connie walked down the hill to the edge of the cemetery and the old stone wall that overlooked the gorge. There was a flight of stone stairs (all of these beautiful stone structures were built in the

1930s to employ people on public works projects during The Great Depression) that went down to a viewing ledge and then down to the bottom of the gorge. From this vantage point, you could see the dinosaur bone excavation site on the opposite side of the gorge where tents covered the old marl pit. Connie wondered if in another few million years someone or something would be excavating the human bones that rested above it.

Connie watched as Sutton made her way up the stone stairs to the cemetery and away from the small crowd still gathered near the scaffolding. Sutton was winded by the time she made her way up to Connie, and the wind ferociously whipped her gray hair.

"How was the meeting?" Connie asked.

"Not important right now," Sutton said. "I just got off the phone with Sheriff Van Patten. They've officially ruled out homicide. It was an overdose. They're prepared to release the body."

Connie gave a huge sigh of relief.

"There's other things to still sort out, like the assault. But you can bring Carl home now."

≈

Sunday Afternoon
Hap

The cheesesteaks at Connie's were the best on this side of the bridge. Hap did his best to enjoy this staple of his diet while he sat at the bar, nursing a beer as well. He hadn't had a good night's sleep all week, tossing and turning and lost in thoughts about Robbie and Carl. He tried to focus on the football game on the TV above the bar, but not even that normally relaxing ritual could settle his mind, or stomach.

Hap's older brother Pete, normally all jokes and smiles, came into the bar somberly and sat down on the stool to the right of his brother. Pete put his hand on Hap's shoulder, gave it a gentle squeeze, then patted his back and sighed.

Amie approached them. "The famous Wolinski Brothers, together again," she said, as part of her traditional greeting to the pair, but without the normal flare, as if she was saying it in slow-motion in a dream.

"The famous Ms. Wren," Pete said, forcing a smile. "I'll have what he's having."

"You got it," Amie said

"I saw the sign on the door," Pete said to her. "Connie's closing the place for the funeral tomorrow?"

"Yeah, and then inviting anyone who wants to come back here after the burial."

"It's nice she's putting him out there on the hill next to his folks."

"I guess…I heard they weren't exactly the greatest set of parents to have."

"Yeah, I guess Connie would know better than anyone else," Pete said. "They were older than most parents, ya know, and most assumed they were sick or something. Other kids never really saw them much, and Carl was usually with Connie's dad. He's the one that brought him to school and Little League practice and all that. Man was a saint. But when you're a kid you don't think about why or what was going on with another kid's parents. You just accept it. Still, it's nice he'll be out there with family."

Hap chimed in to stop Pete from rambling like he always did. "Is Connie expecting a big turnout?"

"Who knows. I wouldn't think so." Pete pondered.

"Well, the three of us will be there," Hap said.

"You never know whose gonna crawl out of the woodwork at times like these," Amie mused. "Anyways, let me get you that beer and put in the sandwich order." She disappeared into the kitchen.

Hap turned to his brother, "Have you heard from Freddie Elms at all?"

"Someone said he was on Facebook under an alias awhile

back but never posts," Pete said. "Doubt he knows about any of this, wherever the hell he might be."

"And Laurel…do you ever hear from her?"

"Somebody was saying she was on Instagram and Twitter for like work shit. But I don't mess with that. I never heard from her directly…not since the day she left."

Hap nursed the beer some more. He hadn't meant to bring up a sore subject, but he couldn't help but ask in the wake of Carl's death. He thought Freddie and Laurel should know, but it was unfair to think notifying them should be Pete's or anybody's responsibility. There was probably a better chance of Hap or Pete being struck by lightning than there was of Freddie or Laurel showing up in West Falls again.

Pete had pulled out his phone and was checking his texts, always his sign of not wanting to talk about the subject at hand anymore. He smiled and laughed as he scrolled through some group chats.

"What's so funny?" Hap asked him.

"Oh, it's just this poor bastard who accidentally wound up in my fantasy football league group chat," Pete said.

"Oh, I remember being part of that league before I couldn't take it anymore," Hap laughed. "You guys are brutal. How did this poor soul happen upon your own little sad corner of hell?"

"Remember Bill? He was in the league when you were, and he moved to Houston for that big new job last year. Well, we still had his old number in our group text, but turns out he changed his number, and the number that used to be his was recycled and being used by some poor dude from Belgium, no less, who comes to this area for work a lot, and so…voila…there he is bustin' into the group text one day and sayin' 'Uh, hey, just so you know, this isn't Bill, but you guys are cracking me up.'"

"What kind of sadist is this guy?"

"I know, right. So we start busting his balls and saying how once you're in our league you can never leave, and that was Bill's mistake. You know, like we killed Bill. Anyways, long story short, this guy is actually going to be in the city for work near the season closer so we're inviting him."

"Oh, that poor son of a bitch."

Amie came back with Pete's beer and placed it down in front of him.

"Yup," Pete said.

The brothers lifted their bottles and drank slow, long draughts in unison and then placed the bottles back down, the glass bottoms clanging on the bar top like the rare splashes of synchronized swimmers.

"I think I'm gonna start a petition to keep that fucking piece of shit Darrel Strayer in prison. You know, something we can take to his next parole hearing," Hap said.

"I'm in," Pete said. He turned to his brother and their eyes met, his hand gripping Hap's shoulder. "Just tell me what you need me to do."

≈

Monday Morning
The Funeral

There was no church service or viewing at the funeral home. People were told to meet at the cemetery. It was a beautiful day, sun shining, blue skies dotted with whimsical streaks of fluffy clouds. A strong breeze kept the top of the hill in late autumn's grasp, and the ground was becoming hard. The crowd was thin and streaky like the white clouds above them, but it was there, the community forgiving Carl for his lot in life, wanting to close another dark chapter and support Connie in moving on.

Hap and Pete stood on the periphery while the people gathered near the tent over the open grave where Connie stood with the closed casket. Mayor Jackson and Amie were at her side. Hap noticed Sam Vaughan, a guy he had done some handyman jobs for in the past and who was quite active on *Under the Falls* standing on the far opposite end. Sam looked a little lost, like he wasn't quite sure he should be there.

"I'm gonna go say hi to that guy," Hap said to Pete.

Pete nodded and stayed standing like a statue on the hard ground while Hap walked around to the other side and approached Sam.

"Hey, man, it's nice of you to show up," Hap said as he extended his hand. "I didn't realize you knew Connie that well."

Sam shook Hap's hand and said, "Yeah, well, you know, I don't really, but I saw all the posts on *Under the Falls* and it just got to me. I wanted to show up, do something. It's just all so tragic."

Hap nodded approvingly. "Well, it really means a lot. I know you guys are still relatively new to the community, but that's what we do for each other, you know, show up."

"It's literally the least I could do. Oh, god, I'm such a fool. I'm so sorry for your loss. I know, I mean I read, how you and Carl were good friends."

"Thank you. When we were kids, yeah, but…well, you know. He took a different path in life." Hap paused and then said, "Hey, you're in marketing or something like that, right?"

"Yeah," Sam replied.

"Do you do like websites and stuff?"

"Well, I mean, I have experience with that. It's not really what I do now, it's more complicated…"

"No, no, I get it. It's just I'm wanting to start a petition to keep Robbie's killer, Darrel Strayer, in jail."

"Yeah, I saw you posting that last night. Tell me where to sign."

"Well, I kinda need help getting the word out. I mean as good as *Under the Falls* is for that stuff, I wanna do it on the up and up, ya know. I don't know if there are petition websites I could use, or if I should do my own website."

"Oh my god, yes! I can help with that…I mean are you asking

me to help with that? I totally would."

"Look, Sam, I don't mean to impose on you. But yeah. We got some time, you know, before he's up for parole. But I really want do this right, put this fucker on blast, and get the whole community involved."

Sam nodded his head enthusiastically, but then toned it down a little, given the setting. "Yeah, look, you still have my contact info from the work you did for us, right? Let's set up some time to talk it through and get started."

"Oh, I would be forever indebted to you if you helped with this. If there's still shit you guys need done around the house…I mean, I'll hook you up, you know."

"Don't say another word. You don't owe me anything. I haven't done anything…yet. But, oh man, I love this kinda grass roots stuff. And if I can help the community find some peace…"

The two men hushed when they saw the funeral director hand Connie a microphone.

"I'm going to keep this brief," Connie said, her voice shaky under the wind, but still loud enough. "Carl did not have an easy life. For most of our childhood I was more like his older sister than a cousin while he spent as much time staying with us as not. His father, my uncle, used to tell these crazy stories about being a roadie for Jim Croce, like that was his proudest accomplishment. And Carl listened to Jim Croce songs all the time, thinking maybe if he loved the music, his father would love him, too. I think this song speaks for itself. I'm sorry, Carl."

Over the small speaker set by the coffin, Jim Croce's "I Have to Say I Love You in a Song" played while the casket was slowly lowered into the ground.

≈

Connie's Place

An hour later, a decent sized crowd, more than what had

shown up at the burial, gathered at Connie's Place in support of Connie. Sutton had to take care of some official mayoral business back at town hall, but promised to stop by later and take Connie home. Meanwhile, old and new friends had crawled out of the woodwork, as Amie had suspected, waxing about old times and new problems. Connie was in her element without Sutton's official presence. It was like the good ol' days when her dad was at the helm. The drinks were plentiful. Stomachs were full. Cheeks were red. Laughter was hearty. The music was loud.

But the mood shifted as the Wolinksi brothers started talking about Robbie. They were in the corner of the bar by the entrance, and at first Connie couldn't hear them. Amie was the first to tune in. She tried to give them a look, like, *hey guys, try to be sensitive here*. She started to move away from Connie and towards them to intervene on their topic of discussion, and that's when Connie noticed. Connie looked over at Amie and the brothers. She started to nod with her whole body, this look of defeatist knowing crawling across her brow and her mouth. It seemed like no one from those years could gather in this town without the pall of Robbie Elms hanging over the place.

Hap saw Connie's face and the change in her demeanor. The other conversations in the bar went quiet. There was just the music, Tom Petty's "Learning to Fly", and clearing of throats. Hap started to get blubbery, the bar like his therapist's office. "Robbie loved this song," he said, and he started to cry.

Connie nodded. "It's okay, Hap. It's okay."

"It's been a long, hard day," Amie tried to intervene. "Maybe we start clearing out? Let Connie get some rest."

"No, no, Amie, I know it's hard for you to understand. This is tradition," Connie said, turning herself toward the larger crowd. "Did I ever tell you all the story of when Robbie and Laurel were younger...like maybe eight and ten, and I had just turned old enough to start babysitting. And Mr. and Mrs. Elms, oh man, they still loved going out back then. To a show in the city, a movie, dancing, drinking. And I would go over there and watch Robbie and Laurel on Friday or Saturday nights. Even though Freddie was the same age as me and sure as hell old enough to watch them, but they didn't trust him." She laughed at the thought of a thirteen-year-old Freddie, well before they started dating.

Connie went on, "Well this one night, Freddie was just up in his room listening to music. Shit, it might've been Tom Petty. Or more likely something harder. Guns & Roses maybe. And Robbie and Laurel were with me in the living room watching scary movies. It must've been summertime because I remember the windows were open, and there was that smell in the air, ya know? Electric and warm. And the curtains were suddenly blowing, and the wind whipping around, and a huge thunderstorm rolled through and knocked the power out. I fumbled around in the dark to the kitchen, and got a flashlight to go check the circuit breakers in the basement. Now, most of you probably know the old stone Elms house overlooking Ramble Lake, well over a hundred years-old…and that basement was creepy as hell in the daytime let alone at night during a thunderstorm. But what else was I supposed to do? Freddie was no goddamn help, that's for sure. God knows what he was doing up in his room. So, of course the kids are grabbing on me and coming down with me because they're too scared to be left alone in the living room. And I knew the fuse box was in the one corner because Vera had showed it to me the first time I babysat telling me about the crazy old wiring in the house and sometimes you just needed to flip a breaker. So, I'm shining the light on the fuse box and fussing around with it to no avail, and one of the kids is pulling on my shirt and I drop the flashlight. And now it's on the ground shining a light directly on the oldest, dustiest, cobweb-covered corner. And wouldn't you know it…their names…Robbie's and Laurel's are carved into the damn stone. But it looks old as hell. And I turn to them like *when did you little brats do this?* But they said they didn't do it.

"The lights came back on not too long after that. And the kids fell asleep on the couch. And when Mr. and Mrs. Elms came home I asked her about it. She tells me the story, at first I thought just to spook me, ya know, but then I realized she was dead serious…those names were carved in there when they bought the place! Now most of you probably know they bought that place when it was all dilapidated and they learned that *way back when* it was owned by the original Elms family in like the 1880s or something. So, it seemed like fate. And then those names carved in the block…that was like fate, too. Apparently one of those relatives from back then had a middle name Laurel, and they assumed there was a Robert, too, probably, ya know, it being a pretty common name. But that's where they got their names from. When they bought the house they only had Freddie. Then came Laurel and Robbie. Now how many of you knew that? About how they came up with their names?

"Of course, there were plenty of other times Mrs. Elms tried to spook me with stories about that old house. At times she swore there was a ghost there. She thought it might be the original owner. And then, of course, years later after everyone was gone but her, she and I did that séance. To see, ya know, if she could talk to Robbie. But that psychic was a nut job so of course she didn't sense anyone…not the original owner…not Robbie. But I dunno, sometimes I still wonder…"

The crowd had been hanging on Connie's every word, and she had been so focused on telling the story, that no one noticed Hank and Sheila Carter had come into the bar. Well, no one except Amie, who nudged Connie and broke the spell that had been cast on the hushed crowd.

"Oh, that's rich," Hank's words were slurred and angry. "Here she is, everyone's favorite storyteller, Connie Strong. But she's full of shit, always been, always will be." He pushed his way through the crowd up to the bar as close as he could get to Connie and Amie. Sheila feebly tried to pull on his arm and bring him back. "I didn't do nothing to that piece of shit cousin of yours…nothing he didn't deserve. But I sure as hell didn't kill him!"

"No one's saying you did, Hank," Pete offered.

"But you sure did beat the shit out him, just like you always did," Hap followed.

"Why can't you two just ever shut the fuck up?" Hank turned to them. "This is between me and Connie." He turned back to Connie and Amie.

Amie looked beyond him at Sheila shrinking back into the crowd. "Can't you get him the hell out of here?" Amie pleaded.

"Fuck you!" Sheila shouted back.

"Shut up, both of you!" Hank screamed. "All of you!"

"It doesn't have to be like this, Hank," Connie said.

"You thought you were hot shit back then, but you took advantage of me," Hank spat as he pointed his finger at her. "I'm not going to let other people take advantage of me anymore. Not you, not these damn punk kids in this town, not anyone!"

The main entrance to the bar behind the crowd creaked open. "Hank, why don't get out of here before you make any more of a fool of yourself," Sheriff Jim Van Patten Jr. boomed.

Sheila grabbed Hank's arm and pulled him back towards the door where Sheriff Van Patten stood. The sheriff took his other arm and leaned in close, whispered something in Hank's ear.

Amie watched closely at the interaction. By the look in Hank's eyes, she imagined the hair on the back of his neck was standing on end.

Hank and Sheila slinked out of the bar, and someone turned the music up. Another Tom Petty song.

Amie turned to Connie, who gave Amie a look like *get rid of him, and fast, girl.* But Amie couldn't help but wonder what Hank meant when he said Connie had taken advantage of him back then…when they dated briefly…and then the remark about the punk kids. What the hell was he talking about?

≈

Amie & Hank

Hank showed up at Amie's door around midnight with a swollen right eye, bloodied lip, and just all around looking like he'd been beaten to hell.

After the melodrama at Connie's Place, he was honestly the last person Amie wanted to see, but she instantly went into doting girlfriend mode as she quickly but gently ushered him inside. "What in the world happened to you?" she asked.

"Some black kid jumped me outside the shop," he said.

Amie had him sit down on the couch as she grabbed some ice from the kitchen. She wrapped cubes in a dishtowel to place over his eye to hopefully keep it from becoming completely swollen shut.

"What in the hell for?" she asked as she sat down on the arm of the couch and leaned against him. She didn't know if she should touch him or rub his back. She didn't know where else he might have injuries. He didn't wince as she leaned.

"Because I stopped dealing to them," Hank said, exasperated and still obviously drunk. "I can't have the cops pulling me in for that while they've been questioning me about Carl."

Amie leaned way back, as far as she could without falling off the arm of the couch, a shocked look on her face mixed with anger. "*Dealing what*, Hank Carter?"

"Don't start on me. It's not like I'm selling them hard stuff or fucking fentanyl. Just some pain pills I get with the prescriptions Sheila and I have had for years…and some weed. Can you believe this kid jumped me because he couldn't get his fix of fucking weed? Like he can't get that or anything else under the sun right down the road in Hampten? Shit, Amie, I've been doing this for years to try to keep these damn kids safe. I'm their safe dealer. I coached 'em when they were in pee wee football. Their parents bring their cars to my shop to get fixed. I don't want them out there on the streets of Hampten trying to score shit."

Amie was shaking her head in disbelief. She got up off the couch and went back into the kitchen. She began to vape while pacing back and forth in the confined space. "This explains a whole lot. Jesus Christ, Hank."

Hank just sat there holding the cold, wet dishtowel to his eye with his head down. At a loss for words. Then his shoulders started heaving up and down. It took a moment, but Amie realized he was crying.

"Jesus, Hank," she said more softly now as she came back over to the couch to put her hand on his shoulder.

Amie comforted him, neither of them speaking, until the sobs subsided. She then helped him out of his clothes and lead his bruised body into a steaming hot shower. Afterwards, she nursed his wounds in bed with more ice, and she laid down beside him.

"How fucking pathetic am I?" Hank asked her, or himself, or nobody at all, as he stared up at the cracks in the ceiling. "And it all goes back to Robbie. Nobody ever wants to talk about Robbie, but then anytime anyone else dies, people talk about nothing but Robbie. This whole town is still all fucked up over what happened to Robbie. I should've left like his brother and sister did. They were the smart ones. They didn't want to end up losers in this loser town. They knew the only way they could ever escape their brother's ghost was to get the fuck out."

Amie inched a little closer to him but didn't want to roll over and lay her head on his chest because of the bruises on his ribs. She regarded the cracks in the ceiling and imagined them opening up into the sky full of light pollution. She wanted to ascend beyond and disappear into the stars. She came back down to the room, to the sound of Hank's heavy breathing, and his deep, pregnant pause. She took a deep breath, and then said, "Tell me more. Tell me everything. You gotta get this out."

"If you think I'm gonna tell you that priest molested me…" Hank was quick to level-set.

"Then tell me what happened. If that wasn't it, Hank, what

the hell happened? I know this kid Robbie was murdered. I read the stuff on *Under the Falls* from Hap. I mean, I know you picked on Carl back then, but all of you…Robbie, Hap, Carl…you were all friends, right?"

"I mean we were all from the neighborhood…not sure we were friends. Robbie was friends with everyone. After he was killed in that way he was killed…it tore this town apart. Everyone was affected. We couldn't believe it could happen here, and to him. Of all people…of all us kids. He was the best of us, and the rest of us were rotten. His parents divorced. His dad went off somewhere for a job…Europe, I think. The sister Laurel, I think joined the dad. And Freddie, the older brother, got the fuck out of dodge after graduation…like I'm talking the night of. Left Connie laying in her graduation gown in the middle of the night after partying hard out in the woods, as he sped off in his piece of shit car, like something from a damn Bruce Springsteen song. And I know the details of this because she told me this a few years later, when I was seventeen and entering my senior year, getting served by Connie at her dad's bar. And she knew I was vulnerable and still all fucked up, and she knew Shelia and I had been hot and cold and she took advantage of me, Amie. People think girls… women…can't take advantage of boys like men have done to girls for all of time, but they can. And she did it with that in mind, to get back at every man that had ever taken advantage of a girl, and to get back at me specifically because of how I had treated Carl. And I was young and dumb and raring to let her do it, and, boy, did she do a number on me."

"Look, Hank, I get it. There's some bad blood between you and her because of some star-crossed torturous fling when you two were kids…" Amie said.

"I was still a kid. She was a grown ass woman."

"And what, it pisses you off she wanted to be with women after that?"

"Don't trivialize this. Don't let her off the hook because you think she's some god-damned saint."

"I don't think Connie's a saint. I think she's like everyone, seen her fair share of shit, done her fair share of shit, but when you look at the ledger of her life she's probably one of the best of us like this kid Robbie was…as fucked-up as we all are anyways."

"And what do you think of me?"

"I don't know, Hank. I think you're a guy who has been through some shit and is going through a midlife crisis, and your wife…I mean, Sheila is a mess, and you two are either perfect for each other or absolute poison for each other, and you gotta figure out which one it is, quick, before you both spiral into the abyss."

"Wow, ain't you deep? Ms. Out-of-towner therapist/barmaid. *The abyss.*"

"Oh, I'm sorry. Do fancy words scare you? Apologies for reading. And c'mon, Hank, am I lying?"

Hank lay there silent for a moment. He startled to sniffle, like he was holding back more tears. "Sheila was my rock after Connie did what she did to me. I really loved her. Never quite understood why she loved me. Maybe she saw something broken she thought she could fix. I mean, ain't that always the way with women and bad boys? And we were pretty happy in those early years. But you know, as time went on, the honeymoon faded and she really wanted kids. I said I wanted them, too, but only because she said she did. I wanted her happy. *Happy wife, happy life,* as they say. But deep down the idea horrified me. What if we had a kid and something horrible happened to them like what happened to Robbie? Or what if I did horrible things to them and fucked 'em all up like Carl's parents did to him? And so, when she struggled to get pregnant, I thought, maybe this was the way it was supposed to be. But she wanted to get treatments, ya know, and we did the whole nine yards, and she got pregnant, but then miscarried. And it was just too much for her to bear. So, we stopped trying after that, and were in big-time debt now from all that fertility stuff."

Amie offered softly, "I had no idea."

"But we were still in love, ya know. Like we had gone through it together, even though all the pain was on her end. I was just…there. And we made plans to save up and travel and find other ways to fill the hole left behind. I guess, though, she was just fucked up like me now. And slowly, over time, it was the little things that just started building up. The little…I dunno, resentments? I got her flowers, she would just let 'em die. I took her out to a nice restaurant on the strip, she would just sit there staring out the window at the people passing by on the sidewalk, barely touching her food. I would always take her car in the shop and get it detailed and make sure I put in a full tank of gas…man, she is horrible about letting the tank go past E. And I swear to god…*not once*…not once did she ever thank me or even acknowledge it. I mean, sure, your husband owns an auto shop, it's expected he take care of your car, but the full tank of gas, that was a little something extra I did because I knew how forgetful she was about it, and I thought…I just wanted her to appreciate it."

Amie was sitting up now, her back propped against her pillows. "I dunno, Hank. Maybe she did but was just too depressed to express it. And maybe two people just fall out of love over time. Maybe two broken people just can't be together."

Hank strained to sit up, to be at the same level as Amie, but he was too sore. He resigned himself to being on his back. "Are you talking about Sheila and me, or you and me now?"

Amie laughed a little under her breath. "Shit, Hank. I ain't broken. I'm just passing through and was looking for a good time. And this sure as hell ain't it anymore."

"What are you trying to say? You don't wanna do this anymore? Is it because I couldn't get it up the other night? There's stuff to fix that, easy. I ain't ashamed. I'll get rock hard for you and we can do it all night long."

"Hank, please, stop. It's not that." She gestured to his battered body and then to the air between them. "It's *this. All this drama.* What the hell are you doing? My advice: stop messing with those damn kids. And get some therapy. You and Sheila. Figure your shit out."

Amie got out of bed. "You can stay here tonight. I'll sleep on the couch." She grabbed her pillows and a blanket draped over the chair in the corner.

"Amie…wait…c'mon!" Hank was sitting up now, wincing, and clearly in excruciating pain.

In the bedroom doorway, Amie turned back to him. "Good night, Hank. I'll see you in the morning."

Hank laid back down and shifted until he found the least painful position. The gentle patter of rain could be heard on the windowsill. He wondered when had it started raining? It quickly increased in intensity and sounded like hail on the roof. He stared up at the crack in the ceiling by the far corner closest to the window. He swore he could see water seeping in, darkening the ceiling around the crack. He was waiting for a drop of water to hit the floor underneath the crack. He closed his eyes, waiting for that drip. He imagined the rain ceaseless, and then coming in through the roof like a waterfall. Flooding the room. Taking his battered body away. It was the most peaceful feeling he had in years.

EPISODE THREE – CONFESSIONALS

December 1992
Laurel

Whitney Houston's "I Will Always Love You" overwhelmed the gymnasium. Laurel Elms sat in the half-dark at the top of the bleachers on the far end of the gym, free from the spinning lights of the glittering disco ball dangling from the ceiling over center court, and far from the pull-out stage on the opposite end where the DJ lazily went through all the current hits. Most kids were congregated on the dark edges of the gym, gossiping. A few slow-danced over-passionately under the ball as if this moment, this song, was what they had been waiting for all their young lives to make a statement of their unending love for each other. A couple sloppily made out on the top row of the bleachers about twenty feet from Laurel. Beneath the bleachers were the familiar sounds of kids giggling and sneaking drinks from flasks or tiny airline bottles, thinking the music was providing cover for the sounds of their misbehaving. Teacher chaperones shined their flashlights around in hopes of squashing any fun. Laurel simply watched it all.

This was the West Falls High Winter Dance - or Jam, as it was called this year by the planning committee trying to be cool - less formal than homecoming, traditionally a big deal for freshman and sophomores, but upperclassmen usual only went as a goof. Laurel, a freshman, hadn't planned on going, but her brother, Freddie, and his girlfriend, Connie, both juniors, convinced her to go.

"Come with us…ironically," Connie said. "Forget about those other little kids in your class. Hang with the juniors."

"Yeah, what else do you have to do on a Saturday night?" Freddie teased. "Gonna just sit at home and wait for Mom and Dad to get into a huge fight again?"

They were decked out in their grungiest wares. Connie lent Laurel an AC/DC t-shirt, and Freddie gave her one of his flannels to go over it. The ripped jeans completed the look. Connie helped Laurel tease and style her hair in that big, flopped-over-to-one-side look.

"You look like Shelly the waitress," Connie said, delighted by her work, and referencing the character from that TV show they all watched awhile back, *Twin Peaks*, about the murdered homecoming queen. Freddie and Connie thought it was hilarious, but Laurel just found it sad, especially when it turned out the dad did it. Nobody watched it after that. It made Laurel feel queasy, as in the epic war of the Elms, she had been firmly planted on Dad's team, but now all dads – all men, really – were suspect to her. She started calling Dad and Mom by their first names, and everyone just accepted it as a surly, freshly-minted high-schooler quirk.

Finally, the Whitney Houston ballad-to-end-all-ballads was over, easing Laurel's suffering. There was that odd ear ringing clamor left behind, like you could suddenly eavesdrop on a hundred different conversations that had been happening in the shadows and now echoed off the gymnasium walls. The tongue smashing of the couple on the bleachers was nauseatingly loud, and the giggling shot takers below might as well have been yelling, "Hey, here we are! Drinking schnapps! Come over here and give us detention please!"

A ruckus emerged from somewhere, and suddenly Freddie and his obnoxious best friend Pete were rampaging up onto the stage with some other fools from their class. Freddie went over to the DJ and got him to go along with whatever their plan was, and

Pete took the microphone and yelled, "This one's for you, Laurel Elms!"

Laurel flipped them the middle finger thinking it unlikely they could see her.

Nirvana's "Smells Like Teen Spirit" was now blasting beyond the capabilities of the speaker system like some screeching anthem for the soon-to-be-deaf. A whole swarm of juniors came out of nowhere and attempted a mosh pit in front of the stage while Freddie and Pete thrashed about like madmen. It was complete pandemonium.

Laurel descended from her perch atop the bleachers. Some of the *I'm so drunk from just a few sips* kids from underneath were stumbling out.

"Laurel! I can't believe they just said your name!" the bright, chirpy redhead from her algebra class exclaimed as she came out from under the bleachers. She was wearing a puffy, white winter coat with a faux-fur collar and hood over a ridiculously too-tight mini-dress. Sensibly, at least she had on sneakers. The coat was apparently to hide her flask.

"I love your coat!" Laurel yelled over the loud music with a big, fake smile plastered on her face. "Can I try it on?"

"Sure," the girl said as she slipped it off and handed it to Laurel.

Laurel took the coat and ran. Ran as fast as she had ever run, down the brightly lit hallway outside the gymnasium. Behind her a teacher yelled, "Hey, no running, young lady! Where are you going? You need to sign out!"

Laurel spilled out the front entrance into the cold December night. It had started to snow, and a light dusting coated the grass and cars but wasn't sticking to the sidewalks or roads yet. Laurel slipped comfortably into the coat, but her hair was almost too big to fit under the hood. She struggled to get it situated. She then reached into the inside pocket and pulled out that dumb girl's flask. Laurel knew that old teacher wasn't going to follow her outside, so she boldly sat down on the top of the front steps under the awning protecting her from the falling snow and took a swig of whatever nasty drink the girl had in the flask. She was surprised to find it tasted like her dad's whiskey. She could still faintly hear Nirvana behind the closed doors, filtering out into the hallway.

"No moshing!" Laurel imagined the disciplinarian yelling over a bullhorn, trying to break up the mayhem.

Suddenly the door opened behind her. Laurel quickly capped the flask and concealed it in the coat. She stood up and started walking down the steps, not looking to see who it was that came out the door.

"Hey, Laurel, wait up!" a familiar, hoarse voice called out behind her.

Pete sidled up beside her as she began walking down the sidewalk. "I saw you flip us the finger back there," he said in a fake stern voice. "You think we couldn't see up there in the dark, but we could."

"Don't you need to get back in there with your mosh pit buddies?" Laurel said as she tried to walk at a faster pace.

"What're you doing? Can I walk you home?"

"Pete, I'm not in the mood."

Pete gently grabbed her arm and stopped in his tracks, almost slipping on the wet pavement. Laurel turned around and allowed him to balance himself on her. "You know it's not so bad, high school. It'll get better. You just gotta stop thinking you're better than everyone, that it's all so boring, and find ways to make your own fun."

"Gee, thanks for the pep talk, Dad," Laurel mocked him.

"Why are you always so sad? I can't stand to see you so sad. It makes me want to kiss you." Pete leaned in to kiss her, but Laurel forcefully shoved him away. He almost lost his balance again.

"Damn, you been drinking? I can smell it on you." Pete said, trying to deflect from the rejection.

"Go back to the Winter Jam, Pete. Tell Freddie and Connie

not to worry about me. I'm just tired, and I'm going home."

"Okay, okay. You don't have to tell ol' Petey Boy twice." Pete slowly backed up, pivoted, and then ran back to the high school.

Laurel pulled the coat more tightly closed around her neck. *What the hell?* It smelled like Freddie's Coolwater cologne. She walked briskly down the sidewalk and rounded the corner at St. Mary's Catholic Church. The steepled bell tower looked meditative against the backdrop of the night sky gently speckled white by the lightly falling snow. It was eerily quiet, except for Laurel's sloshing footsteps. She stopped to breathe in the cold, fresh air. Laurel found some sense of commiseration with the world at this time of year. That odd, rushed calm between Thanksgiving and Christmas, where time sometimes stood still trying to decide. *Would winter break be peaceful or chaos?* Adults running around planning, shopping, spinning. Kids preparing for midterms trying not to explode with the anticipation. When you were little, it was all about the gifts to come, but for teenagers it was all about the break between Christmas and New Year's. The anticipation of either sleeping in and choosing to be dead to the world, or partying like it's the end of the world.

Hushed boyish laughter close by broke Laurel's train of thought and pierced the peaceful quiet. Laurel stealthily traipsed across the snow-covered side-lawn along the far end of the church and braced herself against the stone wall. She crept slowly to peer around to the front of the church where they had put out their manger scene. She saw two boys with their backs to her standing over the baby Jesus. One she instantly recognized as her younger brother, Robbie. She thought at first the other must be Hap Wolinski, who was inseparable from Robbie, but she then realized it wasn't Hap. It looked like that weird kid, Carl Strong. She watched as they both unzipped their pants and began to pee all over the baby Jesus. They were both trying to muffle their laughter as they did it. Once they were done, Carl said, "Fuck you." The boys zipped up and then ran as fast they could down the street.

Laurel couldn't believe it. What would possess them to do that? It was completely atypical behavior from golden child Robbie. And what the hell was he doing hanging out with Carl Strong on a Saturday night? She wondered if her parents even knew he was out, or if they just thought he was at Hap's house like he always was.

Laurel walked the rest of the way home and went to the basement to watch TV. About three years ago, her father decided to finish the basement, which around here was quite an endeavor because of the high water table. It was all too common for basements to get water in them, and most of these older homes had unfinished basements with low ceilings and dirt floors. But her father dug down to get more headspace, installed French drains and sump pumps, and then fully finished the space to be a teen hangout area complete with a big sectional couch and big-screen TV. It took god-knows how much money to complete. It had become a huge piece of contention between her parents.

"These kids are gonna drink and wanna party," Burg said to Vera. "I'd rather them do it here in our home and be safe."

It was essentially Freddie and his friends' space, but they would be after-partying at Connie's house tonight since her dad would be working until closing time at the bar. So, Laurel could have the basement to herself watching MTV and enjoying the stolen booze from that dumb girl's flask.

At some point she heard her parents starting to argue upstairs. She wondered how many plates and glasses would get smashed tonight. She turned up the volume on the TV, but then Robbie must've just come home, and he was now coming down to the basement.

"Hey, where did ya get that coat?" Robbie asked loudly over the din of the TV.

It was pretty cold in the basement so Laurel had kept the stolen coat on.

"None of your business," Laurel replied. "Where have you been?"

Robbie shrugged his shoulders. He took off his shoes but kept his coat on and plopped down on the couch next to Laurel. He had that mischievous grin on his face, his charming trademark since he was a little boy. "I dunno, just out."

"Out with Hap?"

"Naw, Hap chickened out. I was with Carl. We had all planned to sneak down to the dig site tonight and try to see some of those dinosaur bones. But Hap backed out at the last minute, so it was just me and Carl."

Laurel nodded her head. "Oh, I see."

"What, you don't believe me?"

Laurel turned the TV down a bit so they didn't have to talk so loudly to hear each other. At this point she didn't care if they could hear their parents upstairs. She pulled her legs up criss-cross and turned to face her brother. Robbie did the same. She pulled the flask out from the coat, uncapped it and took a big swig. She held it out to Robbie.

"Naw, I'm good," he said.

"Oh, c'mon. Stop being such a good boy," Laurel teased him. "Everybody in this house is getting drunk on the regular except you. Take a little sip."

Robbie bounced his head back and forth weighing his options, then smiled and took the flask. He took a little sip and winced. Then he took another.

"Hey, hey, now, don't get carried away." Laurel grabbed it back from him. "Okay, it's confessional time."

Robbie sighed and then laughed in that aw-shucks style he had honed. "Ya got me, sis. But you first."

"Fair enough. Pete Wolinski tried to kiss me!"

Robbie threw his whole body back and then threw his hands up to his face and shook his head. "No, no, no, no, no, no! Say it ain't so!"

"Oh, it's so. Don't tell Hap his brother tried to kiss me."

Robbie brought his hands down from his face. "Your secret's

safe with me. Did you let him do it?"

"Hell no, I wouldn't let that fool kiss me! Now tell me, what did you and Carl do after you checked out the big dig?"

"Nothing. That was it. The secret was Carl had snuck some rum from his parent's stash and was pretty much drunk."

"And that's it? Just innocent little Robbie and his drunk weirdo friend checking out dinosaur bones?"

"Yeah, typical Saturday night for two twelve-year-olds, I guess."

"*Robbie*, I saw you two at St. Mary's on the way home."

Robbie sighed and his shoulders sank. "Really, you did?"

"Yeah, how stupid are you two? You know they got cameras! You're gonna get caught. And pissing on the baby Jesus? What the hell?"

Robbie looked something between forlorn and scared. He looked away from Laurel and over to the dark corner of the basement where the stone block with their names carved in it was now covered by drywall. The sounds of their parents yelling at each other grew louder. "You know what Father MacShay did to him, right?" he said quietly as he turned back to his sister, his eyes moist.

"So, you pissed on baby Jesus to get back at some perv priest?" Laurel said.

"I told you Carl was drunk. He wanted to do way worse. Smash windows. Go spray paint shit on the door to the rectory. I told him let's just piss on the manger instead."

Laurel shook her head. "You're so getting caught."

Robbie shrugged his shoulders. "It's about time I got into some trouble. Take the heat off you and Freddie." He smirked.

"But seriously, Robbie, you would tell me if Father MacShay ever did anything to you, right?"

Robbie nodded. "Of course I would." He paused thoughtfully, weighing how much to reveal. He leaned in closer to Laurel. "He would make us do confession before every mass we served as altar boys. And he would talk about the common temptations and sins of boys our age. He was obsessed with talking about the sin of touching ourselves, how we could go to hell just for that alone. But if we felt the urge to do it, and did it in the presence of a priest, he could absolve us right then and there."

Laurel winced as if she just swallowed something gross. "Fucking hell, Robbie! God, men are pigs."

"Look, when he would say this to Hap and I, we were like, 'You gotta be kidding. This guy is a joke.' We never took him up on the offer. But poor Carl and Hank…"

Laurel's eyes widened. "He did it to Hank, too?"

"That's what Carl says. They served together like Hap and I did. I believe Carl, though Hank would never ever admit it."

"Did you ever tell Mom and Dad about what Father MacShay said in the confessional?"

"Yup, why do you think they pulled me out of being an altar boy and we stopped going to church? Same story with Hap."

Upstairs a plate crashed against a wall.

Both Laurel and Robbie swung their legs out and sat facing the TV while she turned up the volume. She reached her hand out to his and held it, like they used to when they were little kids watching cartoons.

"You're a good friend to that poor kid Carl, Robbie Elms," Laurel said.

"He ain't got nobody else," Robbie said.

Laurel started to laugh a little. "Man, are Vera and Burg gonna flip when the church comes to them with that video of you two pissing on baby Jesus!"

Robbie laughed, too. "I think they'll understand."

Laurel shook her head. "Stupid boys."

"Hey, if boys are so stupid and all men are pigs, why are you always siding with Dad instead of Mom?"

"Might I remind you that Vera cheated on Burg first." Laurel explained. "And who are you to talk about taking sides? You try to play up the middle, taking both sides. Vera's got Freddie and

Connie firmly on her side. Burg only has me. It's not fair. You should take a side."

"I feel bad for both of them. I don't want them to get divorced and we have to split time between two homes, but I don't want them to stay together either if it's gonna be like this all the time."

Laurel wanted to change the topic. "I think Freddie might be cheating on Connie," she blurted out.

Robbie let go of her hand and then turned to her, "*Whaaaat?*"

"I stole this coat and this flask from some stupid girl in my class. The flask is filled with whiskey that smells just like Burg's. And the coat smells like Freddie's Coolwater."

Robbie shook his head. "C'mon, sis, stop making up stories. Everybody's parents have the same cheap whiskey, and every boy wears Coolwater."

Laurel shrugged and then playfully shoved him in the shoulder. "You're no fun. I'm not playing confessional with you anymore."

"Not everything has to turn into one of your big soap operas just because you're bored."

"*Eh, go take on a piss on Christ.*"

And then they both cracked up. It was that infectious uncontrollable laughter they had shared since their earliest days together. They always knew how to make each other laugh. The laughter drowned out their parent's screaming, at least for that moment.

The pair ended up falling asleep on the couch, the droning white noise of MTV turned way down mixed with the gas heater cycling through a cold night.

Laurel woke up sometime in the middle of the overnight hours. The staticky glowing buzz from the television was in the peripheral of her vision to her left, and the right side of her face pressed up against the couch cushion obscured the enveloping darkness on the other side. She instantly went into a panic when she realized she couldn't move. Her pounding heartbeat continued to increase the size of her anxiety and dread. She swore through the white noise she could hear a shuffling sound in the darkness, and she had this overwhelming sense a presence was there just on the other side of the couch. She wanted to lift her head up over the back of the couch and see, but she couldn't move.

In the corner of her eye, Laurel could see a woman there, by the corner, where the engraved stone bearing their names used to be exposed, dressed in old-fashioned clothes and saying something in a whisper she couldn't make out. Her dread amplified as she sensed the woman was standing up now and approaching her. Laurel could hear the woman's breathing and feel her warmth coming down over her. It was a dark shadowy figure enveloping her, suffocating her with its presence. It was trying to tell her something, something assuredly horrible. Laurel felt like she couldn't breathe, like she could choke on her own dry breath. Then suddenly Laurel sprung up gasping for air.

Robbie's hand was on Laurel's shoulder, and he had a look of fear in his eyes that matched what she imagined the look on her face must've been when she felt that dark presence bearing down on her.

After Laurel caught her breath, she said to him, "It's okay. It's okay."

Robbie's eyes were misty, and he leaned in for a big bear-hug. "I thought you were going to choke to death. I didn't know what to do."

"It's okay," she said again like a mantra. Her heart was still pounding but it began to calm with him pressed against her.

Robbie broke the embrace and then looked her in the eyes. "What was happening?"

"It was just sleep paralysis. I get it sometimes."

"Holy shit, sis, it must be awful."

Laurel smiled faintly. "There are worse things."

"Like what?"

"Like what happened to Carl. Or Death. Sometimes I fear that's what death is like. A permanent sleep paralysis. Where you can't move, can't breathe. And something is weighing down on you. Forever."

Robbie nodded his head and caught a little glint in his eyes, considering this deeply, thoughtfully. He leaned back against the pillows and blankets on his side of the couch, knitted his hands behind his head, and stared up at the ceiling.

He said, "Do you remember when we were little and Mom and Dad would have those big parties on Saturday nights? All their friends and our neighbors, listening to music and drinking and talking and laughing. And me and you would sometimes fall asleep on that couch in the side room by the stairs?"

Laurel nodded wistfully as she leaned back onto her pillows. "Yeah, I remember."

"Dad would come in and carry us up one by one. And that feeling of him carrying me, and my head resting on his shoulder while he climbed up the steps. Feeling so warm and safe and happy, half asleep, but still awake enough to hear the distant laughter from the other room. That's what I think death will be like."

Thinking about this, a shared memory of theirs, and remembering their dad always took Robbie up first, Laurel could almost hear that distant comforting laughter, just as much as she felt the dreadful presence of that woman in the corner moments ago. She always got to hear more of the laughter before their dad came back for her. It was enough to make her want to cry. "I hope you're closer to right than I am," was all Laurel could say before they both drifted off to sleep again.

≈

April 1993
Laurel

Following an eerily civil family Christmas celebration, Vera and Burg Elms announced their separation to their three children over the winter break. By New Year's, Burg had moved out. When Laurel first imagined their dad's new place, she pictured a cheap, bland, sparsely furnished efficiency apartment in some beige complex outside of town. The reality was bachelor Burg was kinda hip, and he rented a spacious, eclectic two-bedroom flat in a trendy updated old brick building downtown along the high-speed line. From the sliding glass doors that opened up onto a small wrought iron balcony, you could see the train whiz by and people-watch as passengers got on and off at the station a few blocks away. Although this train was only taking commuters along its suburban stations back and forth into the city, Laurel liked to imagine it could take her far, far away from here and all the family drama, and she began to have fanciful daydreams about her life beyond West Falls.

Their dad's apartment was easy walking distance to the middle and high schools and their house. Laurel and Robbie would go there after extracurriculars on Thursdays and Fridays to do homework and have dinner with Burg. Some Friday nights Laurel would sleep over, and she and Burg would hop the train into the city for adventures on Saturday mornings. The second bedroom was set up with two twin-beds for Laurel and Robbie, but Robbie always went home so their mom wouldn't be alone. Freddie pretty much lived at Connie's and only saw the apartment once when they helped their dad move in.

"Freddie can always crash on the couch if he ever wants to," Burg told them, with a look in his eyes like he hoped maybe one day he and Freddie could bond in a new way, like friends, or roommates.

Meanwhile, Laurel's prediction about Robbie and Carl getting caught for defiling the church's manger came true. But apart from having to write a performative apology to the church, Robbie got off pretty much scot-free. His parents were understanding of the motive, and passed it off as pre-teen shenanigans. Robbie didn't hang out with Carl much after that, and no one was sure how Carl fared with punishment, but it was probably safe to assume his parents, if they cared at all, were not as understanding as he was seen on multiple occasions in school with fresh black eyes no school bullies laid claim to.

This all coincided with Father MacShay being removed from the parish and sent off to god-knows-where. Reports varied widely amongst the parishioners, everywhere from just over the river to South Africa. The church tried to quickly quell the gossip by bringing in a charismatic, freshly ordained priest who preferred to be called by his first name, Father Daniel. This changing of the guard at church, combined with the dissolution of her marriage, compelled Vera Elms to rejoin the fold, and she and Robbie started going to mass again on Sunday mornings, which Laurel couldn't believe given what they knew about Father MacShay and how the church simply tried to sweep it all under the rug by transferring him. But their mom found comfort in the familiar, and was drawn to Father Daniel. And Robbie, as always, was supportive and didn't want her to sit in church alone. "I don't believe in any of it," he told Laurel, "but what's the harm if it helps Mom feel better about things?"

Father Daniel's first sermon was a lightning rod of a tale that held parishioners rapt. He weaved a scintillating story of a young man who got caught up with the wrong crowd in college, leading to partying and drugs and an obsession with money, sex, and material things. Ultimately the young man was living in the city in a high-rise, and fueled by drugs and despair, took himself to the rooftop and to the ledge and almost jumped…until Jesus spoke to him and saved him. The shocking plot twist: that young man was Father Daniel.

Laurel rolled her eyes while Robbie demonstratively and passionately told the tale second-hand in the basement later that Sunday afternoon, adding colorful embellishments about hot girls and fast cars and the whole partying scene. "Don't go thinking he's any different than the others," she told him. "They're all pigs. And his backstory kinda proves it. They're all the worst kind of sinner."

Their mom fell for Father Daniel and his stories, too, and she started to see him for counseling, specifically about her failed marriage to Burg. As if a supposedly celibate priest knew anything about marriage and relationships, but maybe she figured he had some insights from his decadent, wordly life before he became a priest. Laurel rolled her eyes at this as well, as in her mind her parents were never getting back together.

One Thursday evening, Laurel was sitting on their father's balcony watching the rush hour trains come and go. The outside temperature was right in that mid-April sweet spot of about sixty-five degrees. The sliding glass doors were open behind her, and a vernal breeze blew into the apartment where Robbie was doing his homework at the counter that separated the kitchenette and the living room. Their father was at the stove making dinner, and the smell of sizzling ground beef in the skillet for tacos wafted out onto the balcony, mixing with the spring breeze. It took Laurel out of her trance watching the trains, and she could now hear Burg and Robbie having a conversation.

"Robbs, you're the only one who gets both sides," Burg said.

"I know, Dad, but what do you want me to do?" Robbie said.

"I mean, what the hell is she talking to that young priest about?"

"I don't know, I'm not there with her."

"Yeah, but I know she talks to you about it."

"Well, obviously she's talking to him about you guys, and I'm sure other stuff, too. *Saving her eternal soul.*"

"Do you think she wants to get back together?"

Robbie rolled his eyes. "Dad, *please.*"

"Can ya just talk to her, ask her? That's all. I mean, if there's even that smallest chance..."

"Okay, Dad," Robbie conceded. "I'll see what I can find out."

"Thanks, buddy." Burg started to pile the meat into the hard taco shells. Then he said with a sidelong glance, "Does she ever ask about me?"

"*Daaad!*"

Burg laughed. "Sorry, sorry, bud."

Robbie shrugged. "It's okay. And, of course she does."

That following Friday, after Robbie walked home, it was just Laurel and Burg sitting out on the balcony watching the lights of downtown come on in the darkness beyond the high-speed line. He was drinking a beer, and Laurel had a Coke she wished was spiked with rum.

"You know," Laurel began, "I overheard your conversation with Robbie last night while you were making tacos."

Burg raised an eyebrow. "Oh yeah?"

"It's not fair to put him in that position as a middleman between you and Vera. He's gonna stop coming around here if you keep pressuring him. You want him to end up like Freddie? To never see him?"

"I know, I know," he took another swig of beer from the bottle and shook his head. "I just don't know what to do anymore."

"C'mon, Burg...*Dad*. You and Vera don't love each other anymore," Laurel said, her voice sounding more like an adult friend than a child. "You hate each other. I couldn't stand listening to you two fight like you did. And now you're separated, and you don't fight anymore. You don't really wanna get back together."

Burg sighed and exhaled through his nose. "But how can you say we don't love each other anymore?"

"You know what I mean," Laurel said firmly. "Yes, yes, I know. I've talked to a therapist. You both still love all three of us, *maybe not equally*," she winked at him with a smile, "*I mean who really likes Freddie right now?* And you both still hold a love for each other because of the life and family you built together. But it's time to move on. You're better separated. And you need to figure out how to be alone."

"I don't know, Laurie-girl. Maybe you're right." Burg paused and squinted, almost as if he was fighting back tears. "You usually are. But maybe you're wrong. I mean this is a nice, place, right? But I miss the old stone house. I miss your mom."

And Laurel couldn't help but think she missed her, too.

≈

July 1993
Robbie

Friday, July 2nd

Robbie sat stiffly atop the crinkly paper with his feet dangling, like he was a little kid again, from the high examining table in the ER while the nurse wrapped the splint for his broken left hand. He had gotten into a fight with his dad out on the apartment balcony about not wanting to play middleman anymore between his dad and mom. His dad stormed back into the living room and went to close the sliding glass door behind him, not realizing Robbie was trying to follow him, and his hand got crushed as the door slammed shut.

Burg Elms stood there, white as a ghost, amazed at the fact Robbie seemed neither angry nor in any terrible pain.

"It's okay, Dad," Robbie said. "It was an accident. Though I'm still pissed at you. But I'm madder about this screwing up my movie plans to see *Jurassic Park* with Hap and the guys." Robbie had been dying to see the movie since he first saw a trailer for it in January.

Just then, Vera Elms came rushing into the scene, arms and hand-bag flailing, out of breath, "Oh, Robbie, my baby!"

The nurse calmly pushed her off, "Hang tight there, Mom. We're just finishing up wrapping the splint. You can then give him all the hugs you want."

Vera turned to Burg with the fire of rage in her eyes. "*How could you!?"*

"Mom, mom, please," Robbie said. "It was an accident. He didn't mean to do it. Did you call Hap for me?"

Vera turned from Burg and nodded calmly at Robbie. "I told his mom what happened. Luckily I just caught her on her way out. They were already loading up in the car to go to the Cineplex."

"Bastards went without me!?"

"Robbie – language!"

"Christ, Vera, cut the kid some slack," Burg said. "He did just break his hand. Look, Robbs, it's playing at the Rialto, too. I can maybe take ya sometime this weekend."

"Don't bother," Robbie said.

Saturday, July 3rd

It was 11am and starting to get stifling hot in Robbie's bedroom despite the air conditioning working overtime, so he stumbled down to the basement where it was cooler to watch TV. His hand still throbbed in pain, and he wasn't in the mood to do anything else. He was surprised to find Freddie sitting on the couch looking like he had just woken up and was nursing the usual hangover.

"The phone woke me up, why didn't you get it?" Freddie asked him.

"I'm not answering the phone anymore," Robbie said as he sat down perpendicular from Freddie on the sectional.

"It was your boyfriend Hap," Freddie said. "You two still not talking to each other?"

"Jesus, it's been one day," Robbie cursed. "Do I have to talk to him every day?"

"He was asking if you were going to the fireworks downtown with him and the gang tomorrow night."

"Well, you can tell him I'm not going with him. I don't wanna see any stupid fireworks anyways."

"All this because he went to see a silly dinosaur movie without you?"

"Can't I just not want to see any stupid fireworks?" Robbie huffed.

"Look, I agree with you, fireworks are lame, but isn't Dad gonna take you to see that movie?"

"No, last night apparently work called him, and then he called earlier this morning and told Mom he wouldn't be able to take me this weekend because he had to go out of town."

"For work, on July 4th weekend?"

Robbie shrugged. "Look, I dunno. If you ever talked to him, you would know he got a big promotion and a lot more responsibilities now. Maybe he has to prep for some big meeting on Monday in some other city."

"Well, hell, bro…maybe Connie and I will take you to see *Jurassic Park* tomorrow night. We weren't planning on watching the fireworks either."

Robbie's eyes lit up. "Really?"

Freddie smiled and tossed a pillow at him. "Really. I kinda wanna see the dinosaur movie, too."

"*Dinosaurs are still cool, man,*" Robbie said in his deep, silly voice.

Freddie laughed. "Robbie, I hope you never grow up. You keep loving dinosaurs. Growing up ain't all it's cracked up to be."

Sunday, July 4th - Daytime

Yesterday it got up to 89 degrees. The weather forecast said it would reach 95 today and was likely the start of another heat wave. Robbie had been sleeping in, especially since breaking his hand and taking a max dose of ibuprofen at night for the pain. The heat roused him from his slumber this morning. Foggy-headed, he opened his bedroom door to find a note taped to it.

Robbie the Robster — sorry, dude. Connie came up with other plans for me and her tonight. No movie. I left money on the kitchen counter for you. For pizza or whatever. — Freddie

Robbie ripped it down and crumbled it up.

Laurel just happened to be passing through the hallway, coming from taking a shower wrapped up in an elaboration of towels. "Can't say I blame him. I overheard him on the phone with Connie last night. Sounds like they're planning on using Burg's place since he is away."

"For what?" Robbie asked. "A party? Without us?"

"Not a party. *Just the two of them.*"

"Oh."

After showering and getting dressed, Robbie went down to the kitchen and found the money Freddie left him. *Maybe I'll just go see Jurassic Park by myself,* he thought as he shoved the money in his pocket. But he instantly felt weird even just thinking about going to a movie alone. Still, he was just mad enough to do it. Laurel was sitting at the kitchen table dressed for the pool, eating toast and drinking coffee.

"Mom knows you drink that?" Robbie asked her.

Laurel shrugged.

"Where is Mom?" Robbie asked.

"I dunno," Laurel said between sips of coffee, "it's Sunday. Church? Shouldn't you have gone with her? She's probably out shopping by now."

It seemed odd to Robbie there would be mass on July 4th. He hadn't even thought about it being Sunday. Vera must've thought it was better for him to get more rest. "You going to the pool?" he asked Laurel.

"What does it look like?" Laurel threw him her mocking eyes.

Robbie wanted to go, too, but it was a pain in the ass with this splint. He had to wrap it in saran wrap just to take a shower. Also, he knew Hap and the guys would be there, and he was still in no mood to be around them.

"What are you gonna do with your pitiful self today?" Laurel asked him.

Robbie shrugged. "Roast."

"Have fun." Laurel took her final bite of toast and drank down the last of the coffee. As she passed by Robbie she said, "It'll be alright. Watch whatever movies you want here. Or do whatever it is boys your age do when they're alone." She smiled, lightly punched his shoulder, and then left.

After eating some cereal and having his own coffee, Robbie went out for a walk. It was already blistering hot, but he wanted to check out the dig site down at the gorge as he assumed everyone else would be at the pool, and he could have the whole place to himself. From the little trail atop the gorge, you could see down to where the waterfall used to empty. There were tents and tarps set up blocking the view of what mysteries and fossils were being excavated underneath.

Story was way back in the day, when the town first dammed up the creek and stopped the falls in the 1920s, one of the workers discovered a giant dinosaur fossil. It was excavated, and they found a nearly full skeleton of a dryptosaurus, which meant "tearing lizard" and was a smaller cousin of T-Rex. The area was then filled in and left untouched for over eighty years, until just over a year ago after a torrential storm washed away some of the top layers of soil and a kid discovered another fossil. Now it was a major dig site. The kids would try to sneak down to the bottom, but no one had ever successfully gotten a good peek at anything beyond some tools and dirt and stones. As he sat down on the ledge overlooking the site, Robbie's imagination ran wild with what might be underneath those tents and tarps.

"Hey, Little Elms!" a familiar but unwelcome voice called out. It was Hank Carter.

"Why do you call me that?" Robbie asked as Hank plopped a seat down beside him. "We're the same damn age. In fact, I think I'm older."

"You're the littlest Elms I know," Hank said. He was wearing swim trunks that were still wet and a slightly wet t-shirt. "Have you seen that little pissant, Carl, around here?"

"Man, I haven't seen him all summer. Why the hell do you keep bothering him, though? Just leave him alone. You know he gets enough shit at home. He doesn't need it from you, too."

"Damn, Little Elms, I didn't know he was your boyfriend. Sorry."

"Fuck off."

"No seriously, I'm sorry. You look kinda down. I heard about your hand. That sucks. You should come back to the pool with me."

"Naw, I'm good here. I kinda wanted to be alone."

"Hap and them are there. And some cute girls, too"

"Fuck those guys."

"Daaaaaamn, Little Elms. You're feisty today. But that's okay. I get it. Hey, you wanna go down there and rip off some of those tarps?"

"Not with you. Man, why couldn't you ever admit that Father MacShay did the same thing to you that he did to Carl? Instead, you make his life a living hell." Robbie turned to look sternly at Hank as he said this.

Hank instantly went red in the face, which was hard to tell through his sunburn. He looked like he was about to punch Robbie, but he held back, gritted his teeth, and then let out a big sigh.

"There's something about you, Little Elms," Hank said. "You think you can see right through people, huh?"

"What's the big deal admitting what happened?" Robbie asked him. "No one would blame you."

"What the hell do you know? You know how Father MacShay helped my dad and me when my mom died! How could I? How could *he*?" Hank shook his head, like he was trying to shake off a desire to cry. He held his head down low.

Robbie's face and eyes softened. He put a hand on Hank's shoulder. Hank turned to look at Robbie, and it was possibly the saddest face Robbie had ever seen. Hank leaned in and kissed

Robbie on the lips then instantly recoiled and turned away. Robbie's hand was still on his shoulder, but he let it slip off, trying not to recoil as quickly.

"It's okay," Robbie said, followed by a deep breath, but he had no idea what to say after that.

"I just wanted to see what it was like to kiss someone I actually cared about for once," Hank said, still looking away. "It's not a gay thing. I'm not gay. You're not gay."

"I know. It's okay."

Hank stood up, looked down at Robbie one last time, and then ran up the path disappearing into the hazy, blazing glare of the midday sun.

Robbie stayed at the gorge for a while and then anxiously wandered around town, playing the scene over and over again in his head. He was overheated and exhausted by the time he made his way back home, where he found Laurel lounging in the basement.

"How was the pool?" he asked her.

"Hot and boring. Pete and Hap were there," Laurel said. "What've you been up to?"

"Just walking around."

"In this heat?"

Robbie shrugged. "What are you doing tonight?"

Laurel sat up excitedly. "I had this idea. Hop the train and go see the big fireworks show in the city. Forget about this rinky-dink town for a night."

"Would Mom and Dad be okay with you doing that?"

"Who cares? How would they ever know? You wanna come?"

"I dunno. I'm really not feeling like any fireworks tonight."

"Oh, c'mon. Ride the rails with me. RIDE THE RAILS. RIDE THE RAILS."

"I really just wanna go see *Jurassic Park*. Sit in a nice air-conditioned theater and ignore the fireworks and everyone."

Laurel's voice went higher. "RIDE THE RAILS. RIDE THE

RAILS."

Robbie sighed. "I'm serious, Laurel. I just want to see my dinosaur movie finally. I've been waiting to see it forever, and everyone has been pissing me off and ditching me."

"Fine then." Laurel shook her head. "You just gonna walk down to the Rialto by yourself?"

"Yeah, why not? Who's going with you into the city?"

"Oh…just a few of my girlfriends. If they don't chicken out."

"Be careful out there."

Laurel laughed a little under her breath. "Ok. You be careful, too."

Robbie just stood there for a minute, like he wanted to say something else. Like he wanted to tell her about what happened with Hank. Like he wanted to ask her if she really was going with friends or if she was just going to ride the train alone. He wanted, most of all, to ask her to come to the movie with him. Or for her to ask if she could come with him, so he wouldn't be alone…so she wouldn't be alone.

"Okay then, *weirdo*," Laurel said to break the awkward silence.

Robbie smiled at her and then ran back upstairs.

≈

The Night Of
Freddie

Freddie couldn't believe it was finally going to happen. He and Connie had been a hot and heavy item all year at school and been dating exclusively since freshman year, but tonight, this hot summer night, they were finally going all the way. They had gone about as far as you can go without actually going all the way plenty of times, as teenagers often do, and their friends thought for sure they had done it already. They had done nothing to dissuade their friends of this notion, as teenagers also often do. It wasn't as if there weren't plenty of opportunities, as they both had relatively permissive parents, and they could've comfortably been having sex all this time in either house. They didn't have to sneak around, but they did anyways. Maybe it was more fun that way? And here they were, finally, sneaking around to do it. Using Freddie's dad's bachelor pad. He got roses and candles and tried to make it all romantic. Connie laughed when she walked in around 7pm to the candle-lit apartment, which was still bathed in bright natural light. She shrugged her shoulders as if to say, "Okay, if we're finally doing it, let's just do it right now." Freddie excitedly led her down the hallway littered with rose petals to his dad's bedroom where he had the bed sheets already pulled down.

Freddie stripped down completely naked, almost tripping getting out of his jeans and boxers. Connie laughed again. She stripped down to her bra and underwear and laid down in the bed. Freddie climbed in on top of her and pulled down her underwear. He sloppily kissed her on the lips and neck. She spread her legs, and he fumbled to get it in until she guided him to the right spot. He saw her make a face.

"Am I hurting you?" he asked.

"No," she said.

Freddie wanted it to be like what he saw on one of those porno tapes. He went fast and hard wanting to make her moan, but she stayed silent, and he ended up going so fast he was finished after less than a minute of thrusting. He rolled off her, sweaty and exhausted and stared at the ceiling.

"Was it good for you?" he asked.

She pulled up her underwear and rolled onto her side facing him. She rested her head on his shoulder but said nothing.

Freddie's heart was still pounding, and now he wondered if he did it all wrong. All that build up and for what? He felt amazing as it happened, but it was all so quick, and Connie just lay there silent. The sound of the train going by outside drowned out his thoughts.

Finally, after a few minutes, Connie sat up. "I'm gonna take a shower," she said. "What time are the fireworks?"

Freddie ordered them a pizza to be delivered while Connie showered. They ate it in the living room watching MTV. Later they sat on the balcony and watched both the city fireworks show that could be heard but barely seen in the distance to the west, and then the local fireworks which boomed overheard about twenty minutes later. Freddie wondered if Robbie was down there in the crowd. He felt a twinge of guilt over not taking Robbie to the movies instead.

It was 9:30pm by the time the fireworks were all done, and the whole town seemed to let out a collective sigh that could be heard from their perch above the crowds. Freddie and Connie were no longer virgins heading into their senior year, yet their lives hadn't really changed all that much that night. They weren't suddenly gifted with a new worldly wisdom. If anything, they were more confused than before. It wouldn't be until later in the wee hours of the morning when they went through Stabler Woods that their lives would change forever.

≈

Laurel

Laurel took the 6:35pm train into the city. Alone. It was musty inside the car, but there was a feeling of relief and rush as the train rattled down the line with West Falls and Hampten appearing as blurs and then gone. Underground it went, then over the bridge, the river below sparkling under the hot glow of the scorched sky above, then underground again before reaching the first city stop. She hadn't really thought about which of the city stops she would get off, but she figured this one must be closest to the riverfront, and it was so stuffy in the train and in the station, she just had to get out onto the surface to breathe in different air. It was hot and stank up there, too, but at least air seemed to flow as people and cars rushed by, stirring up the stagnant summer swelter. Laurel had no map, so she took careful note of the cross-streets and landmarks that would lead her back to the station that would take her home at the end of the night.

At first she had been leery of actually doing this by herself, even though she had explored some of this area with her father, but walking the streets alone gave her a newfound confidence. She didn't have anyone distracting her, trying to pull her this way or that. Everything sprawled out just for her. Tourists were everywhere visiting historic sites before the fireworks, but she felt like this was her city. She was no tourist. The places she knew so well from coming here with family or on school field trips took on a new appearance. She wandered around with equal parts renewed curiosity and poise. She sat on a bench and watched people in the public gardens. She got some kind of fancy juice at a juice bar on the corner across the street from the park.

As twilight came she wandered through a historic cemetery and then traversed the precipitously stacked shelves of a used bookstore. On the second floor in a nook with a smeary window overlooking the street, there was a cat curled up on a chair in the corner and a section with French language books. She ran her fingers along the worn spines, whispering to herself the titles. Some she recognized as classics. Maybe she would switch to French sophomore year. She petted the cat which purred sweetly in response. Her dream grew a little bigger on the cat's encouragement. Maybe she would go to France, study abroad in college. She looked out the window at the people on the street below. She saw some kids Robbie's age rough-housing and teasing each other playfully as they made their way down the street.

Laurel made her way to the riverfront promenade as a hazy night gently fell. She was with the throngs leaning over the railing at the river's edge waiting for the show to begin. As the fireworks went off, the crowd went hush. She looked up, never having been so close before. This show put the local West Falls show to shame. She felt like she could climb up inside the explosions and splatter herself as light and ashes over the water.

Laurel thought back to one of her earliest memories from when she was maybe three or four and Robbie wasn't even a toddler. It was July 4th. Their parents took them across the river and just beyond the city to some kind of plateau from where you could see down into the skyline. How crazy her parents must've been to be taking three little kids out that late to watch fireworks. She remembered running around like a wild child through the grass atop the hill, cooing at her baby brother while their mother bounced him up and down trying to stop him from crying. When the fireworks started, everything went silent, even baby Robbie, except for those explosions. She vividly remembered their mother letting her hold Robbie, and she could see the reflections of the fireworks in his eyes as he looked up in ignorant wonder, and she then turned her eyes to the skyline and wondered what it would be like to be right there in the city underneath them.

Now here she was, right there, in the thick of it. Before Laurel knew it, the show was over and the crowd dispersed as smoke lingered in the air, adding to the already sticky haze. She meandered quickly through the city as she made her way back to the underground train station. She thought there was supposed to be a 9:05pm train, but the regular schedule must've been altered by the holiday and firework shows all up and down the suburban line. It felt like an eternity standing there on the platform waiting for the train. By 9:30pm she was finally on the train heading back to West Falls, and the city and the world and all it might offer her one day were just blurred lines fading in the distance. She suddenly realized, sitting there, while the whole world vibrated and moved, how badly she had to pee.

≈

Vera

Vera normally didn't drink that much wine…well, she used to. Like all the time. But not for the past few years. She had really cut back. But she needed it tonight as she was going to come clean to the Wolinskis, Peg and Gene. She felt she owed it to Burg, who was no longer inside any of their once shared friendships and could no longer defend himself. Yes, Burg had been a pig and an asshole, for sure. She wasn't letting him off the hook, but it also wasn't fair how in his absence he was being blamed for everything, and she had won the battle for the hearts of all of their friends. He really had no one now. So here she was, on her third glass of wine at the local "white table cloth" Italian hotspot with her best friends telling them it was she who wandered first in the marriage. She was the initiating adulterer. And she regretted it.

Peg and Gene took it well. They both looked a little like deer caught in the headlights, but then they smiled and nodded and assured her they still thought what Burg did after was way worse. It didn't make Vera feel any better. She wondered what Burg was doing tonight. Was he really alone in some hotel room in some strange town on a work trip?

After dinner and desert, they were all a little bloated and drunk and walked down to where the whole town was gathering for the fireworks. Vera felt especially embarrassed, sweaty and confessional, her full stomach turning and her head already aching. She didn't really want to run into the kids like this, but at the same time she wanted more than anything in the world just to see them and tell them all how sorry she was for what was happening.

Inevitably, they ran into some other parents and neighbors and chit-chatted in that bland neighborly way one does when they run into someone they run into too much already. Eventually the fireworks went off, and as the show came to a close, Hap came galloping up to them, excited to see his parents.

"Hi, Mrs. Elms," Hap said politely and formally, as if he didn't half-live at her house and she hadn't wiped his butt when he was little and cook him dinner countless nights and even tuck him in on occasion.

"Hi, is Robbie with you guys?" Vera asked.

Hap turned around to look at the rest of the gang goofing it up behind him, as if he didn't know if Robbie was with them or not. He then looked back up at Vera sheepishly. "No. I haven't seen him all day."

"Oh," Vera said. She wondered, the poor kid, had Robbie just stayed at home all day and night? Maybe the pain from his hand was still bothering him and he just needed to rest. She turned to Peg and Gene. "Well, I better get home and check on him then."

They nodded in response.

Hap called out as she walked away, "Tell him I said I'm sorry and to call me!"

Vera stopped, turned around and smiled back at Hap. "Oh, of course I will, sweetie. And just come on over tomorrow. We'll drag him out of bed together if we have to."

"Deal!" Hap called back, and then he waved goodbye.

Was it the wine? The indigestion? The heat? Vera found herself anxious and walking briskly back to her house, which was all dark. No signs of lights on inside or out. As she came through the front door she flipped on the porch light and then walked through all the rooms downstairs, flipping all the switches. "Robbie!" she called out. "Robbie, I'm home!"

Was he asleep already? She thought about the last time she saw him, this morning, as she was on her way out to church and she peeked into his room where he still soundly slept. In the hazy light of dawn, she went over to his bed and petted his soft dark hair and kissed his forehead like when he was a little boy. Now in the evening darkness, she found herself racing up the stairs to his room and swinging his bedroom door open. Empty. She raced back downstairs and to the basement. She opened the door and called down into the darkness, "Robbie? Anybody?"

Vera came to the realization it was almost 9:45 at night, and she had no idea where any one of her three children were. Sure, Freddie, he was almost eighteen; she never knew where he was. Laurel, she still kept pretty good tabs on her, but she was known to wander about and then always show up safely before bedtime. But Robbie, he was the youngest. The most innocent. The one needing protection. She always knew where he was. Or thought she did. He was hardly ever home anymore. But it was summer, and that was normal, right? He was with Hap all the time…until the last few days.

Panic struck as she rushed out onto the front porch and screamed out into the night, "Robbie!"

"Mom, what the hell? Are you drunk?" Laurel came casually walking up the front path to the porch, seemingly having materialized out of the dark, musky night.

"Where the hell have you been?" Vera demanded.

"Out. *What?* It's not even 10pm, and I'm home already."

"Where's Robbie?"

"I'm pretty sure he went to see *Jurassic Park*."

"With who?"

"No one."

"By himself?"

"Jesus, Mom, he's twelve. He's a big boy now."

"He went to the Rialto?" Vera asked, her anxiety rising in her voice.

"Yeah," Laurel replied.

"Come inside," Vera said quickly. "Check the movie times with me."

Laurel followed Vera in and then combed through the messes in the kitchen and living room until they found the movie section of the newspaper.

"There," Laurel said. "The movie was at 7pm and the runtime…a little over two hours."

Vera pondered this. She looked at her watch again. It was 9:47pm. "He should be home by now. It doesn't take that long to walk back here from the Rialto."

"Maybe he met up with some friends."

"All his friends were at the fireworks. I saw them."

"Maybe he's with Carl Strong."

Vera fretted. "I'll call over there. He better not be over there. But lord knows there's probably no one there to answer. And then I'll call the Wolinskis in case he showed up there after they got home."

"And Mr. Carter," Laurel added.

"Right. I didn't see Hank downtown. Maybe he's with Hank for some reason."

Three calls in a matter of five minutes. No sign of Robbie. Nobody had seen him or knew where he was.

"Stay calm, Mom," Laurel said. "Maybe he went and grabbed an ice cream cone. It's probably packed down there. Hell, he might still be standing in line."

Vera took a few deep breaths and then sat down with Laurel on the rockers out on the front porch. She looked down across the road and small field into the lake and up the opposite hill into Stabler Woods. The lingering smoke from the fireworks had dissipated into the summer evening haze, leaving a waning gibbous moon hanging high over the trees. "It'll be okay," she said quietly out loud as she anxiously rocked, feeling like some strange old woman out of time. "He'll just walk out of the woods like he always does and come traipsing around the lake and back home in a few minutes."

But he didn't. By midnight, she called the cops, and despite their reassurances they were sure he was just out and about like so many other people and kids in town tonight and would show up soon, she had this sinking feeling she would never see him again.

≈

Robbie

Robbie didn't see the note from his mom on the fridge until he went to get a TV dinner out of the freezer to heat up in the microwave.

Went out for dinner and drinks with Mr. and Mrs. Wolinski. See you down at the fireworks later. Money for pizza on the counter. – Love, Mom

Robbie guessed she didn't know he was still not speaking to Hap, and that Freddie left him money, too. He'd be rich by the time everyone ditched him for better plans. He ate his turkey meal in front of the TV in the living room watching the 6 o'clock Action News. He checked the newspaper for the movie showtimes. *Jurassic Park* was playing at the Rialto at 7pm. He washed his face, combed his hair, reapplied deodorant and put on a clean red polo shirt and beige shorts. With money lining his pocket, Robbie stepped out into the humid early evening and walked down to the Rialto.

The Rialto may have been a shadow of its former glory, but to Robbie, stepping up to the ticket booth underneath the old-fashioned marquee (even with a third of the neon bulbs blown out) always felt like coming home. His dad took him to see his first movie at the Rialto when he was five years-old – *Flight of the Navigator* – and the story of a boy who was thought to have disappeared only to have actually traveled into the future left an indelible mark on his ever-growing imagination. There were always rumors of the Rialto closing down, especially since the new twelve-screen Cineplex opened up just outside of town last year, but Robbie still preferred the charms of being able to walk to the neighborhood theater and get unlimited off-brand soda and stale popcorn for two bucks.

He felt a little weird entering the darkened theater room alone. At first he thought to hide and sit in the back row, but it wasn't terribly crowded with most locals out celebrating the 4th, so he sat down in the center seat, center row and enjoyed his popcorn and soda while the previews started. After the first preview, a noisy group of girls came in and sat down in the back row.

"Hey, Robbie!" a hushed voice yelled out from the back.

Robbie's stomach sank. He slouched down in the seat, as if he could disappear, but then slowly turned around to see the gaggle of girls from his class giggling in the back row. When he turned forward, one of the girls had plopped down right next to him. It was Jennifer Alvarez, the stylish, athletic, but mostly stand-offish girl who loved to whup the boys at basketball.

"Hey, Robbie, what's the matter?" she said, her mouth smacking with gum. "Looks like you've seen a ghost."

"Hi," was all he could say.

"I've missed seeing you down at the pool that last couple of days."

Robbie thought that was a strange thing to say. While he often saw her there, she never gave him the time of day. He pitifully lifted up his wrapped hand.

"Damn, how did that happen?"

"Playing basketball," he said nonchalantly. "Brought the rim right down and onto my hand."

Jennifer laughed. "Yeah right. I've seen you play. You can't hang, but that's alright. Mind if I sit with you? They've been getting on my last nerve. Surprised you're not here with Hap."

"Eh, he's been getting on my last nerve." He passed her the popcorn. The theater darkened and finally – what Robbie had been waiting for all summer – *Jurassic Park.*

When it got to the most suspenseful part where the kids were trying to hide from the velociraptors in the giant industrial kitchen, Jennifer grabbed his arm and didn't let go until the finale where the T-Rex came rampaging through the lobby and the giant banner came floating down from the ceiling.

Outside the theater on the street, Jennifer and Robbie breathlessly went through their favorite parts while her friends hung in the background chattering and laughing. Robbie hadn't realized it, but he had been rubbing his arm where it was sore from her holding onto him so tight. Jennifer casually lifted up the sleeve of his polo to look at the mark she left.

"Sorry about that," she said. "But hey, you're growing some muscle there."

Robbie blushed. She offered to show him some moves on the

court sometime. She then asked if he wanted to come with her and her friends down to the ice cream parlor.

Robbie wanted to go with her more than anything, but he said instead, "I really can't. I forgot to leave a note for my mom telling her where I went. I should get home. I don't want her to worry."

Just then the fireworks started going off in the distance on the other side of town. Everyone jumped a little, and the girls in the background were giggling again.

Jennifer nodded. "Aww, I get it. You're a good kid, Robbie Elms." That's when she grabbed his arm on the sore spot again, leaned in, and kissed him on the lips. The moment seemed to last longer than Robbie ever expected, and they were suddenly doing something he thought might be a French kiss, mouths open. When the girls in the background went, "Woo-ewww..." they pulled apart. Robbie staggered backwards a bit with a sly smile and his eyes darting all over the place and then down at the ground.

"I'll see ya around," Jennifer said with all the confidence in the world. Then she leaned into him again and whispered, "Watch out for the creeper that was in there." Her eyes indicated someone behind him.

Robbie's smile wiped from his face. He took a few steps back as he watched Jennifer and her friends disappear down the street heading towards the ice cream parlor. Fireworks continued to go off as he turned around and saw standing in the opening of the alleyway between the theater and the next building a shadowy figure. His heart started to pound thinking about what Jennifer had just said. When the figure emerged, he breathed a sigh of relief. It was just Mr. Strayer, a nice, quiet guy who had fixed up a few small things around the house for his mom since his dad had moved out. Robbie approached him.

"Hey, Mr. Strayer," he said. "Did you see the movie?"

"Oh, yes. It was amazing," Mr. Strayer said. "Looks like you kids really enjoyed it. Where's your girlfriend going?"

"Oh, she's not my girlfriend. They were just going to get ice cream, but I need to get home."

"Oh, it's getting kind of late." Mr. Strayer looked down at Robbie's broken hand. "How about I walk with you?"

Robbie didn't like the way Mr. Strayer was looking at him. He hadn't noticed him in the theater, but apparently Jennifer did, and she clearly didn't like his vibe either. Wanting to remove himself from this awkward situation, Robbie carelessly said, "Oh no, that's okay. I have my shortcut through the woods I can take. Walk it all time."

Mr. Strayer nodded. "Okay. Tell your mom I said hello when you get home."

"I sure will, Mr. Strayer. It was good seeing you." Robbie calmly walked past him, and then after he was down the street about a block, he sprinted to Stabler Woods.

Fireworks continued to go off, casting an intermittent glow over the trail through the woods, but Robbie felt like he could've walked it blindfolded. Plus, you were never really so deep in the woods where the distant ambient glow of street lights on the paved walking paths didn't provide some sense of where you were headed. At some point, Robbie thought he heard laughter coming from up on one of the paved paths. Had Jennifer and her friends secretly followed him, or was it just in his head because he wished they had? That flicker of potential joy was replaced quickly by fear. He heard some sticks crack under foot behind him, and then in front of him, and he now felt a presence in the woods with him. He thought he heard a hawk overhead but maybe his mind was playing tricks on him. He wondered, as his heart quickened along with his steps, was this what Laurel felt when she suffered through an episode of sleep paralysis? As his pulse began to pound in his ears, he suddenly thought he heard a woman's voice in the distance calling out his name. He stopped in his tracks to turn around and look up. Sadly, he was mistaken.

EPISODE FOUR – THE AFTERMATH

July 5, 1993

The phone rang intermittently every few minutes a little bit after midnight. Both Freddie and Connie were in a deep sleep by then, which was atypical as they often stayed up far later than that, but it had been an atypical night. The strangeness of staying in Burg's apartment and the new weird distance between them, in spite of having finally gone all the way, made them just want to sleep. The phone rang again a little after 12:30. It woke Freddie up, but he didn't want to pick it up and reveal to whoever was on the other line that he and Connie were secretly crashing there, which was ridiculous, because no one would care that they were, and Burg especially would be thrilled his oldest son wanted to stay there. Finally, Freddie's beeper went off. It was Laurel's personal line at home. He picked up the phone and called her back.

"Jesus, Freddie," Laurel said in a frantic, hushed tone.

"Laurel, what's going on?" Freddie asked groggily. Connie was up now, too, pressed up against his back with her head on his shoulder while he cradled the phone against his opposite ear.

"Vera has the cops here. Robbie never came home. I've been trying to call you, obviously. Please tell me he's there with you so Vera can call off the search party. It's getting ridiculous over here."

Freddie pushed Connie off and stood up. "He's not here with us."

There was a hot silence on the other end of the phone. Then

Laurel thought out loud, calmly. "He's not here. He's not at Hap's. He's not with you. Where the hell is he?"

"Did the cops check Stabler Woods?" Freddie offered. "Maybe he's partying it up in there."

"Robbie? Party? With who?" Laurel paused. "Freddie, what are we gonna do?"

"Seriously, though, have they checked the woods?" Freddie said again.

"They haven't checked anything," Laurel replied in a flustered tone. "Not enough time has passed. They don't consider him missing yet. They just keep asking Vera the same damn questions over and over."

"Fuck those cops then," Freddie decided. "We don't need to wait for them to go looking for him. Connie and I will check out downtown and the train station and then head out to the lake and Stabler Woods."

"Make sure you leave him a note at Burg's, in case he shows up there, telling him to come home."

"Of course. We'll find him, don't worry. *And, boy, will he be in big trouble*. Little brat. Making us all worry like this. *I'll show him* when I find him."

Laurel didn't want to say out loud how scared she really was, but it came out in the tone of her voice. "That didn't sound very convincing. But thanks for trying."

"We'll find him. Now go check on Mom and tell those fucking cops to do their jobs and get off their lazy asses to start searching."

Downtown was a ghost town littered with the debris from the July 4th celebration. The only signs of life were the stragglers getting off the late-night trains and slipping down the dark side streets or into their shadowy cars and floating away. The only thing open at this hour was Connie's Place out on the pike, not far from the Rialto. It made sense to head there next and canvas the neighborhood in between. They stopped at Connie's Place and told

Connie's father about Robbie.

"I'll make an early last call and canvas along the pike, and then check in on Carl in case Robbie's over there for some reason," her father said confidently, trying to reassure the frightened teenagers. "You head back home. Chances are that's where he'll show up, right? That's where you should be waiting for him."

Freddie and Connie took solace a responsible adult was on the case with them. "We're gonna check out Stabler Woods and then head home to check on my mom and Laurel," Freddie said.

Connie's dad pulled two flashlights out from under the bar. "If you're cutting through the woods, take these."

It was 1:37 a.m. when Freddie and Connie entered Stabler Woods. Their flashlights' panicked beams cast spotlights onto looming branches, up towards the sky, and down to the ground as the teenagers made their way across the unsettled earth and deeper into the trees.

Suddenly, there was a commotion of light – other flashlights – and voices. They could hear the distant crackle of a walkie-talkie and a voice that sounded like it was from beyond a grave tell someone who might as well have been in outer space, "Better get homicide down here to Stabler Woods."

Connie grabbed Freddie's hand. They dropped their flashlights as another flashlight's beam cast an ungodly blinding brightness over their faces.

"What are you doing out here, son?" the authoritative voice asked.

"We're looking for my brother," Freddie said, covering his eyes from the light.

"What's your name, son?"

"Freddie Elms."

"Connie Strong, is that you?" the officer asked.

"Yeah," Connie answered.

"You both need to come with me."

"Where to?" Freddie asked.

"Back to your house," the officer said briskly.

"What about the others out there?" Freddie said.

"You both need to come with me," the officer said with a sense of finality.

Freddie's voice strained to relay the thoughts speeding through his mind. "What's out there? Did you find him? I need to see."

"Son, trust me," the office said calmly but firmly. "You don't need to see this. You need to come with me. Your mother and sister are going to need you there."

Freddie's knees buckled. Connie tried to hold him up. The police officer pointed the flashlight away from them as if to give them a moment of privacy. "I think I'm gonna be sick," Freddie whispered to Connie.

"Freddie, let's listen to him," Connie said. "Let's go home. Let the cops do their job."

Freddie pulled himself back up. The police officer walked past them and said, "Follow me, please."

It was Connie who started to cry on the way back to the Elms' house. As they walked up the pathway to the old stone house and passed through the threshold to where Vera, Laurel and another officer waited, it was as if a black curtain came down behind them and the heaviest, darkest pall settled over the house. The officer from the woods couldn't, wouldn't tell them anything yet. Freddie, Connie, and Laurel circled around Vera on the couch, in a state of suspended animation weighed down by this black curtain.

Vera felt like she was under water with them. When Freddie, Connie, and the other officer came inside out of the blue, it was if they were deep sea divers, slowly moving through water at the bottom of the sea and coming across a shipwreck. She kept wanting to say something to them, but words stayed trapped deep down in her throat, and they accumulated there until she couldn't breathe.

It was 2:47 a.m. when Detective Jim Van Patten came upon

the shipwreck. Vera couldn't hear what he said, as if the weight of the ocean clogged her ears, but she knew why he was there. She knew they had found something out there in Stabler Woods. She could see images of her little boy in the air bubbles that came out of his deep-sea helmet and danced up to the ceiling of the living room until they popped. The last bubble was so big, and Robbie's beautiful face and eyes so vivid, that when it popped, suddenly her ears were cleared and she could breathe again, too. Now, all she could hear was a blood-curdling scream. Dear God, was it hers? *Was it Robbie's?* Was it Laurel? Connie? She didn't know. It didn't matter. She felt wet and cold, and hands clawed at her. Hands searching for an embrace. It was Connie. She hugged Connie. She hugged her so hard she thought she might squeeze the life out of her. Connie Strong. *Was she strong enough to survive this embrace?* Vera wondered. In Connie's embrace, she melted into a mass of black ooze. It was like she was looking down on the scene from above, disembodied for a moment, then suddenly back in her body, and as Connie pulled away, Vera's voice said calmly. "Someone needs to call Burg."

≈

In the following days…

It took them longer than anyone anticipated to finally track down Burg Elms. He was not reachable at the hotel he had told Vera he would be staying for business. Nobody had any idea where he could be otherwise. Finally, he showed up at his apartment on Wednesday morning, unbeknownst to him his youngest son had been murdered, and he was default suspect number one.

People gossiped. *They always look at the parents first in these situations,* they reasoned. But the rumors grew more cancerous, as it was commonly thought Detective Jim Van Patten, chief on the case and former high school sweetheart of Vera's, was the person in question with whom she had cheated on Burg with, and that conflict of interest was perhaps clouding the investigation. By the following Sunday, however, Burg was able to clear his name, and his alibi – he was with a married woman just over the bridge in the city the whole time – was reluctantly corroborated. Meanwhile, Robbie's body had yet to be released.

During this time, Vera stayed cocooned at home. If a stream of disconnect had been slowly making its way between Vera and her two older children, a vast gulf now separated them. Vera had no idea where Freddie and Laurel were from one day to the next. Vera found comfort in Connie, who had practically moved into the Elms' house and became a steady presence there. Connie even helped with the funeral planning as they waited for the body to be released. Vera also found comfort in Hap; poor, sweet Hap. Upon hearing the news of his best friend's death on Monday, Hap went on a hunger strike, locked himself in his room, and was inconsolable. His parents brought him to Vera on Wednesday, and the two became inseparable. Connie made sure they both ate and rested.

Most of the time Hap simply stayed by Vera's side. But on occasion he would tell her how sorry he was. "It's my fault. I should've come over and checked on him. I should've made him come to the fireworks," he cried. Vera would hold him, and they would cry together. She never told him it wasn't his fault. In her mind, it was all of their fault. If only Burg hadn't gotten into a fight with Robbie that led to Robbie's broken hand which put him at a severe disadvantage against his attacker. If only Vera had woken him up that morning and taken him to church, maybe he would've spent the day with her. Maybe she would've cancelled her plans for dinner and had dinner with him instead. Maybe they would've gone to the fireworks together or just stayed at home and watched a movie. If only Freddie had taken him to see *Jurassic Park* like he had promised. If only Laurel had gone to the movies with Robbie instead of sneaking into the city on the train. If only Hap had broken through the silent treatment Robbie was giving him and just showed up, like he had countless times before, never letting a crack in their friendship get too big, always getting Robbie to laugh and forgive and forget. If only Hap hadn't decided this time to let Robbie stew. *If only…if only…*

Meanwhile, any other leads were thin. They were able to confirm Robbie did go to the Rialto to see *Jurassic Park*, but no one could confirm seeing him with anybody. There was some physical evidence found at the scene, but nothing could be tied to anyone yet.

Then on Sunday, one full week after Robbie's murder, Hap said to Vera during one of their crying sessions, "I protected him from Father MacShay. I should've protected him this time, too."

Vera, sparked now to action, told Detective Van Patten everything about Father MacShay and the boys. They were able to quickly confirm Father MacShay was indeed in town over the holiday weekend visiting his elderly uncle who lived in the local nursing home. There was now a new suspect number one as the body was released on Tuesday, July 13th. They were then finally able to schedule the funeral on Thursday, July 15th.

Vera found some solace in this, as they made final preparations. At the funeral home, the day before, she and Burg went over the arrangements with the director. Burg had wanted a closed casket, given the circumstances, but Vera insisted on an open casket, and the director promised Robbie would be presented appropriately. "He'll appear like an angel," were the only words the director could find to gloss over the harsh reality.

"So, his head wounds won't be visible?" Burg asked bluntly.

"We've taken the greatest care to present him how you would like to remember him," the director responded.

"How the hell would you know how I want to remember him?" Burg said. "You think I want to remember him lying in a coffin, like a perfect doll? After what was done to him? *After what I was accused of doing to him?* Making it all seem like nothing happened? Like he just fell asleep or died of some other tragic thing kids die of, something normal and acceptable, like cancer? His killer is out there walking the streets, and we're just playing dress up in here!" Burg stormed off.

Vera said nothing. The director tried to recover. "What else would you like to see, Mrs. Elms?" They were standing in the main viewing room. Vera looked around. There were no windows in there.

"Robbie would want there to be light," she said. "This room…it's suffocating. I want him in the sun."

"The sun?" the director repeated.

"Can we put the casket in the sunroom?"

"Well, traditionally we have these very fine viewing rooms which are designed to accommodate larger crowds of mourners, which we are expecting in this case. And with this heat wave, the sunroom would not be ideal. It would be very hot out there. And, well, we wouldn't want…the makeup…"

Vera said, "What, his face would melt?" She walked to the back corner of the room where there was an emergency exit door. "If we can't put him in the sunroom, I want this door open. I can't have him trapped in this room with no escape."

At the viewing on Thursday, the open door behind the casket became a centerpiece. The loud drone of the air conditioning units working overtime just outside the door filtered into the room, drowning out the dreary church music. Luckily, the heatwave had broken with some rain the day prior, but it was still very warm. Lines formed around the block, and the open door became a welcome exit point for those looking to pay their respects but not linger in the suffocating sadness of it all.

There were pictures of Robbie from infancy to age twelve up in the lobby and next to the casket, collages like school kids would make. Burg, Vera, Freddie, Laurel, Connie and Hap made up the receiving line initially. It quickly became too much for Hap, who then took a seat in the front row with his parents and older brother Pete behind him. The other teenagers eventually joined him, with

Freddie joining him first, staggering and hung-over, the smell of liquor coming through his pores.

Once the receiving line slowed down and those who meant to stay had taken their seats or found standing room in the back, Father Dan approached the podium and microphone in front of the casket while Burg and Vera finally took their seats.

"I hope you can all hear me," Father Dan began over the loud drone of the air conditioners outside and the fans inside. He dabbed the sweat from his forehead with a handkerchief, loosened his white collar, and then took a sip of water. "What can we say about Robbie Elms?"

Freddie said to Connie, "I'm gonna be sick." He covered his mouth and ran out the door. Connie didn't know what to do. Should she follow him?

Father Dan looked over at her. "No, no, stay. Let him be. Again, I ask, what can we say about Robbie Elms? Clearly, by his brother Freddie's show of emotions there, by the grief that has driven that young man to the brink, by this outpouring of support shown by the community, above all else, Robbie Elms was loved. A beloved son, brother, friend. The finest of students. A star Little Leaguer. An altar boy."

"This is bullshit!" Laurel screamed. She stood up and pointed her finger at Father Dan. "One of your own did this to him! You're about to go on and on about his memory and his soul and Jesus and heaven. Well, it's all bullshit! He didn't believe in any of this! He wouldn't want any of this! He's fucking dead. He was brutally, horribly murdered by some fucked-up pervert, and you're gonna try to tell us he's at peace? Well, fuck you! Fuck the church! Fuck everyone in this town who believes it!"

Vera was trying to pull her back down but Laurel resisted. She broke free from her mother's grasp and ran out the door. Vera looked up at Father Dan pleadingly, about to apologize.

"No, no, Vera, don't apologize," Father Dan said. "Your daughter, Robbie's sister, her grief and anger are real. She's telling us in no uncertain terms the truth…*about peace*. Peace we all hope to find one day. But not today. But not today. No, maybe not even when we find out what happened, and who did it, and they are brought to justice. There may be no peace even then."

Father Dan took another sip of water and then stepped down from the podium. He paced back and forth, turned back to the casket, then to the larger crowd, then directly to Vera and Burg and Hap and Connie. He then said, "When I heard something horrible had happened to Robbie, I was in shock. We are all in shock. *We are not at peace*. We must believe he is at peace. But we are not." He walked over to Vera, took her hands in his, leaned over and whispered something in her ear no one could hear, and then walked through that open door.

The befuddled funeral director came up to the podium as others, confused, started exiting, both through the open door and back out into the lobby. "On behalf of the Elms family," he began, barely audible over the commotion, "thank you for coming. The remainder of the service and internment will be private for family and close friends only."

Connie turned to Vera, "I'll go find Freddie and Laurel."

Someone had switched the music to Tom Petty's "Learning to Fly." Robbie's favorite song. It played on a loop for over twenty minutes before the crowd had fully dispersed, and it was just Vera and Burg and the Wolinskis left in the room.

"Turn off the fucking music!" Burg screamed.

It was silent again except for the air conditioners and fans.

Just then, Connie came back in with Freddie and Laurel.

"Close the fucking door," Burg said to Freddie, who still staggered, his suit jacket and tie gone, likely covered in puke somewhere outside, and his white shirt stained through with sweat, sleeves sloppily rolled up, his hair a wet mess.

Laurel pushed Freddie forward to take a seat with Connie and then closed the door before sitting herself down.

They all sat there in hot, uncomfortable silence for what

seemed like eternity, intermittently looking down at the floor and then at the casket. Robbie's corpse and profiled face appeared like a low mountain peak muted in the far distance peering up just over the horizon.

Finally, Hap's parents went out to the lobby to fetch the director. Sheepishly he walked to the front of the room. "I am so sorry," he began. "Please take all the time you need…"

"We've had enough time," Burg said.

"The cars are waiting for you outside to take you to the cemetery. Let us close up the casket." The director turned to step away.

"We want to watch," Burg said.

"I'm sorry, Mr. Elms?" the director said, turning slowly back around.

"We want to watch you close the casket. I'm not leaving my boy's side until he's in the ground."

"Oh, well, it really is quite a process," the director prattled on. "We have to lower it down, with a crank to be able to close it. Most families don't…"

"We're not most families." Burg told him resolutely.

The director nodded slowly. "Of course, you can stay." He motioned for the other staff members to come up to the casket. One of them inserted some kind of turning mechanism on the one side that was then cranked to lower the coffin bed deeper into the body of the casket. It was a slow, arduous, and surprisingly loud process. The body jostled as it was lowered.

"I said to keep the door open!" Vera cried out.

The director ran to re-open the back door.

Vera imagined Robbie sitting up, climbing out of the casket and just walking out the door into the warm summer day. She and Burg met in film class in college. One of the films they watched together was Carl Theodor Dreyer's black-and-white classic, *Ordet*, where in the climax of the film, a previously faithless man's wife, who died following a stillbirth, just casually rose up out of her casket at the funeral, as if waking from a peaceful sleep, and was alive once more. Vera thought maybe that could be Robbie, too. And for a split second, she thought she saw his hand grip the edge of the coffin to lift himself out as they completed the cranking of the casket. But it was all just a fairy tale, a vision. Vera took a deep breath, as hands clawed at her again, touching her shoulders, her arms. She closed her eyes and held that breath at the sound of her son's coffin closing, like a clap of thunder. It startled her like nothing had ever startled her before in her life. It was final. She would never see her son, Robbie, again.

Vera opened her eyes and exhaled. Hap was hugging her, while her estranged husband was beside them lost in his own rage, and her own children bereft in the periphery, left to their own devices. In some ways, she would never see them again either.

≈

The subsequent days and year...

In the back of the room, during the strange spectacle of Robbie Elms' funeral, was Detective Van Patten, observing it all. As the mourners dispersed after Father Dan's brief sermon, a young girl approached him. It was Jennifer Alvarez. She told him she was at the Rialto with Robbie, sat with him even, and there was a strange man watching them as they left. Detective Van Patten had her agree to come in and work with a sketch artist. It would be weeks before she did, as her family was on vacation down the shore following the funeral. While the investigation remained centered on Father MacShay, the sketch was broadcast far and wide. It ended up matching closely to some mug shots on file, one of them Darrel Strayer, who had been charged with indecent exposure three years ago. Strayer became part of a line-up where they asked Jennifer to identify the man she saw that night. She failed to identify Strayer, and the man she did identify turned out to have a rock-solid alibi. He was in a town twenty miles away sitting in a cell all night on July 4th, having been brought in on drunk and disorderly conduct. That lead went dry for a while.

Meanwhile, Father MacShay claimed to have been visiting with his elderly uncle at the nursing home until visiting hours ended at 8pm. The nursing home staff confirmed this. He then said he went back to the rectory where he saw and talked to no one, prayed and slept, and then left in the morning for his new parish over one hundred miles away. Naturally, no one could confirm seeing him at the rectory overnight, but they could confirm he left in the morning. His alibi was shaky at best with the unaccounted hours matching up to the timeframe Robbie was believed to have been murdered, but there was nothing else tying the priest to what happened to Robbie that night. Eventually, that lead dried up as well.

Later in the fall, Detective Van Patten did end up taking the mug shot line up to the Rialto to see if any of the staff working that night recognized any of the pictures as someone who may have been there to see *Jurassic Park*. The ticket booth worker recognized Strayer, saying he was a regular customer, and he was almost certain he was there that night.

Strayer was brought in for questioning that October. He admitted to being there that night. He really enjoyed the movie. He said he saw Robbie and Jennifer. He even admitted to knowing Robbie and his mother, having done some small fixes around their house. He said he noticed Robbie was going to walk home alone, and he offered to walk Robbie home, thinking it was dangerous for a kid to walk alone at that time of night. His calm, self-assured answers, his reference to it being dangerous, and how he wanted to protect Robbie, a kid he knew…*his whole demeanor* made Detective Van Patten's skin crawl. But Strayer may have just been a creep playing games, toying with the cops because the details of the case were so well known by now.

All the evidence pointing towards Strayer was circumstantial and self-admitted. There was nothing concrete or physical that put him in those woods with Robbie. Van Patten attempted to get a warrant to obtain a DNA sample from Strayer to compare to the sample taken from Robbie's body, but a judge did not agree there was sufficient cause. All Van Patten could do now was lay in wait and watch Strayer like a hawk in hopes of catching him slipping up. The guy was a pervert, and he couldn't stay chaste for long.

Van Patten swore to Vera and Burg that he would find Robbie's killer. With all other leads dead-ended, watching Strayer became his life's work.

Meanwhile, for Robbie's family and other loved-ones, life lurched forward. As school started in the fall, Hap fell back in with his other friends, many of them having mourned Robbie in their own ways and to somewhat lesser degrees, but all in tacit silent agreement to act like everything was okay and it was old times again. He and Jennifer Alvarez became friends, voicing to each other the guilt they shared.

"I kissed him that night," Jennifer told Hap.

"That must've made him so happy," Hap said, holding back his tears unsuccessfully. He wanted to imagine Robbie had happy thoughts before he died. He didn't want to imagine what happened out there in the woods. He preferred to picture Robbie under the Rialto marquee kissing Jennifer Alvarez. "I loved him so much. He was my best friend," he told her. Jennifer hugged him, and then kissed him, too. But that's all it ever was. By the close of the school year, they were running in different circles, but still acknowledged each other with a smile or a nod of the head, in the hallways.

At the start of the school year, Hap still visited Vera once a week on Sunday afternoons, but the visits eventually changed to once a month, and by spring he only saw her in passing about town. His parents tried to keep in touch with Vera and occasionally made plans to go out, but Vera always found an excuse not to go, and eventually they stopped trying.

Burg found a new job that fall, working for a military contractor as a director supporting the daily operations of a nearby air force base. It was a little less than an hour away, and he could've commuted, but he chose to break his lease and move to be closer to the base.

Freddie and Connie started their senior year still a couple, but it had become strained and awkward. They were never able to find the right level of intimacy following that night. Freddie was often too drunk or otherwise self-medicated, and Connie blamed it on the stress of Robbie's murder, but deep down she knew something was off that night they first had sex. Still, she convinced herself she loved him, and it was that false sense mixed with sadness and pity that kept her with him throughout the year. His grades tanked, ending hopes of college, and he would likely just skate by to graduation. Teachers pitied him, too, and passed him whether he earned it or not. Connie had never been the best student, but she still planned to go to community college before joining her dad to help run the bar. She continued to grow closer to Vera, revealing to Freddie's mom much of their relationship drama, leading Freddie to drink and self-medicate even more.

Laurel took a different approach to fill the hole in her heart left by Robbie's death. She buried herself in her school work and became a straight A-student just like Robbie had been. She picked up extracurriculars, like debate, photography and French club. She made new friends, but it was only ever surface-level and centered around shared classes or activities. She stayed busy and away from home as much as possible. At parties she mostly observed, and drank just enough to allow herself to voice some cutting, sarcastic remarks and become known as a cool but slightly dangerous wallflower. Her brother's murder hung on her like an invisible medal of honor. It made other kids both afraid and in awe of her. People wanted to be around her but also left her alone, allowing her to occupy this odd high school purgatory where she was expected to say something super witty or super sad, and either way, the other kids loved the mystery of not knowing which Laurel would show up. Laurel hated it all, but she went through the motions to survive.

Meanwhile, after the summer movie season, business at the Rialto continued to tank as it was now tainted as the place Robbie Elms was last seen. People worried his killer still frequented there, and they forbade their children to go. By Christmas, its doors had shuttered, and the owner sold it to their notorious brother, who for a few miserable months that spring reopened it as an Adults Only bookstore, only adding to its infamy. Many businesses along that section of the pike began to shutter as downtown continued to become the mecca of the area (viewed as safer, well-lit, and more walkable) leaving behind abandoned storefronts amongst which only Connie's Place remained as a beacon. Though some would say this was all inevitable, Robbie's murder was a grim marker that precipitated this dark period of West Falls along the pike.

≈

June 1994

Freddie's mortar cap shaded his face from the hot sun, but it felt like a weight atop his foggy, pounding head. He and Pete and the rest of the gang drank beer and smoked cigarettes all night long at the playground down by the lake. Cops drove by and silently displayed their sirens a few times, but they let them be. It was tradition for a group of seniors to do this every year on the eve of graduation, revisit their childhood haunt, and as long as it didn't get too wild or noisy, no one paid them much mind.

Freddie and Pete sat atop the monkey bars and howled at the moon. "Man," Pete said, "Remember when you fell from the top of this thing and broke your arm? And Robbie and Hap, who were like not even in kindergarten yet, ran all the way home to get your mom?"

Freddie looked down from his perch, which seemed so high when he was a kid, but now didn't seem much different than falling off the couch drunk onto the floor. The earth spun a bit below him. He wished the fall was higher, so he could slip off and just fall and spin into nothingness until he was splattered across the ground. Pete always found a way to bring up Robbie. Freddie thought about strangling him.

"Hey, man," Pete went on. "What's with you and Connie?"

Freddie looked up and over at Pete, who appeared to shimmer and break into two. Freddie wasn't just drunk, but Pete didn't know that. Freddie shrugged his shoulders. Then he fell.

Freddie's right side and shoulder were bruised and ached as they called out the names of his classmates to come get their diplomas. It would be his turn soon, but it was a joke he was even getting one. He looked out into the crowd gathered on the bleachers. He could see his mom and Laurel. But his father wasn't there. After they called his name, he walked shakily onto the stage. The principal had that pity look on his face as he shook his hand and handed Freddie his diploma. Freddie just kept walking. He didn't rejoin his class. On the way to his car, parked a few blocks down the street from the football field, he threw his mortar cap into some bushes and stripped out of his gown which he left lying on the sidewalk. At his car he sat on the hood and smoked a joint. He could hear in the distance the names being called. It seemed like forever to get to the S's and for Connie's name to be called.

Connie came strolling up to the car a few minutes later still in her cap and gown and also carrying his.

"Should we wait for Pete?" Connie asked.

"Fuuuck him." Freddie said as he slipped off the hood of the car and squashed the joint under foot. "He can catch a ride with the others to the shore house."

As was also tradition, seniors would rent shore houses, up to twenty kids to a house, to party for a week after graduation, typically paid for by parents. It was considered one of the local rites of passage.

Freddie and Connie didn't even make it to the shore house. After spending a few hours at a dive bar in the middle of nowhere, getting served without even having to show their fake IDs, the car broke down on one of the back roads through the pines just a few miles from the shore. They had joints and snacks, and camped out, laying on the hood of the car, listening to the drone of bugs that covered the woods, letting the radio play and insert its cacophonous music into the discordant melodies of nature.

"We could probably walk the last few miles. It will be cooler when it's dark," Connie said. "I bet Pete and them are already there." But she wondered, wouldn't they have seen them already pass them on the road?

Freddie gave no reply. As the sun went down, the mosquitos came out and started to bite. They got back into the car for cover and rolled up the windows. Freddie got Connie into the backseat to mess around, but they were hot and sweaty and slow and fumbling. Connie tried to give him a hand job, but he couldn't keep it up. Connie suddenly felt this unbearable weight sitting there with him, Freddie half dressed with his pants down and practically passed out, limp, his head on her shoulder, the nakedness and stench of him making her queasy. She felt like she couldn't breathe in there. She decided to take her chances with the bugs outside. She pried him off and slid out of the car.

Outside the car, Connie straightened her clothes and put her shoes on. She popped the trunk and grabbed her bag. She walked to the road's edge with the music and dim light from the dashboard still filtering softly into the darkness behind her. Bruce Springsteen's "Thunder Road" played while she wondered how long it would be before the car battery died, before Freddie woke up.

For a brief moment, she imagined herself going back into the car and shaking Freddie awake. She would tell him it was over between them. She would tell him he needed to get his shit together. She would tell him how much she knew he missed Robbie. She would tell him he shouldn't beat himself up over what happened anymore. Robbie would want him to live his life. Move on. That's what she was going to do. Move on. Without Freddie.

But Connie didn't wake him. She simply walked up the road, batting mosquitos away, waiting for a car to pass. Sticking out her thumb. Hitching a ride to the shore, to any spot, where she could walk to the beach under the moonlight and jump into the ocean. Wash everything away. Sleep out under the stars on the sand. And in the morning, walking to a payphone and calling her dad to come pick her up. That's what Connie Strong did. She never said goodbye to Freddie and never saw him again.

Weeks later Pete and the gang returned from the shore house, and he told Connie that Freddie never made it down there. Vera said he never came home either. Later in the summer, Vera told Connie about a call she got from Freddie asking her to wire him some money. He was out west somewhere but he needed money to get the car fixed so he could drive it to work. He was staying with some people he met along the way. Vera would get calls periodically from different locations for about a year and a half. She would tell Connie about them. Then the calls stopped. Occasionally, a brief letter would come, always saying he was fine and he would write again. One was postmarked from Alaska. A postcard came once from South America. For all those years up until Vera passed, those were the extent of her communications with her oldest son.

≈

October 1994

Laurel hadn't seen her brother Freddie since his graduation in June. She was essentially now an only child. She wasn't terribly surprised he had just up and left. Vera, for a while, acted like he had run away, even though he was eighteen-years-old and in the eyes of the law, an adult.

Coldly, Laurel said to her mother, "Freddie left the day he found Robbie's body."

Vera slapped her across the face. Just slapped her, like in a movie. Laurel assumed she deserved it. She and Vera barely talked after that. Laurel essentially made the basement her own little apartment.

On Halloween, Pete invited her to a party. She dressed as a French maid. She and Pete hung out on the back deck at the house of some senior from her school who Pete still hung out with, even though he was a working man now and going to community college part-time.

"How's Hap?" she asked Pete.

"He's okay. He'll be okay," Pete said. "I miss your brother."

"Which one?" Laurel took a long slow sip from the bottle of beer.

Pete nodded slowly. "You gonna be okay?"

"I'll be fine. Thanks for asking."

Laurel walked herself home a little while later before the party got out of hand. She fell asleep in the basement.

It was the first time since just before the Christmas of 1992, when she and Robbie both fell asleep down there, that she suffered such a terrible bout of sleep paralysis. She felt that weighty dark presence again, and she could hear The Cranberries' "Zombie" playing on the TV. She could hear something, someone, over in the corner again by the old covered up stone in the foundation bearing hers and Robbie's names. It sounded like they were ripping up the drywall to get to the stone. She closed her eyes as tight as she could to the point of seeing a million tiny stars in the back of her brain. Then the paralysis seemed to break, and she was asleep, dreaming, and there was a sudden sense of overwhelming calm and peace. It was on the moon. She saw that stone on the moon.

≈

Summer 1996

Burg Elms never forgave himself for what happened to

Robbie. He was convinced if he hadn't accidentally slammed the door on Robbie's hand and broken it, Robbie would've been able to fight off his murderer. Secondly, if he hadn't been having a secret affair with a married woman in the city and had been home on July 4th, Robbie likely would've been with him. Detective Van Patten swore to him over and over he would find Robbie's killer, but all Burg wanted to do was punch the guy in the face. Burg also knew, if the killer was ever caught, he would find a way to kill him. He didn't trust himself in West Falls or anywhere near it. Hence the first step to move an hour away for his job.

In the summer of 1996, he was offered to lead the security operations of a military base in Belgium. He took it without a second thought. When he told Laurel, she said she wanted to come with him. She had graduated high school with honors and could have her pick of colleges far and wide. He imagined her going off to school somewhere far away, like California. But how could he deny her the request to come with him to Europe?

Burg expected a fight from Vera, but she quietly acquiesced. She helped Laurel pack and told her stories of her time studying abroad in college.

"You could do correspondence school," Vera said to her daughter pleasantly.

They had barely talked during Laurel's final years of high school, but as soon as Laurel announced her plans, Vera just wanted to be friends with her again. Not even her mom. Just a friend. Wishing her well. Seeing her off at the airport.

"I love you, Laurel," Vera said at the terminal.

"Thanks, Vera. I'll write…or email." Laurel gave her mom one last hug. Vera handed her one of those cheesy travel guides to Belgium. Laurel was awkwardly early for the overnight flight because Vera had been so worried about traffic to the airport, but she didn't want her mom to feel obligated to wait with her. "Goodbye," Laurel said expectantly.

Vera took the hint, took a step back as Laurel gave her a faint wave, fought back some tears, and turned and walked away.

At the terminal Laurel read from the travel guide about where to get the best liege waffles and the beautiful train station in Antwerp. She then got Chinese food while waiting for takeoff, thinking whatever they served on the plane would be worse than what could be found in the terminal. She was so nervous, she barely touched the food, spare for some rice, and the fortune cookie. Inside, on the little piece of crumpled white rectangular paper, it said, almost like the writer wrote it with a shrug of the shoulders, *Maybe one day you will live on the moon.* Laurel folded the paper neatly and put it in her wallet where it would stay.

Yes, *maybe.* But first Europe. Where she would make her new home base and a whole new life for herself with West Falls seemingly as distant as the moon.

EPISODE FIVE – AND SO IT BEGINS

December 2019

Hank Carter's auto shop was just down the pike from Connie's Place and the Rialto. If you turned right onto the side street just past it, you could take that all the way down into the newer development where Hank and Sheila's house overlooked what was left of the old Murder Woods.

Not long after Carl Strong's funeral, Hank hired some kid from the wrong side of the tracks to train to do oil changes. He had coached the kid in peewee football years ago, before his family moved down the line to Hampten. He thought he needed a break. He also knew the kid knew that he used to deal, and he got the sense he wanted in on that action, but of course, there wasn't any action to be had any more. He also wondered if the kid was using. Not just weed, but something harder. Still, he wanted to give this poor white boy the benefit of the doubt, as he saw maybe a bit of himself – maybe a bit of Carl, even – in the kid.

It was Friday, December 13th and there was a light, cold drizzle falling that night. Hank was working late in the office at the shop finishing up the books for the week when the kid, soaking wet, and strung out on god-knows-what, came barging into the office wielding a knife.

"Gimme all the damn money, Mr. Carter!" he said.

Hank stood up with his arms outstretched and palms up. "Whoa, whoa, son, let's talk through this. You don't want to do this."

"You don't know anything about me," the words fumbled out of the boy's mouth. "About wha-what I'm capable of."

Hank picked up the petty cash box and walked out from behind the desk. "Look, kid, just put the knife down. I'm gonna take this out to my car, and you can stay here in the office until the rain passes if you want. And we can just act like this never happened."

The boy kept the knife pointed at Hank but stumbled as he side-stepped away from the door.

Hank bolted through the door. He ran past his car and down the side street. The kid followed. Hank couldn't run like he used to. His knees had gone bad years ago, and in the slippery rain he was afraid he was going to fall. Somehow the kid caught up to him just a few blocks from Hank's house, grabbed him by the shirt, pulled him back, and jammed the knife into Hank's neck. Hank somehow broke free – perhaps the kid was in shock by what he had actually done – and stumbled down the street towards his house, blood gushing from his neck. He wanted to scream but couldn't. He made it to his front lawn and collapsed, clinging to the petty cash box. The kid was now screaming, and it was his screams that brought Sheila and some neighbors, who had just put out their Christmas decorations, out of their houses. They all screamed as the kid jumped on top of Hank and stabbed him some more. Over and over.

One of the neighbors ran back into the house to call the police while Sheila was screaming at the top of her lungs, "Oh my fucking god! Stop! Please! Stop!" When the neighbor came back out, the kid had run away with the petty cash box, leaving behind the bloody knife on the sidewalk. Sheila was huddled over her husband, screaming and crying until the police sirens came blaring down the pike and into their quiet little corner of the world. Hank Carter was dead at the scene.

On Saturday, police tracked the kid down in Hampten. The

following Tuesday there was a candle light memorial service at the pizza place next door to the auto shop, where hundreds of people turned out. Most of his former peewee football players. Friends and neighbors who he always gave discounts to on car repairs. High school kids who used to buy pills and weed off him. Amie, who had cut it off with him weeks ago and not heard from him since. Connie, who had forgiven him for the outburst after Carl's funeral. The Wolinski brothers, who in some strange way still thought of him as a friend. On Wednesday he was put into the ground. People lamented, shaking their heads. *All over some petty cash. What is this world coming to?* The police kept it pretty hush-hush about Hank's dealing, though everyone knew and gossip ran rampant on *Under the Falls*, but this didn't seem to be connected to it at all. The kid was just an addict in need of cash to get his fix and thought the auto shop was where he could get it. Or in the darkest corners of gossip, some wondered…had Hank, as a coach, done something inappropriate to this boy?

Sheila made plans to get sober. Sell the shop. Soon after, she developed a really bad dry cough and severe headache she attributed to stress and coming down off the booze, which derailed her plans a bit. Nobody, including Sheila herself, thought anything of her lingering illness and brain fog, considering all she had been through.

≈

Christmas 2019
Amie

A muted hush fell over the town during the holidays. There were the normal seasonal festivities and traditions. Santa descended from the roof of the fire station to light the Holiday Tree in the center of town. The main strip was decked to the nines with lights. There were the weekend holiday bazaars. But after what happened with Carl Strong and Hank Carter, creating fresh wounds over the past trauma of Robbie Elms, combined with the general sense of exhaustion with the world at large, there was a pall over everything. People's spirits were not completely broken, but they were bruised and tired.

Both Amie and Connie were left in a daze. Amie contemplated moving, but her lease wouldn't be up until April. She felt stuck and alone. Connie invited her to spend the holidays with her and Sutton.

"There's plenty more for you here in West Falls beyond just Hank Carter," Connie said to Amie while they closed the bar together on Christmas Eve. But Connie couldn't blame Amie for wanting to leave.

"That's nice of you to say," Amie said. "But you know me, I don't have any roots here. I'm like a rolling stone."

The Bob Dylan classic started playing, Amie having inadvertently triggered the digital DJ assistant.

The women laughed, half-heartedly. Then Amie just lost it. She started to cry with only a dirty bar towel to wipe her tears.

"It's been a helluva year," Connie said as she stepped closer and put her hand on Amie's shoulder. "No shame in lettin' it all out. It's been a helluva year for all of us."

"I've never known someone who was murdered before," Amie said to the older woman.

"I know. I know. It ain't easy, but life goes on," Connie said. "Hank was spiraling. But part of me thinks he wasn't much different than Carl. They chose different poisons, had different crutches, but they had the same pain and the same death wish."

"I just keep looking at those pictures of them people keep posting from when they were kids. Them and that poor kid Robbie. I can't stop thinking about what that priest did to Hank and Carl, and what that other sicko did to Robbie. And poor Hap, the only one of that group left. What's gonna happen to Hap?"

"Whether you like it not or not, Amie Wren, you're one of us now. You're a West Faller. And we got your back. Hap is gonna be fine, just like he always is. I'm gonna be fine. You're gonna be fine. And whatever-the-hell life throws at us, we'll have each other's backs, ya hear me?"

Amie nodded. They hugged. She wiped her tears and snot on Connie's shoulder. She hadn't done something like that since she was a child with her grandmother.

On the walk home to her apartment, Amie stopped under the lighted *Seasons Greetings* sign strung up between two buildings straddling the main strip downtown. There was a nip in the air, and she pulled the collar of her coat closer around her neck. She looked up at the sky, trying to see the stars beyond the lights of town. She longed for a little snow. Her apartment was cold. Empty. She wrapped herself in blankets and fell into a deep sleep.

≈

Pete

Pete Wolinski found solace in his fantasy football league and planning for the upcoming final game of the season on December 29th. That poor sap from Belgium, Jules, who became an accidental member of the league when he inherited a former member's recycled phone number, was going to be in town on business. The league pitched in for his game day ticket, and Jules would be joining them. Pete had even talked Jules into meeting up with him and Hap at Connie's Place the night he got into town.

"I wonder what this guy Jules does for a living?" Hap wondered aloud as he nursed his first beer, sitting at the bar with his older brother.

"Event planning or something like that. Works for an international software company," Pete replied.

"Oh, so he's a Mr. Fancy Pants, apart from being Belgian," Hap joked. "Is he gonna be bringing us some fancy waffles and chocolate up in this jawn?"

"I was hoping more for that Belgian beer."

"Cheers to that!" The brothers clanged their bottles together.

"Wouldn't it be funny if this guy knew Laurel?" Hap said flippantly. "Didn't she end up in Belgium…or somewhere like that?"

"*Yeah, and all Belgians know each other.*"

Someone's hands were on both their shoulders. Cold, delicate fingers. It gave them both a bit of shock. A woman's free-spirited laugh followed. Pete and Hap turned around, befuddled by the woman standing there. She was both familiar yet foreign.

"Did I just make you both almost jump up out of this jawn?" the woman said.

"Yeah, lady, ya kinda did," Hap said. "Do we know you?"

Pete's eyes suddenly grew wide in recognition.

"I'm Jules," she said.

"Wait…all this time, *Jules is a woman!*" Hap wanted to laugh, but then he saw something familiar in her, too. In her eyes, he suddenly saw a flickering of his long dead childhood best friend. Only one other person in the whole wide world had that special glint in their eyes.

Simultaneously, both Pete and Hap started to tear up.

"Laurel?" Pete said.

Laurel Elms, jet-lagged but still composed, nodded and smiled.

They embraced. They laughed. They ordered her a beer and made room for her at the bar in between them.

"When did you know it was me in the league chat?" Pete said.

"It took a few days, but then I put it together," Laurel said. "I used my social media detective skills to link all your names up and then realized, *holy shit*, it's Pete Wolinski and the gang from West Falls. By that time, I had to keep the whole charade going. I was having too much fun as Jules, and I knew you guys all assumed I was just some random Belgian dude. I wanted to eventually have this moment and surprise you guys, see the looks on your faces. You gotta keep the charade going with me until the game."

"Well, consider us sur-fucking-prised," Pete said.

"I want to come with a sign or something. Walk up to the whole crew during the tailgate. And be like, *Voila! Here's Jules!*"

"Your secret's safe with us. The guys are gonna flip when they meet you."

They had a few more beers together. Reminisced. The conversation got a little heavy when they talked about what had happened to Carl Strong and Hank Carter. Laurel had followed it all on social media. They talked about the petition and work being done to keep Darrel Strayer locked up. Laurel would sign it. Laurel tried to turn the talk to the upcoming game, and then said she really should get to her hotel in the city and get some shut-eye.

"Sorry it got so dark," Pete said to her at the curb while she waited with her luggage for her ride-share to arrive.

"No worries," Laurel told him. "Things are dark, aren't they? We'll catch up about more pleasant things, like our jobs, our lives, at the game."

"You've been doing well over there, huh?"

Laurel nodded. "Yeah, yeah I really have. But I'm happy to see you guys. I'm happy to be here."

"I'm happy you're here." Pete wanted to reach out and touch her hand as the car pulled up, but he grabbed the handle of her rolling suitcase instead and helped her put it in the trunk of the car. "Get some rest," he said. "Big game coming up."

"I can't wait," Laurel said. She got into the back seat of the car. Pete closed the door for her and then waved as the car pulled away with Laurel's face obscured behind the window, just a shadowy glare, racing away from him.

≈

Laurel

Laurel spent Christmas with the Wolinskis. It felt both like she had never left, and like she was a complete stranger. They pleasantly reminisced about the good old days and childhood pre-Robbie's death. Laurel wondered why both Pete and Hap had never settled down, started their own families. Peg Wolinski never wondered about Laurel, however.

"You've always been a free spirit and so independent," Peg said lovingly after Laurel gave her the social media headlines version of her past twenty plus years in Europe while helping wash the dishes. "Your mother would be proud of you."

There it was. That pall. That dark curtain weighing down on them. That heaviness of the missing people in their lives.

"Thanks for saying that, Mrs. Wolinski," Laurel said. "I was sorry to hear about Mr. Wolinski."

"Gene and I had a good life together. It was quick. A heart attack. And just like that, he wasn't here anymore. Five years gone now," Peg let her hands linger in the warm soapy water. "I was sorry to hear about Burg."

"Yeah, it was painful. Alzheimer's is one of the worst things I can imagine happening to someone. But I don't really wanna talk about that."

"I'm sorry, honey, but I do have to ask, why didn't you come back for your mother's funeral?"

Laurel nodded at this inevitable inquiry. "I wanted to, but I couldn't leave Burg. He was in real bad shape, and he went not too long after that. Looking back, I wish I had come, but then also, maybe it was a blessing I chose not to. It would've been too much all at once."

"I understand," Peg conceded. "I'm sorry to bring it up."

Laurel touched the old woman's bony shoulder gently with her damp hand. "No, it's okay. God, it's so good to see you." They hugged.

Later, it was cold outside on the front porch, but not too cold. Hap was inside helping his mom finish cleaning up, while Pete and Laurel passed a joint on the stoop.

"You're in Amsterdam a lot for work, right? Like are people

just walking around high all the time and smoking pot in the streets like cigarettes?" Pete asked.

"24/7," Laurel laughed.

"They're legalizing it here, ya know. It's gonna be on the ballot."

"First time you ever took an interest in politics, huh, Petey-boy?"

Pete laughed after he exhaled slowly. Then he took on a serious look. "You ever hear from Freddie?"

"No," Laurel said as she took the joint from him. "And you know what, it never used to piss me off, but it does now. I gotta sell the stone house, and do you know what a legal mess it is to do that with him, as a fifty percent owner, basically missing?"

"Wait, whaddya mean you gotta sell the stone house? I thought there were renters in there."

"There had been, but there's issues with the foundation and the plumbing and god-knows-what else, and I can't rent it out anymore. Flippers want to buy it and tear it down to the studs and rebuild. But I gotta wait a certain amount of time, give Freddie a chance to respond to the lawyer's notices and show up, before I can close on any deal. It's the third reason I'm here and staying a bit longer, besides the work trip that's already over and the big game."

"You can't let them tear that house down! It's historical. It's...it's..." Pete took the joint back from her and shook his head while taking another toke. "I mean, I know you don't care anymore, living in Europe, but that house...*your house*...it's part of the fabric of this town."

"It's falling apart, Pete, and to be honest, it's nothing but painful memories for me."

"Robbie would want you to keep it. Fix it."

Laurel grabbed the joint back from him. It was down to the nub, and she tossed it on the bottom step and put it out with her shoe. "Don't you dare tell me what Robbie would want," she said in a low voice.

Pete leaned in suddenly to kiss her. Laurel pushed him away.

"Jesus Christ, Pete!" she yelled as she stood up and brushed some ashes off her skirt. "Tell your mother thanks for dinner. It really was lovely, until just now."

"Oh, C'mon, Laurel! Let me and Hap take a look at the house. It's what we do. We're handy. We can fix shit."

"You gonna fix a foundation?" Laurel looked out into the dark street and laughed. "Gonna exorcise some ghosts?"

"C'mon, I'm serious!"

"I gotta go, Pete. Need to get back to the city to the hotel."

"You can stay here. I mean not at my place…or well, you could if you wanted to. I mean here, at my mom's."

"Good night, Pete." Laurel stepped down onto the sidewalk and slowly started to walk away.

When she was underneath a streetlight, Pete called out to her. "You're just walking back to the hotel?"

"I'm walking to the station to take the train." She then mumbled low under her breath. "*You idiot.*"

"I heard that, Laurel Elms!" Pete playfully called back to her.

"Goodnight, Pete! Merry Christmas!" Laurel hollered back as she walked further away into the darkness down the street.

She didn't talk to Pete again until the day of the big game. The charade was a big success. The others in the league were shocked Jules was a woman and West Falls' long lost daughter, Laurel Elms, no less! She and Pete yucked it up with everyone, got loaded, took tons of pictures, posted to social media, and one of the guys joked about taking the whole story to a podcaster he knew. It was a helluva game, and a helluva time. It didn't even matter who won and who lost.

Laurel extended her stay as she could work remotely from anywhere in the world, but got a short-term house rental in town for the month of January hoping to close soon on her childhood home. She was easily able to rent out her flat to tourists in Brussels for the month to fund her stay in West Falls. She spent most of her time working odd hours because of the time difference, but she was a regular at Connie's Place and became an adult resident of her sleepy hometown of West Falls for the first time in her life. Yet, despite the hospitality of Connie and the Wolinskis, she still felt like a ghost and didn't want to linger too long.

≈

February 2020
Sam

Sam and Val had found a perfect babysitter for Henry over the holiday break in Tyeisha, the high-schooler down the street. Henry absolutely loved her, and she was a seasoned veteran, having sat for families all throughout the neighborhood last summer. Val had gone out to California that weekend following the holidays to visit his mother. Sam needed some Henry-free time to work on the website to help stop Darrel Strayer's parole, and so Tyeisha had been at the house all day.

"I'm almost done," Sam told her as he moved downstairs to finish the work at the dining room table. "Feel free to stay for dinner if you want. Order pizza."

"Sure," Tyeisha called back from the couch where she was snuggled with Henry watching a movie. "I can stay as long as you like."

A few minutes later, she was peering over his shoulder looking at the picture of Robbie Elms he had placed on the website.

"My mom was the last person to see him alive," she said in that teenage girl matter-of-fact style meant to shock adults.

Sam turned to her, shocked. "Wait, your mom…*is Jennifer Alvarez?*"

"Well, yeah, Alvarez is her maiden name."

Sam took a moment to digest this. "It's a small world. How is your mom, by the way?"

"She's good. Says work is getting crazy."

"She's an ER nurse, right?"

"Yeah, she said lots of old folks are coming in from the retirement home on the pike really sick."

"That's gotta be such a stressful job."

"She likes it enough."

"And how's your dad, Marcus?"

"He's okay. He wishes mom would quit. He thinks it's too much stress."

"Pizza! Pizza! Pizza!" Henry's cries came bouncing in from the living room.

Tyeisha smiled. "Guess I better order."

Sam pulled up the delivery app on his phone and handed it to Tyeisha. "Brick oven. Get whatever pizza you like. And a salad. And the fries for Henry."

After Tyeisha left, and he got Henry to bed, Sam texted Val, whom he hoped was just finishing up dinner out west.

Sam: How's your mom?

Val: Good.

Sam: We should plan for all of us to go out next time.

Val: I don't know about that. Let's stick with video calls for now. You know how she is. She accepts us…to a degree.

Sam: Well maybe just Henry then?

Val: Maybe.

Sam: The website is coming along great. The petition is up. I'm even helping Mayor Jackson solicit the letters to the parole board from friends and family to speak to the trauma Darrel Strayer caused. Come May when the hearing comes up I don't see any way they would let him out.

Val: Damn, the way you guys are working to keep him in jail, you'd think he was black.

Sam: Don't you think he deserves to rot in there for life for what he did? Some of his victims were poor black kids from

Hampten, remember? That's what they actually nailed him for. Not Robbie Elms.

Val: I signed your damn petition. What more do you want from me? I don't know these people. What do I care what happens to one fucking horrible white guy out of millions?

Sam: You know Hap.

Val: The guy fixed our washing machine. I don't know Hap.

Sam: I miss you.

Sam took a deep breath while the eternal ellipse appeared in the message bar…like Val was writing him a novel. He tried not to take the harshness personally. He knew Val always got like this when he was around his mother. She was a lot to handle. And stubborn. Like Val.

Val: I miss you too. Kiss Henry on the forehead for me. I know it's getting late there. Good night.

Sam: Good night.

≈

First week of March 2020
Laurel

The local retro radio station played in the rental car as Laurel pulled up to the old stone house at dusk. As if on cue, The Cranberries "Ode to My Family" played, and Laurel was instantly transported to all those feelings of teenage angst from when she decided to leave this house and her mother at age eighteen. The song continued to loop in her head as she stepped out of the car and up onto the dilapidated front porch, an old beat-up wooden rocker still there. She remembered when it was new and her mother would rock out there at night, always ending with her standing up, gripping the porch railing, and staring out beyond the street, field and lake into the deep, dark woods where Robbie had been murdered.

Laurel could still see Vera standing there, saying to her in a hot whisper, "I sometimes imagine Robbie still out there in those woods."

The stone mason pulled up to the curb in his truck, temporarily relieving Laurel of her ghosts and angst.

"Thanks for coming out," Laurel said as the man came up the front steps. She proceeded to unlock the front door and lead him inside through the dusky dim interiors of the old, empty house. As she led him down into the basement, he flipped on his flashlight, and like a spotlight it shot down the steps to the stage of her childhood. Yet the basement was now stripped, damp, and cold, having been returned to its barest bones when she had the house emptied after the last tenants moved out.

"In the corner, over there," Laurel pointed as they got to the foot of the staircase.

The man proceeded carefully and shined the light on the corner bottom stone where the names of Laurel and Robbie had been etched seemingly at the beginning of time.

"What are the chances of being able to remove it whole?" Laurel asked him.

"You said the flippers are gonna take this place down to the studs?" he replied.

"Total rebuild."

"Damn shame. This is a great old house. I mean, this is part of the foundation, but if they let me, I can carve it out, and I can do my best to preserve the etching."

Laurel nodded.

"This Robbie, this was the kid that was murdered back in the day, right?"

"Yeah, my brother. But the names were etched in there when the house was built in the late 1800s."

"Lady, I don't understand a lick of what you just said, but I can give this my best and see what happens. Can I ask what you plan to do with it?"

"I dunno, maybe I'll take it with me to the moon." Laurel

laughed.

"Whatever you say, lady. Give the flippers my number, and when they're ready to take it down to the studs, I can come and carve this out for you."

≈

Connie

With the assistant manager out sick, Connie worked the rare Saturday night. Amie was on schedule, too, and a cavalcade of regulars flooded through the doors that night. During the dinner rush, Sam and Val and Henry Vaughan came. Connie was profusely thankful to Sam for all the help he was providing in the efforts to keep Darrel Sayer from being granted parole, and she doted on the little boy, Henry. Marcus Williams came in to pick up take-out, and told Connie both Jennifer and Tyeisha were home sick. Eventually the family dinner rush subsided and it was the usual mix of regulars and partiers who came to drink and eat during the lull before a local cover band started around 9pm.

Laurel Elms came in with the Wolinski brothers.

"So glad you're staying in town longer," Connie said.

Connie noticed Laurel interacted with Pete like she would a brother, and maybe that's what Pete had become for her in the absence of Freddie, though anyone with eyes knew Pete would always hold a candle for Laurel. Meanwhile, for the first time, Connie noticed a little playful flirting between Amie and Hap. She couldn't wait to tell Sutton about this very interesting development tomorrow morning over coffee and brunch.

Conversation bounced all over the place, including: the ever-increasing focus on what they were now calling the COVID-19 virus and the doomed cruise ship being quarantined on the open seas outside of Japan, the presidential primaries, the recent impeachment acquittal of the president, the most recent mass shootings, the upcoming trial of Hank Carter's killer, the upcoming parole hearing of Darrel Sayer, and the hubbub over the middle school PTA president allegedly having an affair with the high school gym teacher. Connie tried to focus on the local news buzz and gossip, but couldn't help but wonder if the virus was already here with so many more people than usual getting sick, though the only confirmed cases thus far had been on the west coast.

"This is why you'll never catch me on a cruise," Hap said.

"It's just the flu," some regulars dismissed the chatter.

"This cover band sucks," others ranted.

"Trump should be in jail," some said.

"Until these mass shootings stop, they should just shut everything down," one suggested.

"Why they hell didn't they just execute that sick fuck Darrel Sayer?" some guy said, and he turned to Laurel further down the bar. "I mean, am I right?"

"Not cool, man," Pete scolded him.

"Sorry, sorry, I lost my head and forgot who she was," the man said drunkenly and sheepishly to Laurel.

"I would've liked to have killed him," Laurel said confidently, shocking everyone in the bar into silence.

The cover band broke out into a rendition of Jim Croce's "You Don't Mess Around with Jim."

"More like, you don't mess around with Laurel Elms!" Connie announced. "Now who needs another round?"

At the end of the night, after most had cleared out and the band had disbanded, it was just the Wolinski brothers and Laurel left. Connie and Amie were closing, and Connie was content to let Amie continue to flirt with Hap. At one point, Hap called out to the AI DJ, "Play Amie!"

While Pure Prairie League's "Amie" echoed within the walls of the otherwise empty bar, Connie couldn't help but think despite all the chaos in the world right now…this right here, this bar, this West Falls, these people whom she loved, were gonna be alright. And though, like everyone, she had fallen in and out of love with the world throughout her many years on this tumultuous earth, she was in love with the crazy world right here, right now, in this simultaneously small and unfathomably big moment. Pete. Hap. Amie. Laurel. Oh, dear Laurel, to be sitting there; Connie had never thought it could ever be like this. For a brief flicker, the flaming absence of others was snuffed out and a weight temporarily lifted. Those smiles on those faces around the bar were home for Connie, and she never wanted to leave.

The next morning, Connie woke up with a cough.

EPISODE SIX – THE CRUELEST MONTHS

The Lockdown Months, 2020
The Williams Family

In March, after the first person in their area, a resident of a local nursing home, died of COVID, the schools shut down and haphazardly began remote learning. A full stay-at-home order was released about a week later. Only essential workers were allowed out, and only essential businesses allowed to stay open. Almost all flights were cancelled. The high-speed line ran limited trains into the city.

For most, it felt so sudden, a complete upending of norms, and an extreme response to a huge *what if* situation. *What if it got so much worse?* But the Williams family saw it all happening before anyone else did. Jennifer started masking up at the hospital in February. She still got sick and brought something home to Tyeisha, though there were no tests for COVID yet available to the masses so who knows what that might have been, and Marcus escaped unscathed. When Jennifer returned to work the following week right before the lockdown began, she began changing out of her scrubs in the garage when she got home, bagging them to wash, and showering down as soon as she stepped into the house.

No one knew yet just how contagious it was. It was clearly airborne, but did it travel on surfaces, too? When they started ordering groceries to be delivered, she had Marcus wipe everything down with disinfectant wipes before putting anything away. Any non-perishable deliveries were left on the porch for three days. The Williams family were trendsetters. Most people, out of an abundance of caution, followed suit. But factions started to creep in and crack as the unknown scale of the pandemic created virulent imaginations. Misinformation and mixed messages grew exponentially on social media as people cooped up inside all day and night doom-scrolled for some kind of sign this would end and things would return to normal.

Tyeisha was starving for social interaction by the second week of lockdown. She reached out to Sam Vaughan and said as soon at the stay-at-home order was lifted she would love to watch Henry if daycare was still closed. She masked up and went for walks in the morning before online classes and later in the afternoon, avoiding other masked walkers like a game of frogger. The walks grew increasingly longer, and she traversed through every nook and cranny of town, down little side streets or alleyways previously unexplored, through all the parks, past the empty playgrounds with caution tape around the equipment, past the shuttered stores downtown, in the middle of empty residential streets lined with parked cars, many not having moved for days. A few times a day, the rattling of the mostly empty train down the high-speed line into the city was the only sign civilization was still operational.

Everything seemed so quiet. No traffic. No airplanes overhead in the once constantly droning flight path that had provided the town with white noise before the pandemic. White noise they had never noticed until it was gone. Some people took calls next to open windows, otherwise clandestine conversations sneaking out into the still air along the sidewalks where quiet passersby could stop for a moment, taking comfort in the presence of others, even if they were on the other side of a wall and blissfully unaware of those listening in. Others left silent signs or talismans on their journeys, little painted rocks, encouraging notes in chalk, tiny mementos to remind strangers and acquaintances alike they were all in this together. The only way out was through.

During the third week of lockdown, Tyeisha and a few friends agreed to meet up at a local playground at night after dinner. "Let's tear down the caution tape!" they agreed. They played like little kids. They were dutifully masked up, but the cloth couldn't muffle their hooting and hollering. For a brief moment, in that break in the darkness on the swings underneath the street lights, they were free, swinging up higher into the sky than they had ever been pushed by their parents when they were little. Finally, their cries of *higher, higher* were answered.

Soon people started to develop pods, families agreeing to the same rules and taking on mutual risk by interacting with each other. Neighbors or extended families came together so kids could learn or play with each other. Tyeisha wanted to be in Sam, Val, and Henry's pod, but Jennifer and Marcus were still being ultra-cautious, as Jennifer was on the frontlines.

All the caution in the world couldn't prevent Jennifer from catching it eventually in late April. By the end of the month, she was hospitalized on a ventilator. She was dead by the time May began, leaving Tyeisha and Marcus and everyone who had followed her lead when this all began, devastated.

They hadn't even been allowed to see her. One of her colleagues was there to hold Jennifer's hand in those final hours. That colleague video called Marcus and Tyeisha, and that image on the phone of two gloved hands gripping each other was the last Tyeisha had of her mother. When the news came shortly before lunch time later that day, Tyeisha ran out of the house screaming, hoping everyone would hear her, hoping all would know. She was met with the silent indifference of a midday in lockdown, and all she had for comfort were her own tears, streaming down her cheeks as she ran, trying to create her own wind to sweep her up and take her away from here, *higher and higher.* When she finally came to a gasping stop somewhere downtown, her heavy breathing and crying was accompanied by the daily church bells at noon. The bells calmed her.

Later that week, while wandering the streets as her mother's body was cremated, she traipsed down a back alley between two store fronts atop of which sat apartments. Tyeisha leaned against the brick wall underneath an open second story window and breathed deeply, calmly, as two people inside talked of love as if they were the only two people left in the world, on the brink of some new kind of happiness.

≈

Laurel

No, it wasn't the loneliness of being trapped in her hometown during the pandemic that made Laurel feel like life was at a painful standstill. She was used to being alone. She thrived being solo, especially traveling. Though she had a close circle (and sometimes revolving door) of endlessly interesting friends and coworkers in Brussels and other parts of Europe with whom she spent holidays and vacationed, it had always been those solo trips – to Paris, Amsterdam, Spain, Italy, to Japan and Vietnam and Thailand – where she lived her best life. Soaking it all in, at her own speed, on her own terms, with no one to question her and no one to answer to. Yes, it was the closed world, not the loneliness, that was the worst.

While in West Falls, people, especially other women, who had never branched further than West Falls or the city (with maybe a once-in-a-lifetime family trip to California or Florida), questioned her.

"Aren't you scared to travel alone?"

"Isn't it dangerous for a woman?"

Admittedly, sometimes it was. There was no denying, everywhere was a man's world, and in some places more than others there were suspect strangers, would-be muggers, or worse yet, rapists on the prowl. But Laurel had vowed to herself long ago never to let the bad behavior of men – her father, Darrel Strayer, the pervert on the train, strangers in strange lands, politicians or dictators – dictate how freely she would live her life. She would go wherever and do whatever she damned well pleased. She would be smart about it, of course, as careful and watchful as needed, but she wouldn't let them ruin the big, open, beautiful world for her.

Which was now closed, and she was stuck in West Falls. Working remotely at odd hours due to the time zone differences. Having strained and banal conversations with old acquaintances and curious locals who found her exotic or strange. Waiting for a man, her long-lost brother, to respond to another man, her lawyer, about selling their childhood home. Extending the lease for the people renting her apartment in Brussels, who had originally only meant to stay for a month, but who were stuck now, too. She cooked up dreams of moving somewhere else when the borders opened back up. Truth was, she had wanted out of Brussels for a while now. The longer it took to sell the old stone house, the more its value increased despite its state of disrepair. Maybe she would end up with enough to buy a pied-à-terre in Paris.

It all seemed like a dream, while day to day had become surreal. How many virtual software innovation and networking conferences could Laurel possibly arrange before people just started screaming? *She* just wanted to scream. On social media she read about people having virtual scream therapy sessions where people logged onto calls and took turns screaming. Mostly women. Frustrated working moms who felt trapped and were taking on more of the emotional workload than ever before in this lockdown environment, where all the inequities that had always been there were amplified. Laurel wasn't a mother, but she could empathize. Oh, how she wanted to scream.

On *Under the Falls* a group arranged "Communal Screams" where at agreed upon times during the day, you were supposed to step outside and scream. Laurel set her alarm for these events, and she would step outside hoping to hear other screams in the neighborhood. Any sign of life and shared pain. One time, she thought she heard a scream in the distance. There was a baby next door she heard wailing. A stray cat tiptoeing down the sidewalk mewed. Laurel couldn't bring herself to scream in those moments. She thought about how she wanted to scream for her brother Robbie when he was just missing and not yet confirmed dead, murdered. She thought if she screamed now the world would crack wide open.

Later she realized it already had. She walked down to the cemetery and looked at her brother's and mother's graves side by side. She had no flowers for them. Hap had placed more pictures of him and Robbie and little talismans around the gravestone in the build-up to Darrel Strayer's parole hearing. She had forgotten about Robbie's chain. All the boys got silver chains in middle school back then. How had Hap ended up with it? Maybe Vera had given it to him at some point as a memento. There were things more childish, too – a baseball card, a little army man. As if the importance of Robbie's brief life could be measured by the things he accumulated. Maybe this is where she would lay the cornerstone with her and Robbie's names etched on it once it was removed from the foundation of the house? Or maybe not. She didn't want people thinking she was dead, too.

That's when Laurel walked up to the overlook above the gorge and decided to scream as loud as she could so the whole world could hear her.

"It feels good, doesn't it?" a familiar voice behind Laurel called out.

Laurel jumped and turned around to find a masked Sutton approaching her on the ledge. Laurel pulled up her mask. She was suddenly aware of how windy it was up there, a bit of a chill even though spring was in bloom. She shuddered a bit.

"I didn't think anyone else was up here," Laurel explained.

"Oh, don't stop because of me," Sutton said. "I wanna do it, too.”

Laurel didn't know what else to say in this awkward moment, a rare in-person interaction. She glanced down at the mess of tarps in the gorge. “Are they ever going to finish?” she asked, thinking as mayor, Sutton must know.

“Funding fell through on the current research grant long before the pandemic started. I've just been trying to get them to clear all the stuff out, but you know, with the lockdown and everything.”

“Pete Wolinski was saying there was a push to fill the gorge, turn the falls back on?”

“Yes, somewhat of a re-wilding,” Sutton explained. “It's complicated, though. We would have to dam further up-stream to keep the lake relatively full and not turn all that lakefront property into swamp-front property, which is what it all used to be anyways.”

“The falls would be a draw, though, right?” Laurel wondered.

“Indeed, and would give us our name back. But it would rebury all those bones down there. If anyone cares about those bones anymore.”

“I would think people would be more concerned with the bones in the cemetery.” Laurel shrugged and then said in a mocking tone, “What a lovely waterfall view the town's dead would have.”

“Were you visiting your family's graves?” Sutton tried to change the subject.

Laurel nodded.

“Could I still compel you to write a letter to the parole board?” Sutton asked.

“You haven't yet.” Laurel almost laughed. “What makes you think you'll compel me here standing on this ledge?”

“It would help for them to understand the hurt he continues to cause.”

“He doesn't hurt me none,” Laurel said, standing firm against the ledge. "Look, I signed the petition, of course, and I'm thankful you maintain such an interest. But what does it matter to me living in Belgium what becomes of him over here? Of course, I want them to keep him locked up, but a letter from me will not decide that."

Sutton looked away, as if a better reason was out there in the wind, and then turned back to Laurel. "I'm just worried with the overcrowding issues they're having in the prisons, and as long as the pandemic is raging, they might just let him go to free up space "

"And what if they do?" Laurel asked, folding her arms across her chest.. "Maybe he'll get COVID and die before they can do that."

"Connie told me about what you said in the bar…about killing him yourself."

Laurel rolled her eyes. "It was a joke."

"Would you though, if you had the chance?"

Laurel looked the older woman dead in the eyes. "You think I would tell you, the former prosecutor? Are you trying to entrap me?"

Sutton stepped back. "Of course not."

"Settle down, that was a joke, too," Laurel put her arms down. "Look, I just want to sell my parents' house and go back home as soon as the borders open up again."

"I understand," Sutton said.

"Do you? Really?"

Sutton shook her head. "I'm sorry I bothered you." She turned to walk away.

"Wait!" Laurel called after her. "What about you? Would you kill him yourself if you had the chance?"

Sutton paused, looked back at Laurel with her eyes strained atop her masked face. She shrugged her shoulders and walked away.

After enough time passed, Laurel turned back to the gorge, the gaping hole in the earth seemingly screaming back at her as she lowered her mask and screamed again.

≈

Amie & Hap

When lockdown began, Amie had already provided notice she did not intend to re-sign her lease in April. Even though she was flattered by Connie's "You're one of us!" speech back in March, her gut told her it was time to move on, just as it always had anytime she was getting too close to someone or settled in somewhere. Here, it wasn't any one person she was getting too close to, it was the town. She liked it here, in spite of all the drama. Her affair with Hank Carter made her a point of gossip, but his brutal murder endeared her to people. The regulars at Connie's Place enjoyed her company. Others pitied her. Connie had grown to love her like a younger sister. After Hank's murder, in Amie she found a kindred spirit. As different as the circumstances were between Robbie's and Hank's murders, they both understood now what it was like to lose someone like that so violently and suddenly. Then, of course, there was the added layer of Connie's past connection to Hank. Yes, there was something to be said for the anchoring powers of pity, love, and shared tragedies, Amie admitted to herself. But her gut still told her to get the hell out.

Then there was the pandemic. A week into lockdown, Amie messaged her landlord she changed her mind and wanted to re-sign her lease. While Connie had no choice but to let go of the part-time help, she kept Amie on full-time, paying her an assistant manager's wage to make up for lost tips. Together, with the full-time kitchen staff she kept on, and the busboy turned delivery driver, they kept Connie's open for take-out. Sam Vaughan helped Connie set up a make-shift website to handle both take-out and grocery orders so they could sell the excess stock of perishable food that had been pre-ordered months ago through the supplier when they were still trying to run a bustling bar and restaurant.

"It makes no sense for it to go to waste," Connie explained to Amie. "We're not even going to make a profit on it. We'll give it to people who need it at the same wholesale prices we bought it for."

Amie couldn't help but linger on the *we* Connie used whenever talking about Connie's Place. Meanwhile, giant blocks of cheese, jumbo sized cartons of eggs, tubs of butter, and bags of rolls headed out the door in droves to people looking to buy in bulk or too scared to go to the grocery stores.

So here Amie was, going against her gut, a victim of circumstance, staying. Connie was thrilled, naturally.

In May, Amie's refrigerator at home went on the fritz. She had to keep stuff in a giant cooler full of ice. The landlord told her to do whatever she needed to do to get it fixed or replaced and then send her the bill. She went on *Under the Falls* to ask who people recommended, and she should've realized everyone would unanimously recommend Hap Wolinski.

"I can put the mask on or not, your choice," Hap said at the door, maskless but with one dangling in his hand.

Amie had her mask on already, as it was becoming force of habit. She didn't know what to do in this situation. She shrugged her shoulders but kept hers on.

"The lady of the house votes to mask," Hap said as he strapped his on across his nose and mouth.

Amie lingered in the kitchen as Hap pulled the fridge out in one swift movement and began tinkering with stuff in the back. She was surprised how easily he moved it. Hap wasn't a terribly big guy, but he must've been fit and knew how to move his body to get things done.

"I miss you guys," Amie said.

"You and Connie and the place seem to be doing alright," Hap said.

"I know. I mean, I just miss you and Pete being there. You're both so funny, so much alike. Same sense of humor, body language, and voice even…but then…"

Hap paused and peeked out from behind the fridge. "*Oh…*" he said in a mock theatrical voice, "The lady of the house noticed my brother has the pasty skin and privileged bloat of a fourth generation Polish American, and I…well, I look more like *Slumdog Millionaire.*"

Amie laughed. "I don't even get that reference."

"I'm adopted, you know." He searched for something in his toolbox on the floor beside him.

"I didn't want to presume. You know me. In my head I cooked up a juicy little story where you mother had an affair with a dashing Indian doctor."

Hap laughed, maybe a little too loud. It made Amie jump.

"Have you *met* my mother, Peg?" Hap asked.

Amie tried not to laugh. "Sorry."

"No, it's funny," Hap said. "She actually found me abandoned on the steps of St. Mary's church in the dead of winter. It's a nice little Hallmark movie."

Amie was shocked by how casually Hap revealed his origin story, as if he had a preset jokey blurb ready whenever it came up to gloss over the seriousness of it. As if he was protecting others from his sad beginnings more so than even himself. She wanted to know more, but didn't know where to start. Finally, after an awkward pause, she asked, "And your name…Hap…is short for something?"

"It's short for Happy."

"Did other kids ever give you a hard time? As progressive as this place presents itself to be, it's not…abundantly diverse."

"No, mainly because my brother would've kicked their ass. But also, when you're best friends with Robbie Elms, you're golden."

"It must've been pretty nice growing up here then?" Amie coughed a little under her mask. "No, sorry, I mean, well…"

"You don't have to dance on eggshells around me," Hap said. "Despite what happened to Robbie, and what happened to others, it was very Norman Rockwell. Still is. Still golden."

"People love you on *Under the Falls*," Amie gushed. "You're like *the appliance whisperer*. A local celebrity. A hero."

"Exactly. So why would I ever want to leave?" Finding whatever do-dad he needed from his toolbox, Hap went back to tinkering behind the fridge. After a few minutes, he stopped, put his tools back, and stood up.

"So, what's the diagnosis, doc?" Amie asked.

"Well, I don't think I can whisper this one back to health. You're gonna need a new one."

"Oh, shit."

"Yeah, and, umm, just about everything is on back-order due to all the supplier issues. I'll see what strings I can pull, but it's likely gonna be eight to ten weeks at best."

"I might as well just set up a cot at the bar."

"Look, I got a spare mini-fridge in my basement. I can bring it over when I'm done these with next few house calls."

"Really? *Oh, my hero.*"

Hap laughed. "All in a day's work. Let me get something on order, I'll run it by you and your landlord of course before placing it, and in the meantime I'll bring over that mini-fridge. Maybe I'll even stock it with a six pack of beer."

"Only if you're gonna drink it with me." Amie's eyes brightened.

Hap paused. Was he grinning under that mask? "Deal."

Hap delivered and hooked up the mini-fridge, more bags of ice for the cooler, and a six-pack of beer later that evening, but he had to take a rain check on hanging out because there was some old lady who needed her oven fixed right away. They texted back and forth over the next few days to arrange a better time. Eventually, Amie had a day off, and he agreed to unplug, too, and they decided to do a little day drinking. After all, it was starting to get warmer, and Amie could open up the windows and air out the apartment.

Maskless, Amie answered the door upon hearing Hap's rat-a-tat-tat knock. He stood there with his mask dangling in hand, placing it in his pocket upon seeing her naked face. They both smiled awkwardly at each other as he stepped into the apartment and she closed the door behind him.

"How's the mini-fridge working for you?" he asked.

"Just like the good ol' college days," Amie said as she leaned down to grab two bottles of beer out of the little black fridge.

"Oh, where did you go to college?" Hap asked.

"I didn't. I was just joking. I mean, I did a year of community college in the city actually, but it wasn't for me, and then I went off on the first of my misadventures. God, it seems like ages ago."

It was the first time Hap wondered how old she was. She looked young. At least younger than him, but maybe not. Maybe they were closer in age than at first glance. The beer bottle felt ice-cold in his hand. "Welp, it seems to be working pretty damn well."

Amie laughed. "More like a mini-icebox. But it's how I like my beer."

"Me too."

There was a little café table and two chairs set up in the living room underneath the open window where a nice warm breeze blew in gently lifting up the thin curtains, but the view was just of the brick building across the alleyway. They sat down. Hap popped the caps off both beers on the edge of the metal table, and they toasted.

"To lockdown!" Amie said.

"To seeing each other's faces," Hap said with a smile.

It was the first time Amie thought about how old Hap was. Doing the math from Robbie's death, he must be almost forty, but his skin and face and smile made him look boyish. Here she was again with another older man, but there was something different about Hap. At least something very different compared to Hank.

"Business must be booming for you," Amie said. "Everyone at home, noticing all the things that need fixing. Appliances breaking down from over-use."

"I'm doing well," Hap said. "But people are struggling. So, I'm doing a lot of stuff at discount or for free. Anything I can do to help people out."

"You're a good man, Hap Wolinski. And what Connie has done for me is a godsend. She could've easily just let me go. And you know, I was *this close* to not signing my lease renewal and getting the heck out of dodge before the pandemic hit."

"I'm glad you stayed."

Amie leaned back in her chair, enjoyed the beer, and gazed out the window. "Hear that? *Nothing.* I used to not be able to open this window because of all the noise from the foot traffic downtown, but now…"

"It's eerie," Hap said. "But also nice in a way. The silence. I don't know how much longer we can sustain this. Did ya hear about the guy who owns the local gym down the road? He's been opening up against the government mandates. Says gyms are essential. The cops keep having to come every morning and shut him down."

"Are people actually showing up to work out?" Amie wondered.

Hap laughed. "Hell if I know. They'd be fools to. I mean, heck, they can come over to my place and do jumping jacks. Just take a walk or a run, people."

Amie laughed. "I'm all for just waiting it out. I mean, what else can we do? Help each other where we can. Find connections however we can. And wait it out. Eventually it's just gonna be like another flu or cold, right?"

"Yeah, but when is that gonna happen? And so many sick and old people dying. And frontline folks trying to save lives are losing their lives. Look at Jennifer Williams. I still can't believe it. Her husband and daughter couldn't even put on a funeral for her."

"You went to school with her, right?"

"Yeah. She was among the best of us. Now she's gone in the

blink of an eye, and no one seems to care."

Amie's eyes softened as she regarded him. "You care."

Hap's face had changed while talking about Jennifer. He looked away, up at the fluttering curtains. He pretended some dirt or pollen had blown into his face. He rubbed his eyes. They were moist. He sniffled. "I'm sorry," he said. "This was supposed to be fun."

"It's okay."

"She was the last person to see Robbie alive. She was my first kiss. Like I said, she was the best of us."

"You know what we need, besides to drink more? Music!" Amie got up and turned on a wireless speaker that sat on the coffee table and began scrolling through her music list on her phone. "Let's see, what do you like?"

"Me?" Hap took a big swig of beer. "I like…no, I love…jazz."

"Jazz? No way! So do I!" She seemed to have found what she was looking for on her phone. "*Speak Low.*"

"I don't think I know that one."

"Sarah Vaughan. Oh, it's an oldie for sure. It was my grandparent's wedding song. They used to play it all the time."

Amie stood by the window and Hap remained seated. They both enjoyed the velvety tones and words, Sarah Vaughan's voice so smooth, the tinkling of the piano keys filling the room and gently dripping out the open window into the alley. Neither one of them said a word until it was over.

"It's wonderful," Hap said. "I love it."

"Shhh…" Amie said. "And speak low when you say you love something."

Hap lowered his voice as deep as he could, "*I loved it.*"

Amie laughed. She sipped more of the beer, looking pensive. "Would you believe me if I told you I've never been in love?"

"Impossible!" Hap slapped a hand on the table.

"I mean, I've liked people," Amie cocked her head. "I've

lusted after far too many people. But love, I dunno. At least not the kind of love people talk about in the most romantic sense."

"Romance is a scam." Hap scoffed.

"No, you know what I mean," Amie playfully scolded. "What about you? Have you ever been in love?"

"Now that's a loaded question. And depends on what kind of love. I've loved plenty of people. But I dunno. Maybe I'm like you. Maybe not in that classical romantic sense. Maybe that's why you and I are both single and sitting here right now talking about love?"

Amie sat back down excitedly and leaned in over the table to get as close to Hap as she could. "Let's talk about all the things we love."

"Okay, sure," Hap swigged some beer and then began. "I love helping people…"

"No, no, no, you don't have to prove to me you're a nice guy. Tell me about the THINGS you love."

"Okay, well…ice-cold beer." He raised the bottle and polished it off. "Jazz. I love the house I grew up in. I love this town. I love history, like prehistoric millions and millions of years ago history. You know about the dinosaur dig site in the gorge right? I love all that stuff, but I could go on and on about that, so stop me. Tell me about you. What do you love?"

"Well, *I love ice-cold beer. Jazz.* I don't love the house I grew up in. I wish it would burn to the ground actually. I think I am starting to love this town. I love being able to just put my entire life in a suitcase and some boxes and getting in my car and driving somewhere to start over. The freedom of being able to do that. Not being tied down. I suppose in a way I love travel, though I haven't done much of that other than the cross-country moves I've made." While she was saying this, she became conscious of Hap looking at her, and it was strange. She was used to men leering or pretending to listen, but Hap was genuinely listening and with feeling. He had this smile on his face listening to her. Suddenly she realized she had just trailed off and was staring at him now.

"Hey, why did you stop?" Hap asked her.

"What came first, the name or the constant smiling?" Amie asked. "You really are Happy."

"Sometimes you become your name. My parents wanted me to be happy. So, they manifested it with my name."

"What was it like having great parents as a kid?"

By now Hap was leaning in as close as he could, too, and their faces met over the middle of the little café table. They kissed. It was like an electric shock. They both jumped back.

"Don't tell the CDC," Hap joked.

Just like that, over a kiss and a joke and two ice-cold beers, it began. Over the rest of the spring their relationship bloomed like the flowers. They talked and texted constantly. Got together for meals and drinks as much as their contradictory working hours allowed. But physically, maybe because of the pandemic, maybe because Hap was uniquely sensitive to Amie's innate hesitation to touch, they took it slow.

Then Hap got COVID, and he quarantined himself. Texting was their only connection for a week.

Amie: It's silly, we've been making out for weeks, so if you have it then I've probably got it too. Let's just quarantine together. Or at least let me come over. We can wear masks. I'll make you soup. Take care of you.

Hap: I can't chance that. If you're not feeling sick yet I don't want you to get sick.

Amie: How are you feeling?

Hap: Like I've been hit by a truck. Like a person is sitting on my chest 24/7. And the worst headache I've ever had.

Amie: Promise me you'll call an ambulance if you have trouble breathing.

Hap: What if it happens while I'm sleeping?

Amie: See! Let me come over and watch you sleep.

Hap: I was just joking.

Amie: How was I to know you were joking if you didn't use a

little smiley face after you texted that? Will you ever use emojis?

Hap: Nope.

Amie: Will you let me come over?

Hap: Nope. Don't worry. I'll be fine. I'm not really sleeping anyway. If I have trouble breathing I'll call an ambulance. I promise. Let's just hope there will be one available to get here.

Amie: Don't joke! It's not funny.

Hap: Okay, I'll just sit here depressed and lonely and sick and not try to medicate myself with humor like we Wolinskis tend to do.

Amie: I miss you.

Hap: I (followed by the endless flashing ellipsis)

Amie: ???

Hap: That was me pretending I wasn't breathing.

Amie: STOP!

Hap: I love you.

Amie didn't know how to respond. She allowed an awkward lapse of minutes while she got ready for work.

Amie: Heading out to work now. I plan to text you all night long when I'm done. Get your rest now while you can still breathe.

It was a busy night for take-out orders, and one of the cooks was out sick with COVID, so Connie was on the line and Amie handled all the packing of the prepared orders and hand off for delivery. She stayed late to help Connie close and clean the kitchen. It was close to 11pm by the time she was heading home. She texted Hap while she walked. There was no response. Her heart started to race. She texted again. Still no response. She even called him, but he didn't pick up. She walked right to her car parked in the small off-street lot behind her apartment. She would just drive to his house, but she suddenly realized she didn't even know where he lived. He always came to her apartment.

How the hell could she not even know where he lived? What kind of girlfriend was she? Was she even his girlfriend?

Amie sat in her car and texted Pete, but she knew from Hap

that Pete was notorious for not responding to texts in a timely manner, if at all. She texted Laurel. Laurel provided his address and asked if everything was okay. She hadn't even known Hap had COVID. Amie drove like a maniac to his house, a small bungalow on the outskirts of town with a small fenced yard and driveway. She ran up to the front door and rang the doorbell. She could hear a dog barking on the other side.

All this talking and texting and the fact he had a dog never came up? Did she really know him at all? Maybe he didn't have COVID. Maybe it was a cover. Maybe he was in there with another woman. Dear god, who the hell was Amie turning into in this moment?

If he was alive on the other side of the door, the first thing she would do was either kill him or demand they exchange keys. She began to pound on the door. Finally, amidst the cacophonous barking on the other side, the door opened. Standing in the hazy darkness trying to hold back the scruffy black lab/mutt mix was Hap looking like hell and straining his eyes to see who it was.

"Why didn't you answer my texts or my call!?" Amie screamed at him.

Hap opened the screen door while still holding the dog back by its collar, almost falling over. Amie came in and steadied him on his feet. The dog jumped on her and barked but then calmed down and stayed close to Hap.

"Jesus, Amie," Hap said in a weak, scratchy voice, "I was so exhausted I put my phone on silent. And you just woke me up from what had been my deepest most restful sleep yet."

"I'm so sorry," Amie said as she hugged him. "I thought you had died. I'm staying here with you, damn it! I don't care what you say. I love you."

Hap gently, weakly pushed her back from him. "Well, if those are the facts, then we better mask up."

Amie spent the next five days nursing him back to health. The severity waxed and waned. He insisted they be in different rooms as much as possible. Their texting conversations continued with

Hap in his bedroom and Amie in the living room snuggled up with his dog, Gus, who had become her shadow, on the couch.

Hap: I wonder if they'll still be able to do the Porch Jazz Fest this year.

Amie: Porch Jazz Fest? What the hell is that? Sounds like something you just made up.

Hap: Weren't you here last September when they did it?

Amie: I must've missed it.

Hap: How could you have missed it? It's only like the greatest thing ever. It's where people let musicians play jazz on their front porches. Like everything from high school bands to quasi-professionals doing jazz and old standards, and people just walk around from house to house listening and drinking and having a great time.

Amie: Sounds lovely.

Hap: God I hope there's not a new wave in the fall. I mean, it's all outside. People can still mask. I hope they still do it.

Amie texted him a link to a post on *Under the Falls* from the planning committee. As of right now they were still going to try to make it happen for the last weekend in September.

Hap: Thanks for finding that so quick! That's why I love you.

Amie: Have you ever done one of these? (She texted a link to a DNA testing/ancestry service.)

Hap: Never been comfortable with the idea of some company having my DNA on file.

Amie: Oh, c'mon, you've never been curious?

Hap: Well, sure, but I've never tried to find my birth parents if that's what you're getting at. Never felt that need.

Amie: Well, yeah, I guess I kinda wondered if you wondered about that, but I just thought this could be fun for us to do. I always wanted to know. Like would it turn out I have some Spanish in me or something.

Hap: Always looking for that spicy story #Drama

Amie: OMG! You used a hashtag! What's next? An emoji?

And actually, I hate drama. Try to avoid it at all costs. It just seems to find me.

Hap: I'll do it with you. Like you said, it could be fun.

After those five days, Hap finally tested negative though he still felt a little weak.

"I haven't been outside in over five days, will you come down to the dinosaur dig site with me?" Hap asked Amie.

"I don't know if that's the best idea. Shouldn't you rest some more? And you could still be contagious."

"Please, I need some fresh air. And I've been wanting to show it to you."

Amie started to laugh a little. "You know I can't believe I haven't told you this yet because you talk about this stuff all the time, but I wanted to be an archeologist when I was a little girl."

"What? Why didn't you tell me?"

"Well, actually it's a little more embarrassing than that. I wanted to be like Lara Croft. I mean, is she even a real archaeologist? And it's funny, because in some ways the dinosaur lore of this town is what made me choose to come to live here."

"And you haven't been there yet?"

"I guess like Porch Jazz Fest last year, I just…I dunno…I've been kinda oblivious to what's here and things I should, could love. And I've been busy…*with drama.*"

"That settles it, we're going. At dusk. There's this ledge you can walk down to and sit on about half way down. And we can watch the sunset behind the cemetery hill. We'll take a bottle of wine."

"*So romantic.*"

But it kinda was. They sat there on that ledge on a blanket, with a bottle of chilled blush wine and two glasses, and they drank and watched the sunset in the warm fresh air. Amie looked down at the mess of tarps at the bottom of the gorge.

"Like, seriously, what is the deal with this place?" Amie asked. "Why is it still an open excavation site after all these years?"

"Oh, it's just one of those things," Hap said. "There's funding to continue digging. Then there's not. One group moves out. Another moves in. Years pass in between. There's still plenty of fossils down there, so they claim. Maybe they'll finally turn the falls back on and just let it flood like they've been talking about."

"Do you think they should do it?"

"I dunno. This was like a magic place for us kids back then. But maybe the town should go back to what it originally was, to what nature had intended. You should ask Connie about it. Sutton, or Mayor Jackson I should formally say, I think is a proponent of turning the falls back on. The university that lays claim to the site is trying to keep that from happening until they can dig everything out."

"Have you ever travelled to other big digs out west?"

"No, I've always wanted to. Have you ever heard of Cerro Ballena?"

"Oh, that sounds romantic." Amie said, wistfully gazing at the sunset. "No, I haven't."

"It's this site they uncovered when they were digging and blasting through some hills to build a highway in South America," Hap explained. "In the strata of the rocks, they discovered layers and layers of ancient whale bones. The name means Whale Hill. It's supposed to be one of the most amazing sites on earth for fossils because they say you can literally see whole skeletons in the hillside When whales die they just sink to the bottom of the ocean, and these natural cemeteries are called whale falls. The site used to sit at the bottom of the ocean, and for millennia whales just collected there in whale falls. It's mind boggling to even imagine."

"I would love to see that. Or any big dig site. Take a road trip out west. I'm surprised you haven't done that before as big as you are into this stuff."

"Maybe we can take an epic road trip together. Even go all the way down to Cerro Ballena. I've heard of people taking their RVs down through Mexico and Central America to South America. Can you imagine that? Maybe after all this, that can be us."

Amie scooted closer to Hap and leaned her head on his shoulder. "I've never thought of leaving with someone before. It's a nice thought."

That night they slept in the same bed, in each other's arms. It was the most restful sleep either of them had gotten in weeks. The next day he tested negative again and felt like a million bucks. Hap was finally in the clear. That night they celebrated by making love for the first time. And it truly was that, not just sex. Hap was slow and gentle and giving and passionate. Amie had never been treated like that by any other man. Afterwards, they both felt like they were in love, in the classical romantic sense, for the first time in their lives. Amie had never felt more vulnerable, lying with him naked, breathless and satisfied, a warm breeze blowing in from the window over their sweaty bodies.

In the middle of the night Amie woke up with a chill. Hap had pulled a blanket up to their waists. His skin was now cool to the touch where they hadn't been intertwined. He was awake, too. She snuggled him a little harder to share their body heat.

"I want to tell you everything," she said quietly. "I've never felt this safe before with anyone. And I want you to feel free to tell me everything, too. Do you feel safe with me?"

"Of course I do," Hap said.

"I want to know your deepest, darkest secret."

Hap swelled his lungs with air and deeply exhaled. His heart quickened a little as he thought about this with Amie's warm head resting on his bare chest. "My deepest secret? I don't know. But my deepest truth would be that Robbie Elms was the love of my life. And no, no, no not romantic classical love or however you describe it. I think you can attest after tonight what *that* kind of love is. Just love, pure and simple. He was the love of my life, and I don't think I'll ever feel that specific kind of way about anyone ever again."

"Well, that's no secret, that's for sure. Anybody who has ever heard you talk about Robbie Elms can instantly tell how much you loved him. And I think that's why I'm in love with you, Hap Wolinski. You wear your heart on your sleeve like a badge of honor."

"Oh, don't go thinking I'm so honorable. I'll always feel responsible for his death. I should've been with him that night. But I was giving him space because he was mad at me, and I let him do his silent treatment thing. If I had just done what I had always done and gone over to his house, we would've been together that night. And he might still be alive today."

"That fucking sucks to still carry that guilt with you. But you know it wasn't your fault, right? You had no control over what that monster did. He alone is at fault."

"I know. And now he's about to be free again. But I can't change that." He sighed deeply, bookending his release and packing his love for Robbie and guilt over his death back into the tiny box inside his heart. "But what about you?"

Amie's pulse increased. She was no stranger to panic attacks, and even just the hypothetical idea of sharing her deepest, darkest secret with someone was enough to set off her anxiety. There was some kind of sense memory kicking in causing her to have those first anxious flutters, but Hap's touch calmed her. He waited, patiently. Holding her still. Not too tight, but just enough for her to know he would hold her tighter if she asked him to.

"My biggest secret is that I was sexually abused as a child." She said it like a quick exhale.

Hap waited patiently again for her to gather her composure and thoughts. "That's fucking terrible. I am so sorry someone did that to you. And I am so thankful I can make a safe place for you for you to unburden yourself of that fact."

Amie was crying, but not in a heightened uncontrollable sense, in more of a natural release. She could still calm herself and talk. "I've never told anyone that. It was my uncle. I don't know how young I was when it began, but I know some of my earliest memories are of stepping outside of my body. I learned how to escape emotionally and mentally long before I got up the nerve to leave physically. It lasted until he died when I was twelve. And my parents knew. But they didn't know how to protect me. We lived in his house after all."

Hap gently kissed the top of her head.

Amie sighed deeply and wiped tears from her eyes and then from Hap's chest. "Jesus Christ, where do we go from here? I mean all of this…in this fucked up world?"

"I dunno," Hap said. "But know this, Amie Wren. You are loved. Whether you stay or you go, you are loved. I can love you like that. Unconditionally. I know how to do that."

≈

The Vaughan Family

The transition to working from home five days a week was not hard for Sam or Val as they had already been working from home more days than not for years. Having Henry there with them, as there was no remote daycare, balancing schedules, and trying to manage their days in halves was a challenge. Henry was still too young to be self-sufficient enough to entertain himself for more than fifteen or twenty minutes at a time, so someone had to be with or near him at all times. The time limits on Henry's tablet were quickly removed even as Val tried to contend this was no reason to relax their parenting style and rules. Val had Henry most mornings, and Sam did the afternoon duty. Unmercifully, Henry was beyond napping age even though the daycare had reported daily naps through their app prior to the pandemic. "I never slept there!" Henry told his dads proudly.

Around 3pm every afternoon, after an hour of tablet time where Sam would attempt to answer work emails on his phone, Sam would take Henry out in the backyard and turn on music and the bubble machine. This was also the time the neighbors brought their toddler outside after her afternoon nap, and through the slats in the tall wooden fence Henry would watch the toddler squeal and try to pop the bubbles that floated over the fence without toppling over.

"Aww, the baby is so cute," four-year-old Henry would say adorably.

Sam would write copy in his head as he watched this daily, the multitude of bubbles taking on a special luminescence on the sunniest of days. *Every afternoon in our backyard our son's bubble machine presents to us the fragile impermanence of infinite universes floating in the air and popping one by one...*and the fragile universe they found themselves in was this one, with COVID and the virulent madness of Trumpism raging. Which bubble was theirs floating up to the sky? When would it pop?

Trump. Downplaying the severity at every turn. Telling people to drink bleach. Fanning the flames of division. As the temperatures rose, so did the anger of people on all sides of the lockdown debate. Previous divisions and institutional and racial injustices were now amplified. The intimate news of Tyeisha's mother, Jennifer Williams' death hit hard. This was followed later in May by more devastating news. Despite the best efforts of all involved, Darrel Strayer was granted parole.

"There was nothing else we could've done given the circumstances," Mayor Jackson explained in a group text to all who had rallied behind the cause, "the prison was overcrowded and they were releasing convicts due to the pandemic." A guilty white man, a child murderer, freed.

This was quickly followed by renewed focus on the societal epidemic of young innocent Black men being killed by cops, with George Floyd's death in May being the tipping point, stirring both peaceful demonstrations and violent riots. Sam took it all so personal, always proud of who he was as both a gay white man married to a half-Black/half-Asian man, and an ally of other minorities, a rouser of good trouble.

At night, after Henry was in bed, Sam would get especially

stirred up while doom-scrolling on his phone. As protests in the city intensified in June, sounds of ATMs exploding and police PSYOP tactics carried across the river and through their open windows, and this spun Sam up even more. Protests and anger so big you could hear it from that far away.

"Doesn't this mean anything to you?" Sam would yell at Val, who remained coldly indifferent - or was it stoic? - through it all. The violence against Asians earlier on (seen by some as the source of the virus), and the ingrained and constant systemic violence against Blacks, seemingly having no effect on him.

"I don't need *anyone* – you, most of all – telling me how I should feel about *anything*!" Val snapped back.

"I want to do something. I need to do something," Sam stated firmly but calmly.

"Why can't you just adopt a rescue dog like every other bored, lonely white person in this town?" What would pass for Val's sense of humor in the past, was laced with bitterness now.

"Don't push me, Val. You know what I mean by doing something."

"You want to leave your son and husband here while you go to a protest in the city about shit you know nothing about so you can feel better about yourself? Go right ahead. Be my guest."

A large Black Lives Matter protest had taken root outside of City Hall and there were calls on social media for more people to come and join. Sam packed some essentials in a backpack and decided he was going to hop the train into the city and join the protest.

"Daddy Val, where's Daddy Sam going?" Henry asked as he and Val watched Sam leaving.

"Daddy Sam is not making good choices right now," Val said to their son.

"I'll be back…soon," Sam said to Henry on his way out the door.

Riding the train was surreal with people masked and trying to remain distant. A palpable sense of trouble, anger, and fear permeated the airspace in between. The train was sparsely filled but packed with emotion. It rattled underground through the darkness beneath Hampten and then rumbled up into the light and over the bridge, descending again beneath the city before reaching its terminus from where Sam would then walk a few blocks up to City Hall. He had heard stories of homeless encampments and muggings. It was dank and dark as he exited the train. Ahead of him he saw a young couple with protest signs. He hurried up to follow them, thinking there would be safety in numbers, brushing aside a few others walking in the opposite direction.

"You better watch where you're fucking going," one of them said to Sam.

On the surface there were sirens, whose wails seeped underground like warnings. *Stay in the darkness. Turn around.*

Sam hurried up the steps towards the dichotomy of light and sirens, but as he did, two teenagers came racing down the steps, and one shoved him backwards. He slipped trying to regain his footing on the steps behind him and tumbled back, slamming his head against an iron post before collapsing on the ground at the foot of the steps.

No one was there to scream for him, or call for help. It would be twenty minutes before a homeless man found him and called for help above, wondering what in the hell was this stranger doing with a puddle of blood around his head lying on this filthy floor of the subway line. *He shouldn't have been here.*

≈

Connie & Sutton

Connie was proud of how she was able to keep Connie's Place alive during lockdown, and more importantly, keep most of her employees fully employed. She did it by strategically pivoting to full-service take-out and food delivery, and without having to apply for a PPP loan from the federal government like so many other small businesses had. She was seen even more now as a pillar of the community – forever made by, and working for all of, West Falls.

There was, of course, a small but vocal minority, who chattered feverishly online about her relationship with the mayor, who these people saw as a flag bearer for the fascist elites who wanted to keep everyone controlled and locked down indefinitely.

"Look who gets to stay open and profit while others have had to shutter their doors and suffer!" they cried on *Under the Falls* or anywhere they could seize space before getting blocked or banned.

Sutton, in her official duties as mayor, was seen by these people as the scapegoat in the whole affair with the owner of the gym who tried daily to re-open during the lockdown only to be forced to close by the police each morning and fined by the state. Some retaliated by spray painting FASHEST DIKE on the outside of town hall.

People on *Under the Falls* rushed to the defense of both Connie and Sutton.

"Mayor Jackson is doing the best she can. It's not her mandates, it's the state's!"

"Connie's Place is abiding by the rules just like everyone else. They were smart to see the need in the community and pivot their business to take-out and delivery. Think of how much they are losing by not having the bar open!"

Within hours people had rallied on *Under the Falls* to meet up outside town hall and clean off the obscenities from the wall. They then painted a rainbow crosswalk at the corner closest to town hall.

In May, both Connie and Sutton shared their disgust with the courts and the release of Darrel Strayer back into the population. There were some heated ramblings online about vigilante justice and tracking Strayer down, but level heads prevailed in quieting them down.

During the early parts of summer while civil unrest and protests heated up in the city, West Falls had peaceful family-friendly gatherings on the main strip in solidarity with Black Lives Matter. A few people grumbled. All Lives Matters signs popped up here and there, but that was mostly the extent of that.

By the end of June, the stay-at-home order had been lifted. Restaurants could return to limited table service. The warm weather welcomed café-style seating. Connie's Place opened back up and served drinks in a new make-shift picnic table area under umbrellas in the parking lot. There was this strange new kind of lifestyle, people still cautious, some still very mad, but they could gather. As they could gather the tenor calmed a bit, at least in West Falls. Most businesses started to pick back up, but people voted with their wallets, and the gym that had so desperately wanted to stay open all along, was quietly, unofficially boycotted. Most of the town held the owner responsible for the hate speech on the town hall wall, and by the end of summer the gym was bankrupt and shuttered for good.

Still, Connie couldn't help but look around at the crowds returning to the bar, laughing and joking, and wonder if she ever really knew her regulars and the people in town at all? Many voiced their support of both her and Sutton one way or another, but there were those who had remained silent, or used cryptic code speak to relay their discontent with liberals in general, maybe with LGBTQ+ in particular, with the mask mandates, and with everything and anything that infringed upon their comforts or closed-minded nostalgic ideals about how others should lead their lives. There had always been old-timers who pined about the good ol' days, but it was more than that now. Maybe it had always been more than that. Connie wondered how many people secretly hated her?

On a particularly hot July night, she was lying awake in bed, sweating, staring at the ceiling, her mind a hot mess of invasive thoughts.

"I can turn the fan on higher," Sutton said to her, noticing her discomfort.

"Was I a fool to think the pandemic would actually bring people closer together?" Connie said.

"It's natural to hope for a silver lining in something like this," Sutton responded after getting out of bed to turn the fan on high and then lying back down.

"But is it foolish? I asked if it was foolish."

"Well, in a way, it made clear yet again who our true allies are. Who will have our back."

"I know, but when it comes down to it, what can our friends do for us?" Connie's frustration grew. "They might say and think the right things, but what can they do? We always have to scrape and fight for our own rights. And now the people who would celebrate taking them away are louder and more emboldened than ever."

"We just have to take it one day and one fight at a time." Sutton paused. She turned her head and edged closer to Connie. Her voice verged on a whisper when she asked, "Do you not feel safe anymore? This town loves you."

Connie sighed. "They love my bar. They love me as long as I play the role of friendly bar owner and storyteller of personal histories. Some of my customers hate the other parts I play, hate who I am, who we are."

"We can't fix their hearts," Sutton said.

Connie nodded. "I can take their money, though."

Sutton just wanted to sleep. She just wanted Connie to sleep. Sutton was consumed with Darrel Strayer. While vigilante wannabes had been silenced, she couldn't help but track him down. She knew where he was living in Hampten. Her own heart wouldn't be fixed until Strayer finally met with justice. Her mind swam with different variations of this justice, but it was always swift and definitive. It's as if the rage she had built up little by little all her life — as a woman, leered at and condescended to; as a prosecutor, feared and reviled; as a lesbian, hated and denied common dignity — was channeling itself into this singular injustice of Darrel Strayer, child murderer, being let out of prison early and walking freely on the very streets where he stalked and preyed on other children. Sutton had built a life on seizing power for herself so she could manifest her own destiny and fix the wrongs of the world – put the bad people in jail, make good and fair public policy – but here was this vile man who she had successfully put behind bars, holding power over her. His very existence and freedom were seemingly all to spite her.

Connie continued talking. Sutton responded intuitively, automatically, or maybe she didn't even respond at all. A nod of the head. Dismissal of the conversation in her mind as she plotted. To what end, only she could determine.

Eventually they both fell asleep and succumbed to restless dreams of their own designs.

≈

Laurel

By summer, everything eventually fell into place for Laurel to finally leave West Falls. Enough time had passed that the lawyer was able to file a notice that a good faith effort had been made to locate Frederick Elms before selling the house, which he had previously been entitled to fifty percent of, and the estate was now officially out of probate. Laurel was then able to sell the house to the prospective flippers at a premium with the pandemic housing market booming. Meanwhile, the mason had been able to salvage the etched names on the basement cornerstone and cut it down to a smaller size so it would meet weight limits in a checked bag for Laurel to take with her back to Europe. Laurel put her apartment in Brussels up for sale and made arrangements to stay with a friend in Amsterdam while she decided where to settle down next. Luckily restrictions between EU countries were lessening, and it was really the hurdle of being an EU citizen coming back to the EU through a still restricted country (the US) that was the only logistical hurdle.

She would have to fly to Canada first, quarantine there for fourteen days, and then fly from there to Brussels and stay there for fourteen days before being able to go anywhere else in the EU.

Laurel sent a final message to the fantasy football league group text, which had gone silent when lockdown began.

Laurel: Well, I fooled them, and they're finally letting me go back to Europe. This number will get recycled and provided to another victim soon enough. Thank you for a great time before everything went to shit.

No one responded.

Pete texted her separately.

Pete: Kurt died from COVID last month.

Laurel: Oh shit. I'm so sorry. That fucking sucks. I guess my group message was in poor taste.

Pete: No one will think that. I'm just glad you saw fit to tell us somehow.

Laurel: Thank you for everything.

Pete: I saw the demo starting on the old stone house.

Laurel: I'm sorry about that too.

Pete: No you're not. But that's okay too. Good luck Laurel.

Laurel: Take care of yourself. Tell Hap I'm sorry we didn't get together for one last farewell. Things just all happened kinda fast once the lawyer said go.

Pete: We understand.

Laurel watched as the trailing ellipses flashed faintly under Pete's last text for a minute. *Please don't write a novel and profess your love for me.* Nothing was written, leaving Laurel to fill in whatever she needed to continue moving on.

Laurel had never been to Canada, and she was put up in a hotel designated for quarantining not far from Pearson International Airport where she had views of strange hour-glass shaped towers in downtown Mississauga. She had never even heard of Mississauga before, but apparently it was a Toronto suburb of nearly three quarters of a million people. From her perch in the hotel, it seemed like a ghost town. There were some signs of life, like empty café-style seating on sidewalks and occasional walking traffic at certain times of day. Like in the US, most people, spare for essential services, were still holed up working from home. And from the hotel she worked, too.

Laurel made imaginary friends with strangers five stories down on the sidewalk, the regular walkers she got used to seeing everyday like clockwork. A young woman pushing a double stroller. An old man wearing a windbreaker even as the temperature soared. Someone dressed like a sanitation worker. A few people in business attire. She imagined conversations with them as she drank her coffee and ate her breakfast.

Laurel's days were surreally monotonous. She would watch home renovation shows on a constant loop as she couldn't bear to watch the news or anything else. She scrolled social media, especially *Under the Falls*, to see if anything new was going on back there. There was more than one rant where someone lamented the demolition of the town's oldest home to make room for some McMansion probably. And these rants lead inevitably to people talking about the history of the house – *her house* – and Robbie. She eventually had to mute it.

Each evening, inevitably, she would stare out at those strange towers and imagine them dancing, undulating as their own increasingly checkered and plentiful interior lights popped like new stars shining in the increasing darkness. The towers' exterior curves were like hips attached to headless, limbless bodies. Forever moving. She tried to let this image guide her to sleep, but it rarely worked. She was constantly restless until around one in the morning when she would start work, logging on to calls or meetings with her European colleagues and clients. They would crack jokes about her being trapped in Canada, and she would crack a smile, laugh even, while shattering over and over again on the inside, feeling like a wild animal was in there trying to claw its way out of her, out of that god-forsaken hotel in god-forsaken

Mississauga, and grow exponentially larger as it stalked the airport and took down planes with one swipe of its massive claws.

Finally, Laurel cleared quarantine, and she thought maybe she could get some real rest on the overnight flight that would plop her into Brussels at 8am in the morning. The plane was mostly empty, and she had the whole row luxuriously to herself. The increasing loudness of the droning engines as the plane taxied for takeoff seemed the perfect white noise lullaby, something familiar and signaling her favorite thing to do in the whole wide world – take off. That comforting sense of lifting off the ground seemed more jarring and ricketier than usual, and for a brief moment she feared the wheels were malfunctioning and not lifting up. Over the years, she had internalized the perfect timing of when this should happen as the plane ascended, but maybe her sense of internal timing was off now. Or maybe the plane was going to come crashing back down in an emergency landing due to the wheels malfunctioning and she would be stuck in Canada forever. Or maybe the malfunction was even worse, and the plane would simply crash back down onto the runway into a fiery ball. *Dear god, of all the places in the world, don't let me die on a tarmac in Canada!*

The wheels came up just as Laurel's panic peaked, and the plane continued its leisurely ascent, the towers and lights of Mississauga and Toronto and the arterial highway in between slowly drifting further down below the plane and eventually completely covered by the clouds. There was no deep sleeping now. Once they were at cruising altitude, the stewardess came by, and Laurel asked for a stiff drink.

"First flight since the pandemic started?" the stewardess asked, a smile obvious under her mask.

Laurel nodded. "Finally going home," she said.

With the overhead lights dimmed, Laurel tried to pass the time with in-flight movies, her face bathed in blue light as she half-watched some disaster flick staring some ex-wrestler with an over-the-top plot and terrible special effects. She watched it in French, as the dubbed accents were soothing while the world on screen literally fell apart with giant earthquakes and tsunamis. *Quaint*, she thought, they hadn't the imagination to think the world might end with a pandemic.

After that, Laurel glanced at some reality show about deep sea fishermen in Alaska. She watched this in French, too, and the rocking of their boat in the gloomy, giant ocean swells allowed her to close her eyes and drift into sleep. There she had a fever dream where Freddie was working on a whaling vessel battling strange and monstrous leviathans from the ocean deep. Then he was trying to call her on a cell phone while standing on the deck, and swells and monsters battered the boat. The boat eventually shattered into pieces and sank with Freddie holding onto a piece of floating driftwood, the illumination from his cell phone as he tried to call her making the only light in the dark, open, deep sea. One of the massive creatures came stealthily up from below, its widening jaw encircling Freddie and the dimming light, and swallowed him whole.

Laurel startled awake. On screen, thousands of pounds of Alaskan snow crabs were being dumped on the deck of a boat. She turned it off. The stewardess came around.

"Last call for anything to drink before we start the descent," she said.

"Just water, please," Laurel said. She had never felt so thirsty.

With so few people onboard, deboarding, temperature screening, baggage claim, and customs went smoother and quicker than ever before. She could feel the stone relic rattle around in her bag as she wheeled it to the taxi. At her apartment, which felt cold and unfamiliar after all this time, like another hotel room, she collapsed onto her bed. Laurel slept for twelve hours straight. It took her awhile to re-adjust to the time difference, but once she did, and finally well-rested, she was a flurry of activity with work and packing and closing the deal to sell the apartment.

When Laurel finally boarded that train to Amsterdam after

two weeks in Brussels, she felt a huge sense of relief. When she got to her friend's apartment she gave her the biggest hug and loved on her charmingly decrepit, old little dog. She hadn't seen this friend in almost a year, and they hadn't been close since the friend had moved to Amsterdam over five years ago. But they had always stayed in touch, and it just all worked out when Laurel mentioned her plans. *Of course, you will stay with me*, the friend instantly proclaimed. The apartment was cramped and quirky and oozing with Dutch charm, and there was a perfect little second bedroom with a bed, small desk, and a tall, narrow window overlooking the street and a canal, and for Laurel it was the most perfect thing. This was her pod. No matter what, they would weather the rest of this pandemic together. And then, after that…assuming there was eventually an after…Laurel would reclaim the world. Or if enough time passed, maybe even leave it.

EPISODE SEVEN – JAZZ

September 2020
Amie & Hap

It was on; Porch Jazz Fest would happen. There were still some mask mandates. Schools had opened for the fall with primarily in-person lessons and virtual learning enacted as needed. The new outdoor café lifestyle that started in the summer was flourishing on the strip. Restaurants that had survived on take-out could expand now with limited indoor seating. Many corporate and office workers still worked from home five days a week, but there were rumblings of return to office plans even as a new wave of COVID spiked. This was what people called "the new normal."

For the earlier festival performances, crowds were scant, and those walking around were like zombies, not sure if this was really happening, if this was really safe. But once others heard music from down the street through their open windows and saw small crowds walking (some people masked, even though it was outdoors), people started to filter out of their houses and stumbled onto the sidewalks as if awakening from a long sleep. Kids were riding their bikes in packs, and small groups of adults leisurely strolled with open containers from venue to venue as the afternoon meandered on, and more performances filled the neighborhoods with music.

Amie and Hap walked holding hands, taking it all in. The music in the air. The cooling autumn breeze. The sun playing peek-a-boo behind bright fluffy white clouds.

"This one group up here on the corner is THE BEST," Hap said excitedly to Amie as they strolled the tree-lined streets off the strip. "Have you heard of them? *That New Jukebox Sound?* They've played in the city a lot and had a small East Coast tour before the pandemic. They're from West Falls. They take classic rock and pop songs and do jazz-style covers."

As they approached the corner house where the band was set up, the warm-up act was just winding down. Their first song was a 1930s New Orleans jazz-style cover of Oasis' "Don't Look Back in Anger" where the female lead singer belted out the lyrics like a burning funereal dirge.

"Oh, man, this was one of my favorite songs back in the day," Hap said with a wide-eyed smile. "Robbie and I used to talk about starting a band. Neither of us was musical so it was joke, right, but you know how kids cook up dreams together. This song came out a few years after he died and it stirred up that dream again. I imagined the girl Sally from this song as a real person, as my groupie or girlfriend. I dunno. I was a dumb teenager. But man, this takes me back."

"Wow, her voice!" Amie remarked over the spooky, sultry din of the musical performance. "They're amazing. This is great."

They listened to two more songs and then walked away from the crowd and noise, down a small side street until they came upon the park in the middle of downtown. They were warm and tired and sat down on one of the benches under the trees. Amie responded to the ding of a notification on her phone.

"Oh, hey," she said, "I got the DNA test results! Check your email. Let's compare." She opened her email and began to scroll through the results.

Hap took out his phone and did the same.

Amie finished reading hers first and then waited for Hap to finish. She was giddy with excitement. "You wanna go first?" she asked.

"No, you go first," Hap said.

"Ok. I'm 45% Irish, 14% Scandinavian, 10% German, 10% French, 6% Polish, and 15% Native American, Cherokee!"

"Wow!" Hap said. He then laughed. "So, we're both Indian."

"Ha ha. Now do you."

"I'm 65% Indian sub-continent - likely the Goa region, 15% Portuguese, 10% French, and 10% Spanish."

"Wow, you got the bit of Spanish I thought I had!"

Hap put his arm around her, and they kissed. "Can you imagine what a beautiful mutt of a kid we would make?" he said to her.

For the first time in her life, the idea of a kid wasn't repulsive to Amie. She knew he was mostly joking, that humor of his, but there was a ring of truth, of hope, to what he said. Still, it made her pull away from him, suddenly sullen and anxious. There were still things she held back from him.

"What's wrong?" Hap asked her.

"I dunno, it just made me think of some things I hadn't thought about in a long time," she said.

"You still feel safe with me?"

"Yeah, of course. Look, this kind of stuff doesn't naturally come up in conversation, ya know? I mean until someone says something like what you just said." Amie paused. "Look, I've been pregnant before. When I was a twelve, I got pregnant by my uncle and had an abortion. And then when Hank and I first started messing around, I took a pregnancy test that came back positive. I never told him. I went to Planned Parenthood right away, and that took care of that."

Hap held her closer. He kissed her on the cheek. "I'm so sorry that happened to you as a child, and the whole Hank thing…I mean, I'm just glad no one prevented you from making those choices. And you made the right ones for yourself."

"Thank you for that reaction." Amie rested her head on his shoulder for a minute. Another weight lifted off her back. How many weights could be lifted just by being with Hap? She sprang forward with a new burst of energy. "Now let's go listen to some more music!"

≈

The Vaughan Family

Sam had suffered from a major head and spinal injury from his fall in the subway and was still in a coma by the time autumn rolled around.

Val was still madder at him more than anything else as he firmly believed Sam had no business being in the city when he was and could've avoided this entirely. But he was also sad, deeply sad, especially for Henry, for whom he tried to keep on a brave, cheery face to help their son regain some sense of normalcy during his last year of preschool before starting kindergarten next fall. Val wrestled with whether or not he should take Henry to see Sam in the hospital, and he decided it was better for Henry to have an opportunity to see his other dad was still alive, and just asleep, getting better…hopefully.

"When will he wake up?" Henry often asked.

"We don't really know. As long as it takes for his body to heal," Val repeated over and over.

The day of the Porch Jazz Fest, Val had been oblivious to its existence, despite signs up all over the neighborhood. Henry, having returned to daycare for the first time earlier in the month, inevitably came down with something. He tested negative for COVID, but the doctor suspected it was maybe an adenovirus, which Val had never even heard of before the pandemic but was apparently a common culprit of many bad colds. It pretty much knocked Henry out, and Val was spread out on his back on the couch in the living room with Henry lying on top of him. The raspy cadence of his son's breathing was the only sound until Val looked up the staircase onto the landing and saw the curtains gently flutter in the breeze, which carried with it sounds of jazz music from down the block. The sunlight, the curtains, the breeze, the sounds, the warmth of his feverish son on his chest…it was a rare moment of peace.

The idea of taking care of this little white boy, whom he fiercely loved like he had never loved anyone before, by himself scared Val even in a peaceful moment such as this. He thought back to the decision he and Sam made about starting a family together. They agreed on using a surrogate so at least one of them could be biologically related to the child. Sam lobbied hard for Val to be the one. In his fragile little idealistic mind, Sam saw a beautiful rainbow child – white, Black and Chinese – but Val knew better. Val didn't want to *other* that child any more than they already would be by having two daddies. He insisted it be Sam so the child would be fully white.

Growing up and even now, Val was predetermined to be *othered* wherever he went. As a child he was looked down upon by his predominantly Black extended family, neighbors and classmates for his lighter skin and slanted eyes. Yet anytime he entered the Chinese world of his mother, or the white world outside of Hampten, he was more than Black enough to be viewed with suspicion and as a potential threat. A Black male between the age of five and incarcerated or dead. *Better keep an eye on him. What do you want, boy? Stay back.* And when he came out as gay, he put another *other* on himself which was met with derision equally distributed across all other labels.

When Val insisted Sam be the one to biologically father their child it wasn't because he hated the Black part or the Chinese part of himself, it's that he didn't want to be forced to have the conversation with his son that all Black parents have to have with their sons. About how to behave if stopped by the police. About the dangers specific to them being Black and male in a world designed to specifically work against them and put them in danger. He didn't want that for his son. He thought often of how privileged he was to be able to marry a white man and use a white surrogate to make a beautiful blond-haired, blue-eyed baby boy for whom this world and society was designed to coddle, protect, and reward.

Here was this perfect boy asleep on him now, with this white people jazz pumping into their beautiful flipped house in this beautiful self-congratulatory predominately white but progressive town where Val was looked on by everyone with a smile of menacing inquisitiveness.

Look at that beautiful, exotic other. That beautiful gay man. That beautiful Asian gay man. That beautiful Black, Asian gay man. That beautiful Black, Asian gay man with that adorable little white child on his shoulders. Does he belong? Oh, yes, he does. What a wonderful welcoming town we have! Stay…but not too close…no, stay…over there. Where we can see you. And look at you. And admire ourselves.

Henry rustled a little as the music continued to gently roll in on the breeze, his warm little body settling in atop Val while letting out a few muffled whimpers. Such a sweet sound. Val could scarcely believe this was his life. That they were living through a global pandemic. That his husband was in a coma. That this was his son. What a strange, strange world he found himself in. He was full of hate and love, and forever further *othering* himself before anyone else could first. He closed his eyes and could hear in his mind Henry's tremulous little voice ask again, "When will he wake up?"

≈

Bike Gang

"Don't let me catch you hanging out with those bike gang kids," Tyeisha's mother would say, in her half-joking but still serious way, before she died. "And watch out for those boys on the basketball team, too."

"Wasn't Dad on the basketball team?" Tyeisha would shoot

back.

"Well, maybe, but he didn't ride his bike around in the middle of the street popping wheelies in front of traffic."

Tyeisha was on the girls' basketball team, just like her mom had been in high school. She wasn't anything scholarship-worthy, but she was decent enough and a good team player, and it made her body athletic and fit. She felt like she could handle her own against any boy, basketball player or bike gang kid, if they got fresh or made an unwanted pass. Not that all passes were unwanted, of course; Tyeisha hooked up with one of the basketball players pre-pandemic, though it never extended beyond that. There was one shaggy-haired white boy who was both on the boys' basketball team and one of those wheelie-poppers, Finn, whose cavalier attitude on and off the court made him oddly alluring and just the type of boy Tyeisha's parents would not want her hanging around. She hadn't thought about him much over the summer as they didn't hang in the same circles, but with school back in session in-person, he reappeared in those hallowed halls, mask loose-fitting and hair even shaggier, as alluring as ever.

Towards the end of the summer Tyeisha was able to babysit for the Vaughans, and Val was especially thankful for her help in the wake of Sam's hospitalization. It was strange, she was helping this family with one parent in a coma, while at home she felt like her father, Marcus, was in a coma of grief since her mother's passing at the end of May. Once school started back up for her, and Henry's daycare re-opened, she was seeing less of them. She took to wandering the streets again, it being too suffocating at home with her father, and she began to see the bike gang kids around town.

One of the boys hooted and whistled at Tyeisha, slowing down beside her like a creepy stalker.

"Grow the fuck up!" Finn scolded his friend as he took up the space sidling by Tyeisha. "Sorry about him, he's an ass," he said.

"I don't need your protection," Tyeisha said to him.

"I know, but he needs to know he's an ass," Finn responded. He popped a wheelie and then caught up with the rest of the bike gang.

One day, after school, it was just Finn riding his bike. He came up beside Tyeisha as she walked and they started to talk.

"I got another bike at home if you wanna ride with me?" he suggested.

Tyeisha texted her dad she was watching Henry after school and then followed Finn to his place. It was one side of those big old twin-homes nestled in the crowded side streets off the main strip, with an overgrown small patch of yard in front of crumbling brick steps leading up to a covered porch with a sinking roof. Dirty old, faded, white siding. A trashed side yard full of old toys, junk, and garden tools. And window ac units hanging out of the upper floor windows looking like a little kid could easily just give them a push from the inside and they would come toppling down.

"Sorry for the mess," Finn said as he dropped his bike on the front lawn. "Wait here." He moved through the maze of junk in the side yard and disappeared around back.

Tyeisha was curious, so she followed him, carefully stepping over the old toys. "Do you have little brothers and sisters?" she called out after him.

"No," he replied, surprised to find her back there with him while he tried to pull another bike out of the old shed. The shed looked like a strong wind could blow it over, and the only thing keeping it upright was the overstuffed junk inside. He was sweating and huffing a bit, out of breath as he turned to face her.

Tyeisha reached her hand out. "Can I touch your hair?"

Finn was startled a bit, but let her run her hand through the hair on the back of his head.

"Seriously, is this a fucking mullet?" she laughed. "How the hell did this shit come back in style?"

Finn just shrugged.

Tyeisha removed her fingers from his tangles but not without first ever so gently caressing his scalp with her manicured nails. "This," she said with a wave her hand and a nod to his hair, "This is some weird white people shit."

"Thanks, I guess," Finn said.

Tyeisha leaned in and kissed him, and they enjoyed the moment, open mouthed, exploring just a little.

Finn pulled back. "Can I touch your hair?"

"Fuck no."

They both laughed.

"Ok, let's ride then," he said, yanking the bike out of the shed.

That's how Tyeisha ended up joining the bike gang. The other guys weren't so bad despite how immature they were. They were just dumb, and sometimes they were actually funny. Tyeisha made it clear not to fuck with her, but they competed to get a smile out of her with their antics, knowing she would never fully approve with a laugh. Finn taught her how to pop those wheelies.

On the day of the Porch Jazz Fest they popped some pills and then rode up and down the streets from venue to venue, slowly, taking it all in. They wove in and out of the crowds, all the sounds and colors blending with the wind whipping through their hair like a hallucinogenic symphony, popping their wheelies when they had open space in the traffic-less side streets or the park downtown. Some people clapped or laughed as they passed.

As the evening emerged, and the festival wound down, the rest of the gang went back to someone's house to drink and smoke weed, but Tyeisha and Finn went back to his empty house and up to his attic bedroom under the slanted roof. The windows on opposite ends of the attic were open, letting in a lovely cross breeze. She was surprised to find his room neat and tidy, the bed made, clothes put away, and a string of twinkly mood lights pinned up along the edges of the ceiling. She almost felt guilty pulling down the covers and ruffling up the sheets as they hooked up. The chattering sounds of cheery people walking home from the festival filtered up through the windows along with some distant music of acts playing on past the official closing time. As Finn sloppily kissed her neck, and she rolled her eyes back to look up into the twinkly lights, which seemed to be dancing, she thought about that couple she overheard through that open window in the alleyway downtown talking about love earlier in the year. *How did that song go? Speak Low?* She wanted to talk about love like that one day, but for now this messy but kind boy would do.

After some snuggling, Tyeisha sat up and began to straighten her clothes and smooth out her hair. "My dad's gonna wonder where I am," she said, bending down to reach for her shoes.

Finn sat up and touched her arm, his hand warm to the touch. "I'm sorry about what happened to your mom," he said.

"I know," she said.

"You know I was the one who found that body in the woods, right? Last November? That druggie who OD'ed?"

"I know," she said again, turning to look at him and give him one last quick kiss before leaving.

Finn nodded. Kissed her shoulder. "We'll ride again tomorrow?" he asked.

Tyeisha nodded. "Sure."

≈

Sutton

Their neighbor on the corner was hosting one of the bands for Porch Jazz Fest, and they asked Sutton to do an opening statement in her official capacity as mayor prior to the festival starting. With Connie working at the bar, Sutton naturally obliged. A small crowd gathered on the corner for the mayoral kick-off early that afternoon.

"Well, we weren't sure if it was going to happen," Sutton began, mike in hand. "But we made it happen. Porch Jazz Fest is here!"

Some mild whoops and clapping rose from the crowd.

"You know, this pandemic might be far from over, but here in West Falls we've done the best we can to get back to normal while still ensuring the safety of each other. I know there have been some divisions and differences in opinion on how things have been handled, but look at us now. West Falls knows how to band together. We understand the importance of community. And we understand the importance of traditions. Porch Jazz Fest is becoming one of those traditions thanks to the passion of all of you. So, thank you for taking care of yourselves and each other. I hope we continue to do so and see level heads and common decency return to the world at large around us come November. And thank you for coming out today. Now let's enjoy some music!"

Her neighbor came up behind her amidst the cheers and took the mike from her. They said a few words before handing it off to the band, but Sutton's attention had been drawn to someone standing by the stop sign on the corner. Someone familiar but menacing.

"Mayor Jackson!" some people called out from the sidewalk. "Mayor Jackson, can we have a word?"

Sutton kept her eye on the man by the stop sign as she came down from the porch and onto the sidewalk to her neighbors and constituents. When the music began, it startled her, but she quickly found herself in conversation and lost sight of where the menacing man had gone.

"It's so great to see you all out here," Sutton said robotically with her official smile, "But I must make a phone call. I'll see you out there later. Thank you!"

Sutton ran back to her house and inside, where she pulled out her cell phone and called Sheriff Van Patten.

"Yes, Mayor?"

"Jim," Sutton said, "I think I might have just seen Darrel Strayer."

"Where?"

"At the corner by my house, leaning on the stop sign while I was giving the opening remarks for the festival."

"Are you sure? Why would he be there?"

"I'm pretty sure. His face is forever seared in my memory. Maybe he found out where I live and he's here to taunt me."

"Ma'am…Mayor…Sutton, if I may, that sounds like a bit of a stretch."

"But if he is here in town, and walking around as a convicted sex offender, he could be in violation of his parole and of the law if he walks too close to a school."

"I can send a few patrolmen out. Drive around the perimeter of the festival. Put a few out on foot."

"Yes, I think you should."

"And Sutton?"

"Yes?"

"Do not try to find him or follow him yourself, do you hear me?"

Sutton's voice went up a pitch. "Of course, yes, I hear you, Jim."

"Go be with the people and enjoy the festival. Or go to Connie's Place. I'll put my officers on watch." The sheriff paused and then said gruffly, "Let them do their job."

"Of course, thank you." Sutton hung up, adrenaline coursing through her blood. She needed fresh air.

Outside it was only the one band so far, but others were setting up. Crowds were sparse, but many people were outside enjoying the beautiful weather. Working in their yards. Kids playing and running around. It appalled her to no end to think Darrel Strayer would have the gall to show up here. Her stomach was tied in knots, her intestines like a boa constrictor. *If he dared…*she would strangle him on the spot, and no one could stop her. She put on her mask to hide her tension from her constituents as she made her way around the neighborhood looking for him. She saw one of the police officers walking the strip downtown. She snaked through the side streets as music began to fill the air and crowds thickened. She thought she saw him at one point, from the back, a few blocks up. She was pretty sure the man she saw initially by the stop sign had been wearing a dark gray hoodie. She tried to catch up to the hoodie, but there were too many people, and then the hoodie was gone around the corner, and by the time she turned the corner, he was out of sight.

"Mayor Jackson?" someone said, startling her. "You look lost?"

Sutton tried to laugh and brighten her eyes above her mask. "I thought I saw a friend go that way, but I was mistaken," she explained to the young man with the scruffy beard and flannel shirt.

"Hey, do you wanna drink?" he said.

"Oh, no, thank you. I'm kinda on duty, ya know, walking around the festival."

"Oh, right, of course. I hope you enjoy it!"

"You too! Don't forget to vote in November!"

The young man was already gone, disappeared into the crowd around the corner from where Sutton came, before she could think of anything else awkward and mayoral to say.

Sutton continued her way down the otherwise deserted side street, the noise from the festival and the strip growing softer behind her as she went. A cat leapt down from a fire escape and darted in front of her, almost causing her to trip. She stopped, and assessed the path before her. This would eventually take her down beneath the overpass, and on the other side would be Hampten. Maybe Darrel Strayer had crawled back to his lair.

Sutton took some deep breaths and tried to clear her head of these anxious and violent thoughts. She made her way back to the main strip and eventually to the park downtown. There she found Sheriff Van Patten surveying the scene by the Veterans' Memorial.

"Mayor Jackson, good to see you," he said with a suspicious eyebrow raised above his mask.

"And you, Sheriff," Sutton said.

"You'll be glad to know everyone seems to be behaving themselves."

"Good, good."

Some teenagers went by on their bikes in front of the memorial, and a few popped wheelies.

"Those kids looked high," he joked.

But Sutton's eyes had turned towards a scene by the playground. She could see a little boy, about five or six, screaming and desperately pulling themselves away from a man in a dark gray hoodie!

"Sheriff, over there!" she yelped.

Sheriff Van Patten turned and walked briskly towards the scene. The child continued to struggle to break free from the man's grip and screamed at the top of their lungs.

"What's going on here?" the sheriff boomed, with Sutton close behind.

Finally, the child slipped out of their jacket and fell hard onto the ground, breaking their fall with their arm. "Oww!" they cried out.

Sheriff Van Patten had drawn his gun.

"Woah! Woah! Woah! Hold on here!" the man in the gray hoodie said. "This is getting out of hand!"

"Don't move!" the sheriff commanded. He kept the gun pointed at the man as he turned his head calmly towards the little boy crying on the ground. "Son, who is this?"

"Mommy! Daddy! Mommy! Mommy! Mommy!" the little boy cried.

"Where is your Mommy?" Sutton intervened.

"I'm his dad!" the man screamed.

Sheriff Van Patten turned back to the man. "Keep your hands up!"

"His mother is off getting drunk right now," the man said, frustrated.

Sheriff Van Patten turned back to the child, "Son, is this your father?"

The little boy nodded affirmatively as he wiped snot from his nose.

Sheriff Van Patten slowly lowered his gun and put it back in its holster.

"Hey, I know this didn't look good, but damn, I was just trying to get him to go home. He struggles with transitions." The man reached in his pocket. "Do you need to see ID or something? I can show you family pictures on my phone."

"No, that won't be necessary. My apologies. There were reports of…*a person of interest*…being here in the park and you fit the description."

"Some kind of kidnapper?" the man asked as he helped his son up off the ground.

The sheriff nodded. "How's your arm, son?"

"It hurts," the boy cried.

"I suggest you get him to urgent care. It might be sprained or broken."

The man swept his son up into his arms. "I'm free to go?"

"Of course."

The man sprinted away to his car parked on the edge of the park.

Sheriff Van Patten then turned to Sutton. "Jesus Christ, I hope no one recorded that. And I hope that guy isn't active on *Under the Falls*."

"I'm sorry, Jim. It looked just like him from afar. And the way he was grabbing that kid!"

"His son, Sutton…*the way he was grabbing his son*…was like any frustrated parent trying to get their kid to go with them."

"But what if that's not what it was? I mean, we didn't know. We saw a child in distress. You did nothing wrong."

"Can I trust you to walk home by yourself, or do you need a police escort?"

At the far end of Sutton's street Sheriff Van Patten pulled up the police cruiser to drop her off, so as not cause a scene so close to her house and the festival venue on the other corner.

Sutton pulled her mask down. She began slowly, "Everyone initially thought it was the priest, Father MacShay, who killed Robbie Elms, including your father. Everyone just kinda assumed that sick fuck of a man would go that far one day and snuff out a kid's life. But then your father uncovered the truth and the real culprit. Darrel Strayer. And he dedicated his life to getting Darrel Strayer off the streets."

Sutton paused and gazed out the window. She turned back to the sheriff. "And when we worked together to finally prosecute him *for something*, I dug deep to find out everything I could about him. I wanted to believe there was a reason Darrel Strayer was the way he was – that his evil was born out of abuse – maybe at the hands of the same priesthood that terrorized Robbie's friends and countless others. But there was no childhood abuse. Strayer just was who he was. Two separate evils preyed upon Robbie Elms and his friends, but one didn't cause the other. And it was upsetting to think these evils were independent and had no cause. They just were. It would've been simpler to believe Strayer was a victim in some way, too."

Sheriff Van Patten lowered his mask, looked Sutton in the eyes, and said, "My father let that evil man completely consume him. He was never around. He was always on, always trying to find a way to nail that guy. My parents divorced over it. I barely knew him, Sutton! You knew him better than I did!"

"I'm sorry, Jim."

Sheriff Van Patten shook his head in disgust, and then was completely still. He put his mask up and returned his eyes to the road ahead outside the windshield. He nodded slightly and then said "Take care of yourself, Mayor Jackson. And let us do our jobs."

"Good-bye, Sheriff." Sutton opened the door and climbed

out.

That evening while the festival wound down and Sutton waited for Connie to come home, she sat in her study looking over the old case file on Darrel Strayer. She remembered interviewing Vera Elms, and she looked over the transcript, but didn't really need to, as some of the things Vera had said haunted her to this day.

The case against Strayer for the crimes he committed against the children in Hampten was over a decade following his suspected killing of Robbie Elms. Sutton recalled Vera mentioning how there was still so much drama regarding Robbie even years later. It was her commentary on the chronic pain and stress it continued to put on her.

Vera said to her back then, while Sutton prepped the case, "Sometimes I wish Robbie's body was never found and his disappearance remained a mystery. One I could write a happy ending to. Or maybe his body just stayed there in the woods and was eventually buried by the natural passage of time, and became a fossil to unearth millions of years later by who knows what kind of intelligent life. Do you ever think about stuff like that? Would they wonder over it – his body, his bones – or would they just simply catalog it? He could be just like those dinosaur bones he loved to look at buried in that pit at the bottom of the gorge."

Now, decades later, all Sutton wanted to do was turn the falls back on and bury everything at the bottom of the pit under water.

EPISODE EIGHT – IT GOES ON AND ON

The 2020s and Beyond
The Vaughan Family - Interrupted

Other couples never asked how they met. Val and Sam were always politely curious when hanging out with other – usually straight – couples and naturally asked how they met. *It was a common go-to question in social situations, right?* Val often wondered, did these straight people assume they met through some gay hook-up app, or maybe something less gay like through work or at a marketing conference? Were they afraid to ask? Or did they just not care?

Truth be told, they met the old-fashioned way, in person, by chance, at a normal (*not gay*) bar in the city at happy hour. It was Sam who first got a glimpse of Val, and he cozied up beside him at the bar, both of them trying to avoid banal work banter with their respective coworkers. It wasn't anything romantic like love at first sight, though Val latter assumed Sam was drawn to him because of his skin color and eyes. They met and started talking out of boredom, as a way to avoid other people, and they found they had some shared interests in movies, music, and careers and agreed to do dinner and a movie later that week. That was it. Nothing spectacular. But they wanted to tell other couples that. They were dying to share their story. But no one asked. Years later, Val couldn't even remember what restaurant they went to or what movie they saw on their first date. It was that unremarkable.

When Sam awoke from his coma in early October of 2020 after over twelve weeks, he couldn't remember anything. Val told him how they met to try to jog Sam's memory, but his own lack of details around their first date left them both perplexed.

Val had long discussions with the neurology specialist and clinical social worker about what to expect, how to help Sam regain his memory, and how to handle Henry in this context. They all agreed seeing his son might be just the jolt Sam needed, but they also understood the delicacy of putting an almost five-year old boy in that situation. Val was caught between wanting to shield Henry from undo trauma and not wanting to lie to their son. He had always believed kids deserved the truth. They were a family. They had to get through this together.

Val worked with the social worker on prepping Henry, explaining to him in the simplest terms that Daddy Sam was awake but still sick, and he might say strange things or act like he doesn't know you when he sees you, but he still loves you very much, and he's working very hard to get better. *It's very, very hard for him right now*, and we need to be patient with him. They told Henry if he didn't want to do it, he didn't have to, and if he wanted to do it, but at any point wanted to stop and leave the room, he could.

"I want to see Daddy Sam," Henry said to them plainly. "I wanna help him get better."

When Val and the social worker brought Henry into Sam's room, Henry lit up, expecting to see the mirrored reaction in his father who had always lit up when Henry entered the room. But Henry got no such response from Sam, who like Henry, had been prepped but was woefully unprepared for this moment.

Sam feigned a smile when he saw the light drain from the boy's eyes. "Come a little closer, let me get a look at you," he said.

Henry slowly approached Sam, still holding Val's hand. From his chair, Sam reached out and touched Henry's cheeks with his cold, clammy hands. Henry shivered a little and squeezed Val's hand tighter. Val pulled him away, sensing their son's discomfort.

Sam looked up at the social worker. "You're sure this is my son?"

Val pulled Henry away. "This was a bad idea." He scooped Henry up and swept him from the room.

"I don't know them!" Val could hear Sam screaming at the social worker as they hurried down the hallway.

And that was the thing. It wasn't like Sam had fragmented or missing memories where he just needed help putting the puzzle together, and he was otherwise still the same Sam whom Val had always known. It was like the slate had been wiped clean. His personality seemed to be gone, too.

"I don't understand how this could happen?" Val said to the doctor, who would proceed to show him images of Sam's brain and where the injury had occurred, and where pressure had remained for some time until the swelling went down while he was in the coma, and none of it would make any sense. The doctor would concede it's always hard to tell how severe the impacts from these injuries could be, and the brain was a mysterious thing, and it all just blurred into nonsense and excuses. All Val knew was Sam was rejecting him and their son, and poor Henry, he should've never brought him to see him, *and what the hell were they going to do now?*

"Will he recover?" Val asked. "Bottom line it for me. Talk to me like I'm stupid. Will he recover?"

"We don't know," the doctor replied.

We don't know? Or we don't care?

In one conversation between Val and the new blank-slate version of Sam, Sam said to him, "I'm not even sure I'm gay."

That's when Val began to suspect one of two horrible possible truths: Sam had been play-acting all along before the accident…or Sam was play-acting now.

Sam also said to Val, "I feel nothing when I see Henry. I'm

sorry. I feel nothing when I see you, and I feel nothing when I see him."

"So, what are you telling me?" Val asked him. This conversation occurred on the eve of releasing Sam to return home and continue his treatments and care out-patient.

"I can't go home with you. I need to stay somewhere else. Alone. To figure this out."

"Figure what out?" Val said. "We're married. We have a son. He needs you at home with him no matter what kind of shape you're in. Where the hell will you go?"

"My parents are helping me get into a highly specialized treatment center…in Minnesota."

"*In Minnesota?* You're just going to up and fucking go to Minnesota?"

"Well, I'm gonna stay with my parents for a little bit, and then go to Minnesota. It's where we think I can get the best help, and maybe get my memory back. Or at least figure out how to carry on."

"Will you be back for the holidays to see Henry at least?"

"I can't do it. I'm sorry. It's not healthy for me. Or him, probably."

"You don't give a shit about him. Do you have any idea what abandonment does to a boy, especially when it's his father abandoning him?"

"You're still his father."

"But you're abandoning him! *Look at me when I'm saying this to you.* Because this is it. *Me.* I'm what happens when a boy is abandoned by his father. You married a very tortured, angry man. And you loved him. And you made a family with him. And we want to help you, we want you to stay with us. Give it a chance."

"I'm sorry. I just can't."

"You know, I want to blame the accident, blame this fucked-up traumatic brain injury that fucked-up your whole…*everything*. But really, I just blame you. It was your careless actions that lead to your injury. It was your choices that put you in this horrible previously unimaginable situation. You risked everything for nothing. I fucking hate you right now. More than I ever hated my father. You don't have to choose this now either. You can let us be your family. You can blame the injury if you want, but you're choosing this. You're choosing to abandon your family. When YOU need us the most. When WE need you the most. How do you not fucking see those needs are intertwined?"

"I'm sorry. I don't know what else to say."

"*Oh, you're sorry alright.*" Val stormed out of the room.

≈

September 2021
Val and Henry

Nearly a year later, Val couldn't believe it was Henry's first day of kindergarten. He was probably more nervous than Henry. The daycare had done a good job keeping COVID mostly at bay with only five confirmed cases in the whole school and only two quarantines throughout the entire prior year. Val had heard plenty of horror stories about other daycares that were carelessly lax with protocols and could barely keep the doors open because staff or kids were always sick. Their daycare was small enough where the kids in Henry's class had become their own pod and the parents trusted each other to be as precautious as possible. Now Henry was going into the wider, much larger elementary school population. His class would have twice the number of kids, at least, and the school went up to fifth grade. There were plenty of debates about whether to mask or not. Most felt another huge wave and spike was inevitable in the fall or winter, so what could you do?

As for that morning, Val was worried Henry would insist on wearing pajamas, but he picked out a reasonable outfit – jeans and a button-down shirt *to be fancy* – and Val took pictures of Henry on the front stoop holding his "First Day of Kindergarten" board with him wearing a mask and without. He was adorable in both versions, and Val just hoped the mask version of the picture could be looked back on as an interesting time capsule, as something Henry proudly lived through and survived.

"Take the mask with you," Val told him, "But it's your choice to wear it or not. If you feel more comfortable wearing it, *you do you*. Don't worry about what other kids are doing."

Val walked him the five blocks down to the school.

"Why does Daddy Sam still not want to see me?" Henry asked as they walked.

Val took a deep breath, pushing all of his anger and resentment into his gut. There had been a lot of questions from Henry last year, but they had settled into a routine as a two-man crew pretty quickly and only occasionally did Henry ask about Sam in the past six months. The start of a new school year in a new school with new kids undoubtedly caused some anxiety in Henry, and he was likely reaching back for the moments of comfort and normalcy he remembered with both his dads. Val wanted to use his most calming and reassuring tone possible. "Well, it's still very hard for him right now," Val said. "He still doesn't remember us."

"Because of the hurting in his head?"

"Yeah, because his brain got hurt really bad and it impacted his ability to remember."

"Will he ever want to be with us again?"

They were coming up to the school. Val stopped Henry at the corner and kneeled down to be more at his level. Here he was – the guy who had been lied to as a boy over and over, and always believed he would be the type of dad who would never lie to his kids – about to lie to his kid. "I sure hope so, buddy."

"Me too," Henry said.

"But that's always been up to him. And I want you to remember something. There are going to be all kinds of people in your life, and some will want to be around you and cheer you on and be on your side, and some will not want to be on your side, and some will be on your side at first but then for whatever reason that has nothing to do with you, they'll walk away. Focus your energy on the ones who want to cheer you on and be on your side. I'll always be on your side. I'll never walk away."

"But what if your head gets hurt, or my head gets hurt?"

"I can understand why you would worry about that. I worry about that, too. But look, we never know what's going to happen. Let's just focus on being on each other's side right now, in this moment." Val stood up as some other families were coming up to the corner behind them. "Now let's keep moving, together." He took Henry's hand, and they crossed the corner and walked briskly up to the schoolyard where all the kids were lining up by grade, and the kindergarten teacher and aide were waiting for them.

Henry was excited to see a few of his friends from daycare. Most of the kids were maskless, but Henry put his on as they headed inside. He waved goodbye to Val as if they had been doing this for years, and just like that, he was gone.

"He's so cute," a mom with a scrunched-up nose said as the kids marched into the building. "Are you the manny?"

"Excuse me?" Val said to her.

"Oh, I'm sorry, I was just trying to be funny."

"I'm his father. Are you a nanny?"

The mom turned her nose up even more, turned around, and walked away.

≈

Later that day…

Tyeisha, a senior now in high school, walked to the elementary school and waited outside until they dismissed the students and then walked Henry home where she would watch him for a few hours while Val finished his meetings from the home office upstairs.

"So how was the first big day of kindergarten?" Tyeisha asked him.

"It was okay," Henry said. "I don't remember all the kids' names. Some of them cried. And some were bad."

"That's okay. You'll learn their names eventually."

"Do you like hanging out with me?" Henry asked Tyeisha while she got him his snack.

"Of course," Tyeisha said. "And we're both only children, so we have to stick together."

"And we both don't have mommies."

"Yes, that's true. But I don't have a mommy because mine died. You don't have a mommy because you have two daddies."

"Do you put flowers on your mom's grave?"

"I do."

Later, while they lounged in the living room on their respective devices, Val came down from the office and Henry announced, "Daddy, don't worry, I'll put flowers on your grave when you die."

Val stopped dead in his tracks, but could only smile at his son's enthusiastic utterance. "Thanks, buddy!"

"You're welcome!"

At bedtime, after Val read Henry a story and snuggled in bed with him, Henry asked, "Why don't I have a mommy?"

"Well, when Daddy Sam and I decided to have a baby, we needed someone's help. So, we were lucky there was a nice woman who wanted to be our surrogate. And she's the one who gave birth to you so we could become daddies."

"How did I get insider her?"

"Well, we had doctors help make you, and then they put what would become you inside her belly so you could grow and become a baby. And, buddy, it was so cool. Daddy Sam and I got to watch as they did it. And we could see on a screen as they plopped you in there. But you weren't even you yet. It was just a speck too small to even see, but there was a tiny flash of light that let the doctors know when they had successfully placed you where you needed to be, and when we saw that tiny flash of light on the screen…WOW…it was like witnessing the start of the universe. It was like our own personal big bang. And you were like our own little star."

"I was a star?" Henry asked, his hopeful eyes looking up into Val's.

"You looked like a little star, yeah, for just that flash, a split second. It was amazing."

Henry looked down at the stuffy in his hands. "But why didn't the nice woman want to be my mommy?"

"Because you had two daddies. She was just helping us."

"But now I only have one daddy." Henry hugged his stuffy tightly.

Val gently squeezed Henry. "Daddy Sam is still and always will be your daddy, no matter what decisions he makes. He just hasn't been able to take care of you this past year. But that's okay, because I have."

"Will you always take care of me?" Henry put his head on Val's shoulder.

"For as long as I can. And for as long as you need me to." Val kissed the top of his head.

Henry snuggled him a little harder. "Thank you, Daddy."

"And I want you to be able to talk to me about anything. Especially if you're scared or angry or confused."

Henry fidgeted. "I don't like talking about that stuff at bedtime."

"That's okay. You can talk to me about anything, at any time. But if you just want to do stories at bedtime, we can."

"Yeah, just stories. Happy stories."

Val's eyes perked up and he jostled Henry playfully. "Oh, wait, I have an idea! How about we make a deal to sit down on the bottom step together? When I come down from work after you get home from school, we can use that time to talk about whatever you want."

Henry furrowed his brow. "Uh, sure, okay. But what if I don't know what to say because I can't describe it good?"

Val's voice softened. "Okay, well how about this…if you've had a good day and you just want to talk about your day with me, sit on the bottom step. But if there's something bothering you, but you don't know how to describe it…the more it bothers you, the higher you sit on the steps."

Val could see Henry was pondering this. Henry said, "So if maybe like one or two bad things happened, like another kid hit me or stole my marker, I sit on the middle step? Or like if a lot of bad things happened, I sit on the landing?"

"Yeah, that's the idea," Val said. "You're getting it."

"And if it was a *really, really, really, really, really, really* bad day and I'm really sad or mad, I sit at the top step at the end of the hallway?"

"Uh huh."

"And if it's *the worst day ever* and I'm so sad and mad and crying, I skip all the steps and coming running into your office?"

"Yes, if it's that bad you can come running into my office. You can always come find me."

Thankfully, over the span of that first school year and subsequent years there weren't many instances of Henry running into Val's office when he came home at the end of the school day. There were plenty of times he was sitting a few steps from the bottom, or higher, or on the landing, or even on the top step. Whether he was on that top step with something heavy weighing on his soul, or that bottom step and just wanted to chat about his day, Val approached every moment with the same intent: to listen, and to just be there on that step with him. Sometimes that's all it took.

Other times, an arm around the shoulder was needed. Or a few choice words of commiseration, or encouragement. Sometimes (in the case of the middle school bully incident) a promise of action. Every school day, and sometimes even non-school days. On those steps. Without fail. If Henry was sitting on those steps, that was Val's invite to come and listen, or just sit.

One of the more memorable moments was that spring day, when Henry was a freshman in high school, and he sat down on the landing, in front of the open window and the breeze. Val came out of his office and sat down next to him.

"I always liked the view from here," Henry said, "I feel like we're giants looking down into the living room."

"What's up, son?" Val asked. "My bones are getting creaky in my old age, like these floors, and I can't sit as long as I used to like this."

"Ok, old man, I'll cut to the chase. You know, I've seen how happy you and Dad are, and how you've always worked through whatever tough spots you've had, and ever since Dad got better you've both always been there for me through thick and thin. And you're both great role models for me, ya know? I want to have a love like that, like you and Dad have. But…I just keep going over it in my head. I've never liked any other boys like that. I can't deny the fact I just like girls, Dad."

Val had been holding his breath through Henry's speech, was touched by his words, and then let out a relieved laugh and jostled Henry on the shoulders. He ruffled his son's hair like in the old days. "Man, you had me going there for a minute. I wasn't sure where that was going. That's great, son. You just came out as straight. I'm happy you figured out who you are."

They told Sam at dinner, together, as a united front.

"We always suspected you were straight," Sam said. "Parents can usually tell pretty early on."

Sam, who after eighteen months of rehabilitation and treatment at the best traumatic brain injury center in the country, returned to West Falls and to his family half way through Henry's kindergarten year. There were still many memories Sam never recovered, like how he and Val met. It became a fun game for them, making up elaborate tales of how they met so they would be prepared whenever someone asked, though people rarely did. He never recovered that magical moment of the "big bang" and that flash of light in the surrogate's womb at the fertility clinic, but Val would tell him and Henry that story over and over through the years. Most of the first five years of Henry's life were still lost to Sam, but they all focused on making new memories, and in that path they found each other again and rebuilt their family.

The final talk on the steps with Val occurred when Henry came home for the holidays while he'd still been living with roommates trying to figure out his path in life after graduating from Princeton. Val came out of his office to find Henry sitting on the top step.

"You're home!" Val exclaimed. "But are you okay?"

"I'm fine, Dad," Henry said, "It's actually good news…or, well, I hope you'll see it that way. But it's big."

Val sat down on the step beside him, barely enough room now for two adults. "Well, buddy, spill it. Don't keep your old man in suspense."

"You know how much I loved studying abroad in France last year, and I told you I would love to try living in Europe at some point, right?"

"Okay. And?"

"Well, I have an opportunity to take an amazing job working for the world's largest AI tech company based in Copenhagen. And they want me to move there and start in January."

"Well, I'll be damned, look at you!" Val laughed, that casual old-man chuckle he had been honing over the years to hide the anger he still felt at the world. He affectionately shook Henry by the shoulders and then hugged him. "I'm so proud of you, son! But, man, how're we going to tell your other father? He won't want to let you go."

Henry smiled. "He'll have to get over it. Because he won't have a choice."

≈

The Ballad of Amie and Hap

As everything began to reopen and mask mandates dropped, Amie stayed on as the assistant manager at Connie's Place, and Hap's business was doing better than ever as the pandemic reinforced his status as a pillar of the community and *the appliance whisperer*. In April of 2021, Amie did not renew her apartment lease and moved in permanently with Hap. If anyone could be happier than the two of them about the whole thing, it was Hap's dog, Gus, who enjoyed late night walks followed by snuggles when Amie got home from Connie's, where return business was booming.

Around town, new places began to open where old places had shuttered earlier in the pandemic, and the circle of life and commerce continued in West Falls. On the day she moved out of her apartment, Amie noticed someone putting up a COMING SOON sign on a shop a few buildings down. She couldn't even remember what it had been prior to the pandemic. *Was that the specialty popcorn shop or the gelato place?* The sign on the outside indicated it would soon be a clothing shop called *Vintage 99*.

After Amie finished loading the small moving truck behind the building, she noticed a woman carrying some boxes inside the store. At first she appeared unrecognizable, but then Amie realized it was Sheila Carter. She walked over to the storefront and the open door. Sheila had placed the box on the only counter left in the otherwise gutted store and then turned around to see Amie standing there in the threshold.

"Oh, hi," Sheila said.

"Sorry, I hope I'm not intruding," Amie said. "I saw the sign and then saw you and…"

"I had forgotten you lived down here."

Amie smiled. "Well, not as of today. I'm moving."

"Oh. Moving in with Hap?"

Amie nodded.

"I couldn't help but see the social media posts of you two. I hope you're good to him. He deserves someone who will appreciate him."

"He's the best of us. I'll do my best to live up to what he deserves."

"Well, I gotta get a few more boxes." Sheila stepped around Amie and back outside onto the shaded sidewalk.

"Oh, like I said, didn't want to intrude. I'll get out of your way. But maybe we could grab coffee some time?"

Sheila smirked and tried not to roll her eyes. "Both of us have come a long way since we last ran into each other. Look, I'm sober now. In a completely different head space. I'm not doing the twelve steps, so don't expect an apology because you'd probably be on the list if I was, but I'm doing it my way. And that way includes cutting ties with that life…my past. I sold Hank's auto shop, sold the house. I bought this storefront and the apartment above it. I'm moving in upstairs, but this whole floor needs to be redone. It's gonna keep me real busy, so ya know, I appreciate the offer, but…"

"No, you don't have to explain anything to me. And if anyone needs to apologize, it's me."

"I'll stop you there. I don't need that either. I'm glad to see you're happy with Hap. I wish you the best. Honestly."

Amie nodded. "I believe you. Okay then. Good luck." And she couldn't help but think. *We made it through to the other side.* So many others didn't. Hank surely didn't. But Amie and Sheila did. *Who could've predicted they would be standing here like this right now a year and a half ago?* "I'll be sure to stop in the store when it opens."

"I'll welcome all business. Take care of yourself, Amie."

"You too, Sheila."

Later that summer there was a huge gala. It turns out Sheila's story was the subject of one of those home improvement shows. It was a compelling hook. Widow and recovering alcoholic finally lives out her lifelong dream of owning an 80s and 90s vintage clothing store. The episode would air later in the fall, but they premiered it at the store the night before its grand opening, detailing her search for the perfect property downtown. Mayor Jackson was there. The whole town was there, including Hap and Amie, though they didn't get a chance to talk to Sheila directly. They were just lost in the crowd. Sidewalk seating had been set up for drinks and food, and then more seating was out back behind the building under twinkly lights.

Hap had been having some really bad headaches, so they snuck around to the back where no one else was.

"Well, this is certainly wild," Hap remarked.

"I know. I still can't really believe it," Amie said. "I'm really happy for her, though."

Hap massaged his temples.

"Do you just wanna go home? Rest?" Amie asked him. "It's all a little weird and awkward anyways."

Hap looked up at the twinkly string lights. "Did you just see that?"

Amie laughed. "See what?"

"Nevermind. Yeah, let's just go home."

At home, Gus was extra snuggly with Hap, nuzzling him and licking his face. Before bed, Hap threw up. Gus slept with them at the foot of the bed, which was unusual as the dog typically stayed in his bed in the living room. In the middle of the night, Amie woke up to find Hap sitting up in bed and quietly talking. He was mostly unintelligible but seemed agitated. Amie wasn't sure if he was having a night terror. She was afraid to startle him, but then Gus gave out a little yelp that broke the spell.

Hap shook his head and looked over at Gus and then at Amie. "I think I'm losing my mind," he said.

"What's wrong?" Amie asked.

"I swear…I mean…I still see Hank and Robbie. They're standing over there in the doorway. But like twelve-year-old Hank and Robbie. That's who I was talking to."

In the morning, Hap could barely stand from the headache being so debilitating, and he was still seeing things…seeing *people*. Amie called the closest Urgent Care, and when she described his symptoms, they said she should take him to the ER right away. They were there all day, and after a series of tests including an MRI ordered by the neurology consult, they were referred to oncology and ultimately sent home after being told Hap had a highly advanced, inoperable, glioblastoma. The brain tumor had been extremely aggressive and tentacled down his spinal cord.

"We can do chemotherapy," the oncologist said grimly, "but the likelihood of it stopping the spread of the cancer or shrinking the tumor is extremely low. The best we can hope for is that if the chemo is successful, it can slow the growth and buy you some time. Without it, we're looking at a few months, up to four maybe. With it, and with success, you might see another year."

How did this happen, just like that? Over the course of twenty-four hours their lives were turned completely upside down. And to be sitting at home, the dog at their feet between them under the table, eating dinner, after receiving a death sentence? Like any normal night?

"Last night at the party, I saw whales in the sky. I looked up and they were up there swimming. I swear I could even hear them," Hap said plainly. "And now I can see an octopus on the ceiling. Is it normal to feel famished? I can't stop eating. I'm so hungry." He shoveled mashed potatoes into his mouth.

Amie couldn't touch her food. "Eat," she said. "You need your energy."

"You too, you haven't eaten all day." Hap paused and seemed like he was about to cry. "Oh, Amie, *I'm so sorry.*"

"What are you apologizing for?"

"I've had this vivid imagination for so long. I never thought anything of it. What if this thing has been growing inside my head for years? The visions, I mean, I guess they started a while ago, but it wasn't until last night that they got so big, like I'm inside some movie. It must've finally hit a nerve…literally."

"Hap, what are we going to do?"

Hap was looking off in the distance behind Amie. His eyes returned to her. "*They're saying fight like hell.* What else can I do? I'll call the doctors tomorrow and tell them to set me up for the chemo asap. Let's blast this fucker. I'm not ready to leave you yet."

Who was *they?* Amie wondered, but it didn't matter. She agreed. *Fight like hell.* Now, who were they going to tell first?

Word spread fast as Hap went through his first round of chemo and summer flowed into fall. He spent most of his time on *Under the Falls* responding to people needing the *appliance whisperer's* help by referring them to other reliable individuals and businesses he had personally vetted. Meanwhile people lamented his troubles. *To have survived a childhood where his best friend was murdered, serving in the U.S. Air Force in Afghanistan, and the pandemic, only to have this happen!* People were beside themselves. Dine & Donate, Beef & Beer, Go Fund Me – all were arranged, mostly spearheaded by Pete and the gang, and supported by everyone from the closest friends to complete strangers. The overflow of sympathy and support was overwhelming to Amie and Hap, who took it all in stride while his insurance covered what it could, but medical bills quickly piled up.

"That's what this community does," Hap told her.

All Amie wanted to do was hold him, make love to him, but the chemo side effects were ravaging him, and she felt like she would break him just by touching him. The dog was his biggest comfort when he came back from each treatment.

After the first round was complete, he had more tests and a scan.

"I'm sorry, but it's continuing to progress," the oncologist said. "It's your choice if you want to begin another round, but given the side effects the first round had, and these results, I would recommend you consider quality over quantity at this juncture. You can be made more comfortable."

"Be honest with me, will I make it to the holidays if I stop the chemo now?" Hap asked as Amie held his hand.

"I can't guarantee, but it's possible. And we can do our best to make you comfortable. At home."

"Keep me off that poison. Tell me what the next steps are."

Hap had always been thin, but he lost about thirty pounds during the chemo. Once he was off it, his appetite came back. He was given medications for the headaches and pain. There were some to help quell the hallucinations, too, but he didn't take those. He started to eat more and feel better. They gave him something for sleep, too, which helped. All in all, he got his energy back and regained a little weight. If they hadn't known better, and known he was terminal, people would swear he was getting better, cured even.

For Amie it was a cruel trick, but she took the joy and bliss where and when she could. They made love as often as possible. They talked about their hopes and dreams. He described his fanciful hallucinations to her in increasingly creative and outlandish ways to make her laugh. And she did. And then she cried. They laughed and cried together. They spent the holidays with Connie and Sutton and Pete and Mrs. Wolinski. Everyone agreed to Hap's request not to talk about his situation. They all played their happy parts in his happy little scene. It was lovely, actually. Living a lie for those few hours together.

Amie and Hap rang in the New Year, 2022, snuggled up at home. The new biggest wave of COVID yet, Omicron, was about to peak, but it felt like an inevitable repeat, and in a way, Hap was happy he wouldn't have to watch the continued reruns. He worried about Amie, of course, but he knew she could take care of herself. She always had. He was thankful he had the time he did with her. They watched the ball drop, had a little champagne, made love just after midnight, and went to bed.

Amie awoke in the middle of the night to Hap talking again and Gus whimpering at the foot of the bed. She gently touched

Hap's shoulder.

Hap turned to her. "Oh, there you are. Robbie's over there again. But he's different. Something's changed. He's not my Robbie anymore." He didn't sound agitated like he normally was when he had visions at night.

Amie gently rubbed his back. "It's okay," she told him. "He's always going to be your Robbie. He'll always be there." And then she said something she herself did not believe, and she wasn't even sure he did as a recovering Catholic, but she said it anyway because she thought it would comfort them both. "And you'll see him soon. He's waiting for you. And if he asks you to come with him, it's okay to go."

Hap nodded slowly. "I know," he turned to her, misty eyed. "But I think this is *your* Robbie."

Amie felt a shiver down her spine.

Hap hugged her. "It's okay. It's okay," he said to her over and over. "I'll always love you all."

The next few days, his headaches and back ache increased to where he could hardly move. His hallucinations escalated, but at least as he reported them to Amie, they seemed harmless fanciful creatures and images of loved ones. She had feared something from the war, or something sinister, would terrorize him, but he seemed at peace with them all. By the following week, after another scan revealed more spread to his spine, the hospice care was increased. He was soon confined to bed, partially paralyzed. He had a DNI order in place, and so as soon as the lungs could no longer work on their own, that would be it. There was a morphine drip Amie could max out herself when the time came. She promised him she wouldn't hesitate. It was the least she could do. She didn't want him suffocating to death. Gus laid at the foot of his bed spare for his walks and feeding time.

"Tell me a story," Hap said to her weakly one morning. His breathing had become more labored.

Amie held his hand as she sat in the chair beside the

adjustable hospital bed set up in their living room. She told him a story about two people so much in love they took their love on the open road. Bought an RV and traveled around the country to famous archaeological digs, down into Mexico, Central America, and South America, and all the way down to Chile and Cerro Ballena. Hap's eyes were closed but he smiled as she told him this.

Later that day, his breathing worsened, and he said, "It's time." Amie knew in her heart he wouldn't make it another night. She upped the morphine drip. Last Christmas, Hap had bought her a small antique record player and records of some of their favorite jazz tunes and old standards. She put on "Speak Low" by Sarah Vaughan and quietly sang along, holding his hand while he drifted off to sleep, never to wake again.

The funeral was on an unseasonably warm winter day out on the top of cemetery hill. Seemingly the entire town was there to see Hap Wolinski – hometown hero, second favorite son, *the appliance whisperer*, friend to one and all – put in the ground just above his beloved dinosaur bones forever trapped in the bottom of the gorge. Amie was again overwhelmed by the communal outpouring. The reception was back at Connie's Place where Connie did her thing to command the crowd and set the tone.

"Ok, here's a good one about Hap that I think perfectly captures what made Hap *Hap*..." Connie began, microphone in hand, sitting on a stool on the stage, the crowd hushed and rapt. "Now most of you probably remember I babysat for the Elms, and that meant Hap was often there because he practically lived there with Robbie, right. So, this one time, the boys were probably seven or eight, and Hap came over on his bike and they wanted to go out bike riding. I felt obligated to go with them even though I knew they went out by themselves all the time. Now, here comes my big idea to challenge them to go up that hill, you know the one on the far side of Ramble Lake before you get to the road...*the Party Woods*. I promised whoever got to the top first, I would buy them ice cream. So, they race each other up there peddling as hard as they could on their bikes through the dirt, and then suddenly here comes Hap and his bike tumbling back down to the path, and thank goodness there's a bush that breaks his fall before he hits the concrete." She paused to take a breath and scanned the crowd before finding Pete. "But it's a sticker bush. And the poor kid is covered in stickers and bleeding and all cut up. I was horrified, of course, hoping he was okay, but then also thinking Mrs. Wolinski *would kill me* for letting this happen under my watch. So, I helped remove those stickers one by one, and then Robbie and I helped him home. He's limping, can't ride his bike, a welt forming above his right eye where he smashed against the bike. He was just an absolute mess, but of course being Hap he's only worried about me.

"So, he tells me he'll tell his mom it was all his fault, and that I told them not to race up there. He just kept saying how sorry he was." Connie focused now on Amie. She smiled and continued, "And that was Hap in a nutshell. Even from the earliest age. Always wanting to protect people. Apologizing for putting anybody out, for being trouble or an inconvenience. I know he apologized to his mom and his brother and Amie and others, too, I'm sure…probably even the doctors, for having this damn brain tumor, this cancer. I hope he didn't feel he was inconveniencing any of us before he went. I hope he felt the outpouring of love this community was willing to give back to him after all those years of him giving to us. And I know he found the right person in Amie. I know she did her best to bring him peace in the end."

Connie looked down at the floor and then back up, looking out over the crowd. "I've got more stories I could tell. Funnier ones. I mean they were good kids, but Hap and Robbie had their mischievous streaks. But the bottom line is Hap didn't deserve this, and cancer fucking sucks. Fuck that tumor. Fuck cancer. He fought like hell at first, to give us all hope, more so for us than for himself, I think…trying to protect us even then."

Connie paused and made eye contact again with Pete. "I can't believe he's gone. But let's keep telling these stories. Let's keep him here a little bit longer with us. Because he would be the first one wanting to provide us some comfort. Let's let him do that."

Others came up to the stage. Everyone had their own personal story about Hap. After a while, Amie couldn't distinguish one from another, and it became all some wonderful montage or mosaic of Hap. But it was overwhelming, and she was exhausted. She hoped someone was recording all of this.

Eventually Pete took Amie home while the celebration of Hap's life and stories continued into the wee hours of the morning at Connie's Place. In the driveway, before she got out of the car, Pete asked her, "So what are you going to do with them…the house…Gus?"

Amie looked at Pete, not at all offended he would ask. After all, she was a wanderer. A leaver of places. She responded with a soft smile, confidently. "I'm gonna keep 'em."

Amie did. Hap had left her both, even though they hadn't been married. He made sure he took care of that with a lawyer shortly after the terminal diagnosis. A few weeks after the funeral she found out she was pregnant. In the past, there would've been no doubt in her mind she would have an abortion. But this time, there was no doubt in her mind she would keep it. Pete and Mrs. Wolinski cried with joy when she told them. It was a boy. And the pregnancy wasn't easy. At age thirty-seven, hers was considered a geriatric pregnancy. The baby was so eager to join the world he came a month early. She named him Robbie, because she wanted the love of her life to have the same name as the love of Hap's life. And though it sounded crazy to her when she told people the story, she was sure this was *her Robbie* that Hap saw shortly before he passed. It made for an amazing origin story whether there was any truth to it or not. But what did it matter what planted a seed of an idea in someone? It was all meant to be.

After Robbie Wren-Wolinski was born, Pete brought them over to his house. "I have a surprise for you, in the old garage out back." As the door lifted, a refurbished vintage RV was revealed, all shiny chrome.

"Hap wanted this to be a surprise. We were working on it together when he got sick. I continued the work and finished rehabbing it after he died. But it's yours. And I also worked with people to make a video of all those stories people told at his funeral, and others that I recorded over the past few months, and pictures throughout his life, and favorite songs…so Robbie will know his father."

"You are an amazing brother, an amazing friend, and now an amazing uncle, Pete," Amie said. "Thank you."

Pete took her and the baby inside the RV. Though it was dark in the garage, Amie imagined sunlight streaming in, and the open road unfurled outside the windows. Their future seemed to flash before her as she snuggled baby Robbie close to her chest, his faint breaths against her heartbeat.

She saw herself watching the video Pete had made to commemorate Hap's life with *her* Robbie as he grew. In that video were pictures of Robbie Elms and stories of their friendship. Amie would teach her son not just about his father, but also about his father's best friend whom he was named after.

"They'll always be with us as long as we remember them," Amie would tell him. She saw them taking the RV out every summer for an epic road trip. The three of them – Amie, Robbie, and Gus, and eventually Gus 2.0 – living wild and free, howling at the moon in the middle of a desert at night, swimming in lakes and hiking in mountains previously unknown, making their own archaeology along the way. Leaving their small trace – ephemeral etchings in the dirt, tiny rock towers destined to fall, a photo from the old-fashioned polaroid camera they took only on these trips, a note with some kind words, the rare etching in stone. It brought tears to her eyes seeing Robbie grow in her mind. Confident and loved.

Amie would raise him to be a better man. Gentle. Kind.

Giving. A lover of the world despite all the hate and chaos that often consumed it. The complete opposite of the toxic men she had known all her life up until she met Hap. Amie would look up at the sky wherever they were and not want to disappear, not want to leave her body like she had done for so many years because that's all she knew how to do to survive. She would savor each moment, each cloud and star and horizon, each place. Each little flower or insect or rock her son brought back for her, cupped lovingly in his small hands rising up to her. *Mom, look at this!* Every time he reached up at night to touch the moon. Every year after each adventure spanning their entire summer, they would pull up in that RV back in West Falls just in time for school to start.

"We're home, Dad," Robbie would say as they pulled into the driveway. *Home.* Something Amie had never had. Something Hap had gifted her. But also, a feeling wherever she and Robbie found themselves exploring. The whole wide world was home just as much as their cozy little bungalow in West Falls. She took comfort knowing Robbie would find home inside himself wherever he went.

$$\approx$$

Connie and Sutton

The chorus of regulars at Connie's couldn't stop going on and on about what happened in Washington D.C. on January 6th, 2021. Some of them had even watched it live at the bar from their stools.

"Not every day you get to see an insurrection!"

"It was a peaceful protest."

"Did you see the jackass with the fur coat and the horns?"

"They're gonna impeach the orange fucker twice now, kick his fat ass on his way out the door."

"Unbelievable what the world has come to."

"I blame social media."

"It's all theater, all for show. None of it is real."

"Did you know Jerry and his kid were on one of those busses going down there?"

"What? *Jerry?* I would've never guessed it. Didn't he vote for Obama…both times? I guess he was dumber than he looks."

"He always was a dumb fuck."

"Say, Connie, speaking of politics and all, how's the mayor doing? I heard a rumor she might not run for reelection this November?"

Connie laughed off the rumor from behind the bar, like she did all rumors. "Where did you hear that crap? You're gettin' to be as dumb as Jerry."

The other regulars laughed.

"I just thought maybe she was sick of all this political theater. Who would blame her."

"Well, West Falls isn't Washington, D.C. ya know," Connie said.

"Amen to that!" A few of them raised their beers in unison.

"But, Connie, what about this Darrel Strayer shit? She's gotta be mad as hell that guy is just walking around. People on *Under the Falls* say he's downtown all the time."

"Well, keeping an eye on people like Darrel Strayer is Sheriff Van Patten's job. Sutton is too busy running the town. And I'm too busy keeping you lot outta trouble."

But the truth was, Connie was worried about Sutton, who had talked about maybe stepping down as mayor, not running for reelection. Connie also knew Sutton well enough to know even though she never talked about it, Darrel Strayer's unwarranted freedom weighed heavy on her mind.

That spring, the excavation site at the bottom of the gorge was officially closed and the equipment removed. In collaboration with the state, county, and local environmental experts, the town council agreed to turn the falls back on and let the site turn back into the pond it originally had been. Some major dredging and rerouting of the creeks feeding into Ramble Lake above the gorge were scheduled to begin in late summer or early fall of 2021, to ensure Ramble Lake would not turn back into a swamp once the dam was taken down and water allowed to flow back into the gorge. They believed with the right engineering, all existing waterways could maintain sustainable levels and a new pond could exist at the bottom of the gorge fed from Ramble Lake above.

The town was hotly divided on this. Some believed the dinosaur dig site was West Falls' claim to fame, and to bury it under water was a crime as there were likely fossils still to be excavated. Others claimed all the fossils that could be found were already excavated, and the water fall had always been West Fall's claim to fame, and thus restoring it to its natural state while still maintaining the beauty of Ramble Lake was a win-win.

In the middle of town there was a bronze statue of the famous dryptosaurus that townies affectionally called *Drippy*, and its neck had become a hotspot from which people hung homemade signs spouting their views on the whole affair. At one point, one of the signs declared, "Don't let dikes drown my family."

I have nothing to do with it, Sutton seethed privately. It was ultimately up to the county and state. The town council was given a voice, but as mayor she could not sway things one way or another, only facilitate the conversations to get the work done that was needed to make it successful.

Meanwhile, Sutton was going down a rabbit hole online, tracking Darrel Strayer to a dark-web forum known to traffic child porn where she posed as a fellow enthusiast. The chatter was all in code speak, and the traders knew not to share any material digitally as it could be tracked. They dealt in old school mediums. Polaroids. VHS tapes. They agreed to clandestine drop offs and pick-ups so nothing could be tracked in the mail either. Sutton was able to lure him into a private chat on untraceable phones, posing as someone with a very specific niche taste, where the code broke down and Darrel began to brag about his crimes as a way to narrow down what this enthusiast was looking for.

Sutton knew from the trial for the crimes he committed against those boys in Hampten that Strayer took Polaroids of them. Finding that stash was the most damning evidence they had against him. He had been so arrogant thinking no one would care about or believe poor little Black and Hispanic children being abused. He didn't have to kill them to keep them quiet because who would believe them or care to do anything about it even if they did speak?

Though he obviously never laid claim to Robbie's murder from years earlier, she always assumed Robbie was probably his first. Given the circumstances, he probably stalked Robbie, and when he saw his opportunity, he took it. Then in the heat of the moment, Strayer knew if Robbie walked away from this attack, he would undoubtedly be caught. He had chosen a child who not only knew him, but who was loved by his family and community. He had no choice but to kill Robbie. It was a unique one-time-only thrill, as he would never put himself in that position again. What he didn't bet on was Detective Van Patten, who would still put it all together and then track him down for his other later crimes done in the shadows. Sutton was banking on the unique thrill aspect of his first and worst crime, as sick as it was to imagine, and she straight up asked him if he had ever killed a child.

Strayer bragged that he did. Just once.

Sutton asked if he had any mementos.

Strayer said he had a Polaroid.

Sutton asked what it was worth to him.

Part of Sutton wondered if Strayer knew it was her. If he was playing into the set-up. Maybe it was a different kind of unique thrill to rub his sickness in the face of the prosecutor who was never able to nail him for his most heinous crime. Maybe there was no Polaroid, and this was all a game to Strayer.

It didn't matter the motives or the truth of Strayer's statement. On August 31, 2021, they agreed to meet at the top of the gorge in West Falls before the remnants of Hurricane Ida were supposed to blow into the area. Maybe it was fate. Or maybe it was a perfectly secluded spot for such a rendezvous because it had been completely closed off in preparation for the dredging and water rerouting project that was set to begin as soon as the storm cleared out.

It was just after sunset when Sutton began her walk down to the gorge, and the sky still had a sliver of pinkish orange hew on the horizon. This week before school started was normally quiet around town, with many families getting in their last days down the shore and those in town trying to get back into early-to-bed and early-to-rise schedules. Kids no longer roamed freely into the evening as the days condensed and nights began earlier. By 8pm it was dark, warm, eerie and still, with a bit of electricity and plenty of humidity in the air as the big storm approached.

Sutton ducked under the blockades put up around the perimeter of the lake's edge, dam, and viewing area down into the gorge. She looked down from the top into the pit which had also been blocked off around its perimeter. Not a soul around. Only the din of cicadas, which was both calming and irritating. Some mosquitos bit at her in the darkness.

"*It is you,*" a soft, scratchy voice came up behind her.

Sutton turned around.

Darrel Strayer stood there as calm and casual as could be in sweatpants, a white t-shirt and a red baseball cap. He carried nothing with him. He was older and frailer than she expected, like a strong wind could blow him down.

In her mind, Sutton imagined some grand speech from him, a boasting confession. Something theatrical. But the moment between them was silent and all of a few seconds, before he simply lunged at her, his bony gray hands reaching for her throat. Sutton grabbed his wrists, and they struggled there on the precipice, both trying to maintain their footing on the gravel. Then Sutton instinctually fell back on her classic defense mechanism against any man over the years: she kneed him in the groin. Strayer let go, and as he buckled over and shuffled backwards away from her, he went with a quiet yelp right over the edge.

Sutton's heart was beating out of her chest. She cautiously looked over the edge, and in the darkness she could just barely make out his body sprawled on some rocks at the bottom of the gorge. She stepped back and looked up at the night sky. Stars were just starting to poke through the black. Tears were forming in her eyes. She took deep breaths to quell her panic. Should she reach for her phone and call the sheriff? Should she go down there and see if Strayer was still alive? *It was self-defense and an accident, right?*

Looking forward, star bursts were entering Sutton's vision. She felt the blood rushing to her head. She had to get out of there. She crawled under the blockade and onto the street. She walked briskly back home, becoming drenched in sweat and guilt. Once home, she poured herself some whiskey, downed it, and then watched the news and weather report, falling asleep before Connie came home from work.

Sutton woke up early the next morning on the couch, her head pounding and her body aching. Rain was starting to come down. She checked her messages and emails to see what was going on with the town, county, and state hurricane preparedness task forces. Flash flood warnings were being issued. All work was paused for the next two days due to the weather, meaning no one would be down at the gorge. She checked the crime and incident report – nothing about a body being found.

Connie came out of the kitchen carrying two mugs of coffee.

"You look like shit, hun," Connie said. "What happened last night?"

"Nothing," Sutton said groggily while massaging her temples. "You know, just worried about how serious Ida is going to be. Making sure everyone is prepped."

"I'm sure it's just gonna be a ton of rain, and everyone's sump pumps will be working overtime."

Connie went about her morning routine and then went in to open the restaurant. Sutton went down to her office in town hall and had a few meetings with the local crews and conference calls with the county and state about preparedness for floods and emergencies over the next twenty-four to forty-eight hours. People noticed she was even more stressed than usual, and her thoughts were scattered.

"Are you alright?" Sheriff Van Patten asked in the hall after a meeting.

"Just haven't been sleeping well lately," Sutton said.

"Hot flashes?"

"I'm going to head home and finish work there before this storm gets any worse. Let me know if you need anything. Everything seems to be covered here, for now."

The rain's intensity continued to increase over the course of the day, and wind gusts of up to sixty miles per hour battered the region. Connie closed up shop early after lunch and sent everyone home. Sutton and Connie both decided to sleep through the afternoon.

≈

Sheriff Jim Van Patten

"Water is flowing over the dam, sir," the officer told him over the phone.

What in the hell.

The falls were coming back way ahead of schedule.

Reports were coming in that the expressway through Center City was flooded. Jim imagined people diving off the overpasses into the filthy flood waters as if it were an Olympic swimming pool.

Once the storm was finally passed, he went down to the scene where public works, county, and state officials were surveying the damage to the dam at the top and the flood waters in the bottom of the gorge.

"You're gonna wanna see what's at the bottom," the primary

contact on site texted him on his way to the scene.

"I'm gonna need back up," the Sheriff said on his walkie-talkie as he approached. "And we need the coroner's office down here."

The body bobbed along face-down towards the edge of the flood waters. Bloated in a white shirt, the corpse resembled the carcass of a stranded beluga whale. When the other officers and coroner arrived onsite and fished the body out, the sheriff instantly knew who it was despite the water-logged damage.

"Well, I'll be damned," he said. "Darrel Strayer."

After passing it off to the detective on site and the coroner, the sheriff wanted to deliver the news to Sutton in person. Connie answered the front door.

"A helluva storm!" Connie said when she opened the door. "Thank god for our French drains. How was it down at the gorge?"

"A fucking mess," Sheriff Van Patten said as she welcomed him inside. "Is Sutton around?"

"She hasn't been feeling well."

"It's important that I talk to her. You should probably hear this, too."

"Sure," Connie said slowly, trying to get a read on the sheriff, "she's in the living room."

Connie led him to where Sutton had been laying on the couch. She sat up and tried to straighten her hair and clothes.

"Pardon my appearance, Jim," Sutton said.

"Mayor Jackson, I don't know how else to tell you this, but a body was discovered floating in the flood waters at the bottom of the gorge."

Sutton breathed deeply, looked down at her hands and then massaged her temples.

"It's Darrel Strayer," the sheriff said.

Connie gasped and then said, "What the hell was he doing around there?"

Sutton looked up at Sheriff Van Patten. "Maybe," she said

calmly, "he was up there at Robbie's grave getting his kicks, and then was walking around the restricted area."

"In the middle of a hurricane?" Sheriff Van Patten offered with a raised eyebrow.

"Well, geeze, Jim, that area has been blocked off for days," Sutton waved a hand at him and shrugged. "Maybe he was up there before the storm hit."

"What makes you assume he was at the top?" He squinted his eyes, trying to make contact with hers.

"Well," Sutton said, formulating her thought, "you said he was found at the bottom of the gorge in the flood waters. I assumed he fell in."

"Is that what they think happened?" Connie asked.

Sheriff Van Patten nodded affirmatively. "It's the most likely scenario. The coroner still needs to do a full examination of the corpse."

"Was there anything on him?" Sutton asked.

"You mean besides his wallet and ID?" Sheriff Van Patten said.

"Yeah, did he have anything on him? You know these sick fucks like to trade. Maybe he was up there meeting someone, in a secluded area."

"Well, that's a theory, isn't it?" The sheriff had a hunch the mayor had been tracking Strayer online.

"So, was anything on him?" Sutton prodded.

"We can't be sure yet, but I also wouldn't be able to discuss such details of an open investigation, either," the sheriff made clear.

"Do you think it might've been foul play?" Connie asked.

Sheriff Van Patten kept his eyes on Sutton, trying to read her. She simply looked worn down, but not necessarily anxious or suspicious in any other way. "I'm sure it will be ruled an accident. I just wanted you to be the first to know."

"I appreciate that, Jim," Sutton said, finally standing up.

"Thank you for stopping by."

"I better be on my way then." He tipped his hat. "Feel better."

Did anyone really care how or why a scumbag like Darrel Strayer ended up where he did? He died from the impact of a fall from a great height. There were no signs of any struggle. As far as anyone could discern, he fell into the gorge, likely twelve to twenty-fours prior to the dam being over-flooded. It was a simple open and shut case. He was simply one of a dozen deaths in the area attributed to Ida.

Neither Sheriff Jim Van Patten nor Mayor Sutton Lynn Jackson had anything else to say on the matter. The mayor ran uncontested in November.

West Falls, meanwhile, breathed a sigh of relief now that Darrel Strayer was dead.

≈

Connie

Over the years, Connie and Connie's Place remained a center point in the life of West Falls. It was there Mayor Jackson's reelection celebrations were held until she finally stepped down and retired at the age of sixty-eight. It was there the old-timers insisted on having the after-parties for their grandchildren's milestone events, from christenings to graduations. Funeral luncheons and wakes then naturally followed when the old-timers passed on. Connie was always there, encouraging someone to give a speech, or giving a speech herself, weaving her tales as only she could. Celebrating the rich tapestry of lives that called West Falls home.

Eventually all good times come to an end, and Sutton finally convinced Connie to sell the place after business had slowed, and that section of the pike had become a blur of medical offices and small shopping centers people from out of town sped past on their way to the main strip downtown.

Almost everyone Connie had known, Sutton included, ended up in that cemetery on the hill with a beautiful view of the restored falls where the steady murmur of the water flowing down into the gorge was like eternal gossip relaying the stories of all who had lived and died there.

During a winter years later when Connie had long since retired and Sutton had been dead for a while, a storm blew down from Canada. For the first time in many years, snow fell on West Falls. Connie, elderly but still feeling spry, carefully bundled up in her old parka, scarf, hat, gloves and snow boots and trudged through the few inches of un-shoveled snow to the main strip downtown. The holiday decorations were still up, and everything was so silent and still in the early morning hours. Looking up at the falling flakes and then at the pristine snow laying gently over every surface, Connie felt like she was inside a snow globe. She could hear the music box in her head. Then she heard the playful screams and laughter of children down the street. She walked and peered down an alley where three kids, probably middle-school aged, were having a snowball fight.

Memories flooded back, and in her mind Connie saw all the places in West Falls that marked her childhood, all frozen in the newly fallen snow. The elementary, middle and high schools. The parks. Stabler Woods. Ramble Lake. The Rialto Theater. The town swimming pool. In her mind's eye, the snow melted with the years, and she could see all these places again in their glory of summers past, swarmed with playing children. She saw herself as a child again. She saw Freddie and Laurel and Robbie, Pete and Hap, Carl and Hank. All of them running wild and free without a care in the world, basking in the sun of an eternal summer. Connie was everywhere with everyone for a blissfully warm flash. As her focus returned back to that moment, to the cold and the snow and children's laughter as they disappeared down the alley and around the backs of the buildings, like physical manifestations of the ghosts in her head, she smiled knowing she was never truly alone.

EPILOGUE

The Future
Elizabeth

Elizabeth Laurel Van Elms could see the future.

When the stone house had been completed and Elizabeth was pregnant with her first child, she dreamt of her own funeral. She saw her grown children, under a pregnant moon and the cloak of night, dig a hole in the backyard where they gently placed her body wrapped in blankets. She saw them fill a coffin with stones and bury that up on what would become a cemetery atop the hill. When she awoke from this dream she wrote it down. She wanted to make sure when the time came, her children knew her wishes for where she wanted to be laid to rest. She wanted to be attached to this land and this house for as long as she could.

On her death bed, Elizabeth saw the boy and the girl again, and while the boy seemed frozen in time as a child, she saw the girl grow to adulthood and eventually old age. She saw things both wonderful and strange that could only be understood through the eyes of the girl, Laurel. Elizabeth died at age seventy-two in 1928, having seen the town of West Falls grow and flourish along with her family. Her children followed her instructions, and evaded the law when they buried her in secret in the backyard. No one knew the body was there until…

≈

Laurel

Laurel received the phone call from Sheriff Van Patten one evening in early 2021 while enjoying wine on the balcony of her Amsterdam apartment overlooking the canal.

"I don't know how else to tell you this," he said. "But the new owners of the house on your former family lot were putting in a swimming pool in the backyard, and they discovered human remains. The coroner has dated the bones and clothing to likely the 1920s. We have reason to believe it's the body of Elizabeth Van Elms."

"Wow, I don't know what to say," Laurel said, mouth slightly agape and eyes widened. "I thought Elizabeth Van Elms was one of the people in the family plot up in the cemetery on the hill, in that row of really old graves behind my mother and Robbie."

"Well, that's why I'm calling. We want permission to exhume the grave, to see what or who is buried there."

"Sure, whatever you need to do. They don't suspect foul play, do they?"

"No, there are clear records of her date and cause of death."

Later that week, Laurel received notice the coffin buried in Elizabeth Elms' grave was filled with stones. The township would pay to have her actual remains reburied in the gravesite. Laurel couldn't believe the strangeness of this turn of events, and she jokingly wanted to ask Sheriff Van Patten to ship over the stones that had filled the coffin so she could keep them with the cornerstone she had bearing hers and Robbie's names.

Laurel knew now the dark figure that visited her when she was paralyzed in her sleep, the person who carved their names in the stone, and this bold Elizabeth who had her family scoff at social mores and the law to bury her in her own backyard were all one in the same. What was it that planted these seeds of Elizabeth's story in Laurel's mind that allowed these fanciful and haunting connections to be made? Had she researched her family's past as a child, her town's history, and saw an old picture of Elizabeth? She had always been aware of the grave in the cemetery and knew that was her father's great-great grandmother. She knew the Elms family didn't always live in the house. It passed through a few different owners, and it was almost by chance that Burg and Vera were able to purchase it when it hit the market just as they were about to grow their family. These little dots were always there in the background of her life, connecting themselves in the recesses of her mind. For those who subscribed to such notions, all of this would seem like fate. Was that really Elizabeth's ghost that had visited her as a child, reaching out from beyond the unmarked, hidden grave in the backyard? It didn't matter. These were now the facts as Laurel saw it.

Laurel hoped Elizabeth's spirit, if spirits did exist, wasn't angry at this turn of events. Hopefully she would be happy to be buried in her proper spot behind her great-great-great grandson, Robbie Elms. What Laurel never imagined was that Elizabeth had seen this all before. Which was funny, because Laurel saw things wonderful and strange, too, before they happened.

Like everyone, Laurel was gutted when she learned of Hap's illness and subsequent death in early 2022. About six months later, she received a request from Pete and Amie to join them on a video call.

"Hi, how are you both doing?" Laurel asked them, waving at them in frame.

Pete tried to smile. "About as good as can be expected. Of course, we miss the hell out of Hap, but you more than anyone can probably understand the hole that's left when a sibling or loved one dies."

"Well, I've been thinking about you both," Laurel said, nodding. "I know even when you see it coming, death and grief, it hits like a tidal wave…and that tidal wave recedes and then comes back again and again over time. It never goes away for good, but hopefully the wave gets smaller and more manageable."

"Yeah, you always had a nice way of putting things in perspective," Pete said. "I imagine it'll be a while before the waves get smaller. But look, we don't wanna take up too much of your time, and you're probably wondering why the two of us wanted to talk to you." He turned to Amie which a soft smile.

"First off, thank you for the personalized note you sent to me," Amie said. "And for the donation you made in Hap's name to help victims of childhood sexual abuse." She took a deep breath, and tried to put on a smile during an obvious holding back of tears. "Well, as luck would have it, I got pregnant before Hap passed. I'm due in six weeks. It's gonna be a boy. And before I get set about naming him, I wanted to run it by you first. Make sure you're okay with it." Amie took a deep breath, and then said, "I'd like to name him Robbie."

Laurel felt waves of joy and sadness, and she hoped she looked hopeful and excited on camera. "Oh, Amie, congratulations, and of course you have my blessing. Look, I don't own my brother's name or memory. I think it's a wonderful idea."

Amie seemed to deflate with a huge exhale. She wiped some tears from her eyes and then smiled. "Oh, thank you. I just felt like you deserved to know, and if Hap had been alive I'm not sure he would've wanted me to name our son that because it might be too triggering, you know. But with both of them gone, and knowing how close they had been, it just felt…I dunno, like a perfect way to remember both of them. Keep them alive in our hearts and memories."

"You're going to be a great mom, Amie. And Pete might end up being an *okay* uncle."

Pete laughed. "Really, thank you, Laurel. How have you been?"

"Good. I've been renting a cute little place here in Amsterdam. The software company I work for promoted me to VP of Experiential Marketing two months ago…and then three weeks later they were bought out by a larger company based in

Copenhagen that is trying to spin up a new cutting-edge AI division."

"Oh no!" Pete and Amie said in unison.

"No, no, no, it worked out because the new company wants to keep me on and *expand my mandate*, as they like to say, and they're offering to pay for my move to Copenhagen. So, next month, off I go again."

"Oh, that's great!" Pete said. "You're really living the life, Laurel Elms. So proud of you."

"And hey, maybe you all can visit one day. Keep me posted on when little Robbie is born. I wanna see all the pictures. When he's older, he has an open invitation to come out here anytime."

"Thank you again," Amie said.

"Good luck, and congrats again!" Laurel said.

Good-bye,

good-bye,

good-bye.

In Copenhagen, Laurel found a new home base for her travel adventures. Based only on a targeted ad that popped up on her phone while she was reading about Danish tourist hotspots, she began spending time in the beautiful and remote Faroe Islands. She took the over thirty-hour ferry ride from Denmark rather than the two-and-half hour flight in order to watch the brutal beauty of the North Sea rollick outside and carry the ferry, that was more like a cruise ship, to the far-flung archipelago. The experience on the North Sea was meditative and occasionally surreal, but it was a quick and lovely dream compared to the two-week long quarantines she survived in the past. There was food and entertainment and strangers to converse with, but mostly, there was peaceful and transformative alone time.

Once docked, the landscapes of the islands were unlike anything Laurel had ever experienced. Jagged peaks shaped by the harsh winds, sloping hills covered in thick carpets of green, and an iconic waterfall cascading down from daring heights into the ocean.

The islands stood like something from an ancient past stretching their giant hands across time. Each time she went, Laurel felt like the ferry ride took her through a portal. The Faroe Islands, often emerging from passing fog thicker than anywhere else in the world, existed in some wondrous, breathtaking, and scary alternate reality where mythological seal-women rose up from the sea to turn to stone and stand sentinel over the land against amazing backdrops of impossible natural beauty.

It was on a ferry ride back to Denmark when Laurel got the email from Pete that Father MacShay was dead. He passed away from natural causes at the age of ninety-one in the advanced care home for elderly and infirmed Catholic priests fifty miles from West Falls. There was no mention in the obituary of the unprosecuted crimes and abuse he perpetrated against the altar boys of West Falls. She had never processed Darrel Strayer's death over a year ago, which she had also learned about from an email from Pete, and the news of Father MacShay's death brought up monstrous thoughts regarding both dead men's evil deeds. On the observation deck she weathered the wind and sea-spray to look out into the roiling icy waves of the North Sea, imaging all of the pain, secrets, bodies, and bones from all of time buried under the water. Laurel screamed out into the droning white noise of the ferry's motor and the sea's mighty swells. She imagined her scream eventually being captured by the fog and burned off the face of the earth by the morning sun rising over the land.

Laurel turned to find a Viking-esque Danish woman of undetermined years, but with multitudes written in the lines on her face and glint of her eyes, had witnessed her outburst. With a knowing nod of the stranger's head, Laurel realized this woman recognized hers not as a cry for help, but as a long overdue release. As Laurel moved past her to get back inside, the stranger placed a firm, comforting grip on Laurel's shoulder and nodded again. Laurel smiled and nodded back, and then left the kind stranger alone on the deck to take in the sea's stunning rage for herself.

Laurel had been going to the islands twice a year, and after five years of living in Denmark, she was legally allowed to purchase a house on the Faroe Islands. She found the perfect little holiday cottage in the village near the seal-woman statue, with a view of a sheep farm, the sea, and the dazzling rockface across the water. Her cottage was red with a sod roof and nestled into a cozy hillside. She had never imagined she would live part-time in such a place, and it was the farthest cry from a Parisian pied-à-terre she could possibly dream of. It was here, now, where she kept the stone engraved with the names of herself and her long dead brother.

Laurel spent much of her holidays on the island hiking, reading, occasionally working when critical meetings could not be avoided, and pleasantly scrolling through pictures of children of friends posted on social media. Including Robbie Wren-Wolinski, a literal golden boy, but with his father's dark eyes and hair, whose smile lit up the hearts of many people from near and far. She watched these children grow up in pictures and reels, like a documentary pieced together over many years. She sensed they had the same wanderlust she had. She saw Robbie on his epic summer road trips with his mother. She saw others choose to study abroad or venture far away from home as they reached a certain age.

These children were born or grew up under the twin traumatic shadows of Trumpism and the pandemic. Many saw them as another lost generation, who in their twenties seemed adrift abroad, scarred and bored. Laurel, however, didn't see a new lost generation; she saw one more resilient, more kind. The ones on the older side of that generation were already in the workforce, and she was delighted to work with them at the AI tech firm where she had risen to senior executive and developed a strong relationship with the chief scientist driving the AI roadmap, Dr. Sara Van Dearling. Laurel couldn't wait for the new generation to take over the world. They had been the ones people were waiting for all along. Older people who thought they still had to be there to coddle them, to steward them — they had to learn how to finally get out of their way. Laurel was convinced, this could be – *this was* – the next Greatest Generation. While they opened themselves to the world, it wasn't to escape from where they came. It was to expand their horizons and then finally get things done. Fix things, if they could. Or if it couldn't be fixed, move beyond it.

Every morning waking up in her cottage Laurel was filled with wonder and gratitude. "How did I get here?" she would say out loud to herself as she took her coffee out to the small deck overlooking the most amazing natural scenery she had ever seen. The bleating of nearby sheep and the sound of the wind was like music. Whether it was sun-speckled and bright, or it rained as it did three hundred days a year. Whether it was crisp but warm or wind-blown and bitterly cold, it felt like different degrees of the same heaven.

In her cottage Laurel had the most astonishing dreams. She began to see a vast, rocky, gray landscape, the beautiful blue and white marbled earth rising on the horizon. She, elderly and wise and kind, stood at the grand entrance to a great dome through which you looked up and saw endless stars. Under the dome was a burgeoning colony of buildings and gardens under construction. She was welcoming people coming off a monorail into the dome from some nearby landing site.

An adult Robbie Wren-Wolinski approached her. They smiled at each other.

"Do I know you?" Robbie asked with a raise of his eyebrow.

Laurel nodded. "Welcome, I have something I want to show you," she said, referring to the cornerstone bearing their names, which was tucked away in her living quarters.

"How did I get here?" Robbie looked around in amazement.

"Follow me," Laurel told him. "We've been waiting for you to come."

CLOSING MESSAGE FROM THE AUTHOR

Thank you for reading *West Falls Revisited*. If you enjoyed this novel, please consider leaving your rating or a short review on Amazon, Goodreads, BookBub, or social media. Word of mouth is the best way to share books with others.

Independent authors love hearing from their readers. You can find me on many social media platforms, including Threads, Instagram, and Facebook as @d.h.schleicherauthor.

ABOUT THE AUTHOR

D. H. Schleicher is the author of the thematically linked short story collections *And Then We Vanish* and *When Come Back* as well as the historical thriller *Then Came Darkness*.

You can follow his blog *TheSchleicherSpin.com* where he shares his views on books, movies, and travel.

He hails from the South Jersey suburbs of Philadelphia where he lives with his wife and son.

He often dreams about the Faroe Islands and the moon.